She Got It Bad for A Detroit Hitta

LONDYN LENZ

© **2018**
Published by *Miss Candice Presents*

Mac

Fall 2017

We're reporting Live from the west side of Detroit on the 1600 block of Evergreen. A house was shot up with six people inside. Two were indeed children a boy and a girl age four and nine. We're updating you as we get information in. From what we have been told three male adults are dead. One male is in critical condition along with the female who owns the home and her two children. It appears the mother had a relationship with a guy who was involved in some street gang.

He is known as Dice and has a criminal record a mile long. It seems the guy brought some friends back to the home. Drinking and drug activity started going on leading to an altercation with one of the guys. The female called police and while on the phone she heard loud popping and glass breaking. As you can see ambulances are still on the scene. Family of the young woman and the children arrived earlier very hysterical.

The Detroit Police Chief will be holding a press conference later as to what he plans on doing about these shootings that have increased in the city. This alone is the fourth shooting within two weeks that involved children. Rather it be intentionally or by accident the bullets that come out these guns have no name on them. Family of the young woman asked if we can all keep her and the children in our prayers. Reporting Live from Detroit westside, I'm Anna Cross Channel 4."

I sat on my bed rotating my stress balls over and over. This was about to be all the city talked about for the next few days. Anytime kids are involved in any crime and or hurt in any way you can bets believe the pigs were going to be heavy with eyes. Shit was going to be bad for business. As I watched the news more and they showed the faces of the two innocent children hit in the shootout. My stress level rose even higher as I kept rotating the balls.

"Here you go, bae." Quinn placed down the plate of food she cooked for me.

"Preciate it ma," I said sitting up to say my grace and throw down. She made my favorite, a cheeseburger omelet, turkey bacon, and fried potatoes. Don't sleep on them cheeseburger omelets, them bitches slap. She came back with some paper towel and a tall glass of Pepsi.

"Yo' bird eatin' ass." I chuckled when she sat down with her plate. Her little breakfast sandwich was an English muffin, egg whites and two pieces of turkey bacon. Like I said bird food.

"Shut up, I have a figure to watch." She took a bite of her food and looked at the TV.

"I see you got them stress balls out. This Maine work again ain't it?" I just looked at her while stuffing my face.

"Well, it's a part of the game right?" I didn't say shit I just finished my food.

I don't even hit bitches, but she was about to piss me off. Before I even let a woman get me off my square, I'll remove myself. I don't argue, choke you up or none of that. In order for me to do that I have to give a fuck. I ain't met a woman yet that I gave that much about to even get my blood pressure high. And before you think you have me figured out, I'm not closed off to finding a real one either. It's just not in the cards for me. I have been cheated on, I done cheated, I been lied to and played even when I come into the shit keepin' it a buck.

So now I'm like fuck it. I'll just be on some chill shit. This airhead wasn't my woman by far. Me and Quinn fucked, chilled, smoked and she cooks for a nigga. I been kickin' it with her for a few months and this is her second time in my crib. Quinn talked and fucked other niggas, and she knew I got down with other bitches and was cool with it. We just did shit like this from time to time, and I'd break her off some change. I ain't no rich nigga, but for a hood muthafucka I do pretty good. I got my own house on the west side of Detroit on Tuller street.

This crib was my grandfather and grandma's. I was the oldest between me and my brother, so when he died, he left it to me. In his honor, I make sure I maintained it. My grandma didn't want to live here; said it was too painful for her. The inside looks completely different now because a young man lives here instead of an older couple. I had this two-story house in my name and shared it with my crazy ass baby brother. That nigga was a mess times ten, but he was mine, and I'd fuck anybody up over him. Quinn cleaned up our mess and walked back in my room.

I had laid back on my bed watching *Judge Mathis* show. She came and straddled me and started rubbing my chest. Shit, it didn't take much for me to respond. Quinn was a fine slim thick redbone. She was the Instagram type I called her. Make-up, lashes and that weave shit bitches like. I had no problem with it either way, but I liked a woman who could do both. Quinn leaned forward and took my stress balls out my hand. She went back to rubbing my chest and stomach. I kept both my hands behind my head.

"How long we gon' do this Mac? I'm ready to be your woman, and I know you want to be with me. So, what's the problem?"

"Quinn if this dick ain't about to go in that mouth then you need to get up. Ain't shit compatible with me and you beyond chilling. I don't trust you, and you should never trust me, so let's keep shit the way it is." She tried to get an attitude, but my expression let her know I wasn't changing my mind. I'd be setting both of us up for failure if I made Quinn my woman. Prime example right now. Her phone started ringing on my nightstand next to me. The word 'boo' with some hearts popped up. I chuckled, and her face got flushed.

"Come on and suck this dick so you can go pick that nigga up from work." She smacked her lips, but in the next few seconds, she had my eleven-inch curve in her mouth just like I said.

***

We need a proper introduction. I'm Mac, short for my real name which I don't disclose to any damn body. I grew up on the west side of Detroit; the better side is what I called it. The streets were what I knew but don't get shit twisted. I wasn't neglected or anything, my mama was a single mother, and my pops was killed in jail when I was ten. That shit fucked me up, but my mama made sure I was close to his side of the family. My brother was seven-years-old and had so much of our pops in him.

He didn't care when he died as long as our mama and grandma was good. Our pops was an ok father. He made sure the bills were paid, me and my brother had designer everything. The relationship with him and our mama was strictly about us. Pops taught us how to stay fresh, get bitches and that's about it. The nigga wasn't much, but he was our father. Quinn left, and I got showered so I could leave and meet up with my brother and cousin. This shootout was still all on the news, and my stress was at an all-time high. The game we were in, I should be used to this shit. But it was hard seeing small kids get caught up in this mess. Still, it didn't stop me from flying off the handle when need be. So as you can see, a nigga was conflicted. I hated the life, but then I indulged in it when I had to.

"This bitch gone get smart with me talem'bout 'My pussy got class.' I told that hoe; yea but how many students been in that muthafucka."

"Nigga you a straight fool." I cracked up at my looney ass cousin. Swear this nigga ain't right in the head. I stopped by our trap to holla at him about last night.

"Why the hell you be entertaining these hoes knowing Alyssa will fuck yo' ass up?" I passed him the blunt.

"Man I'on be stunnin' them bitches. Alyssa knows what's up. Speaking of her I gotta swing by her crib tonight. Lil mama said she got a night planned for us and shit."

"That's what's up I respect y'all rockin' so hard. I gotta work tonight but check it. I wanna talk to you about last night. What the fuck made you think it was cool to move on your own? That ain't how we do shit." He stayed laid on the couch just blowing smoke like what I was saying didn't faze him. Y'all about to learn that disrespect and me don't mix.

"Tha fuck you want me to say?" He shrugged his shoulders while sitting up and started taking his weed out the bag so he can roll it.

"Don't come over here wit' that shit cuz for real for real. You pop kids just like I do and so does Sada." I turned my nose up at this idiot.

"Shut that bullshit up. I pop a muthafucka that's willing to pull heat out on me. I pop uh nigga or bitch that got balls to fuck with my shit. I also don't just spray bullets freely like they got names on them. Let me guess, Spudz and P was down to do that hit wit'chu right." He turned his head in my direction with a nasty ass expression.

"What'chu need to do is get the fuck back. Don't question shit me or my niggas do. You and Sada took to fuckin' long, and them fools needed to be got right then and there." It was at this moment when he fucked up. Blood or not.

"Who the fuck you talkin' to?" I slapped the blunt out his hand and flipped the raggedy ass table all his weed was on sending that shit flying on the floor.

"Huh, who the fuck you think you talkin' to my nigga?" Maine stood up and faced me. I only had him by a few inches in height. I was 6'4, and he was 6'2.

"You the only person standing here bitchin' to me about some shit I don't give a fuck about. Tha fuck you want me to say? You want me to apologize, fuck naw. That bitch shouldn't have had a house full of them Brightmoor niggas anyway."

"I ain't about to stand here and argue wit'chu like you my bitch. You sloppy and you fuckin' reckless. That shit gon' stop." He balled his face up.

"Or what cuz? Tha fuck you gone do?" Ooo wee! My dick gets hard when a muthafucka temps me. I balled my fist up and hit that nigga square in his jaw. Maine fell back while grabbing his now busted lip. Next thing I know he came charging at me, and we started fighting. He got one good hit in my ribs before I hit him in his.

"Ayee what the fuck y'all doing man!!"

"Break this shit up! Y'all family!" P and Spudz came and broke us up.

"Naw fuck that nigga!! Go' come in here like he my fucking father or some shit!!" I didn't have a mark on me. Maine was my cousin, and I loved the nigga like my brother. But he wasn't a fighter.

"P get the fuck off me before I fuck you up next." I wasn't one to yell or scream like no bitch. He knew I wasn't wrapped tight, so he held his hands up and stepped back. I looked over at Maine who was acting all wild trying to get free from Spudz. The way he was acting made me laugh.

"Let that wild ass chihuahua go." P tried not to laugh and so did Spudz.

"Listen, you wanna keep being out here all wild and shit wit' ya two cheerleaders. Then cool, do you. But fix ya self to disrespect me again and watch what I do." I kept my eyes on his while I walked away. Maine started talking shit while I walked out the trap.

"Nigga fuck you!!" I just closed the door and headed to my Dodge Magnum and pulled off. I had a few hours to kill before work. I could go swing by this cutie I met a few days ago. But then I realized it was Sunday, so that meant ma dukes cooked some good ass food. I put my turn signal on and headed over that way.

Sada

"Oooo shit Sada."

"Ooooo my God boy." I was fucking this bitch up with this dick. Her fat ass booty was slapping all on my pelvis. She grabbed the shelf to control her body jerking out of control. I had my tongue out ready to do the dougie on this hoe. This was my talent right here fucking a bad bitch and having her crazy over the dick. She was gripping the shelf so hard the cartons of medicine and towels started falling all on top of her head. I was cracking up while still beatin' the pussy like a drum.

"Damn ma, you gone lose yo' fuckin' job acting like that."

"Ughh I don't give a fuckkk. Ssssss ooo just keep fucking me, Sada." I shrugged my shoulders and started pounding harder. It made me no difference if this bitch was willing to risk her employment. I told her to meet up with me tonight when she got off. But she kept begging and pulling me in this closet. Me being down for whatever, I was like fuck it. I dug my nails deep in her ass cheeks and a few pumps later, I was feeling up the Magnum condom.

"Damn nigga, I gotta make you one of my regulars."
She grabbed some sanitary napkins and started cleaning
herself up. I grabbed some to so I could take the condoms
off. Yup condoms, I strapped up twice when I fucked these
hoes. I didn't need a bitch trying to trap my fine ass.

"We can do that. I didn't get a chance to dig in that
pussy the way I wanted to." I said that shit and this bitch eyes
grew big.

"Don't have me sprung on the dick Sada. You don't
want those type of problems." I chuckled at that shit.

"Baby girl every bitch I meet gets stuck. I met you
fifteen minutes ago and look at'chu now. If you get stuck,
then that's on you. But know this, I will never belong to you
or any bitch. That ain't never been my thing." After I got
cleaned up, I tossed the napkin and fixed my clothes.

"Now get back to work. Make sure my grandma got
some new sheets and give her some jello and apple juice." I
kissed her cheek.

"I'll text you later." I walked out the storage closet,
and two nurses side eyed me.

"I tried to break you off, but you was on some
bullshit," I said to the redbone thick nurse. She smacked her
lips and looked all mad.

"Fix yo' face ma. I tell you what, put'cho number in my phone. Yo' pussy might be better than ol'girl. If it is you can brag to her ass." I licked my lips and smiled. This bitch face glowed up, and she hurried and keyed her number in.

"Oh believe me my pussy, and head game is way better than that bitch. And I always make sure your grandma is taken care of."

"That's what's up good looking out. That's my heart, so I need her looked out for all the time." I winked, and she blushed. Her co-worker kept rolling her eyes and smacking her lips. This bitch always gave me attitude when I came up here to visit my grandma. I knew it was because she wanted me to fuck her.

"I know you feel left out and I would put this dick in yo life if you wasn't built like a damn Charlie horse." Her ugly ass mouth fell to the floor. I took my phone from redbone and told her I'd hit her up. I had to walk past my grandma room on the way out. I popped my head in her room.

"See you tomorrow gorgeous."

"Get'cho little wild ass out of here. I know why you still up here and why I got all this damn jello and apple juice." I laughed at her and blew her a kiss leaving.

My grandma lives in a retirement village in Plymouth. Wasn't nothing wrong with her either. The woman practically ran this place, she still drove and had a smart-ass mouth. I didn't get why she didn't go live with my mama and enjoy her golden years there. But she said she never wanted to be in the way. Me, my mama and my brother Mac always came to see her every single day. Sometimes we'd come together or at different times. But we made sure she seen at least one of us every day. This retirement home had some of the baddest bitches in the metro area, and I wanted to knock all of them down one by one.

So as you know, I'm Sada. Baby brother of that hot temper ass Mac and son of our punk ass pops he told y'all about. I had no beef with our pops. I was just a mama's boy and grandma's baby. So when I'd hear my mama and grandma say he wasn't shit. That's how I looked at the nigga. I'm twenty-one years old. Standing at 6'2 and fine as fuck. My mama and pops blessed me and my big brother. I'm a yellow nigga but with dark-skinned tendencies. I got some long ass dreads I have been growing since I was seventeen.

My body was hard that I kept tight in the gym. 200lbs looked good as fuck on me, and my beard pulled my looks together. I was just the shit and knew it while still being the coolest nigga you wanted to be around. If I even let you be around me. My homies were my big brother, my cousin and a few day-ones. Anybody else was my enemy, and that's just how I looked at it. Bitches were just that, bitches with some pussy and mouth that I would use for a few hours. Don't get it twisted, I respected women. I just like my freedom and fun so relationships I don't fuck with.

It's too much pussy out here to be tied down to one. That's why I strapped up twice and always made sure I dispose of my own condoms. I don't want no lil bastards running around calling me daddy. Naw, that ain't me. I'm the uncle who will sugar ya' kid up, cash out on some toys and then drop they asses back off.

Anyway, I worked at Chrysler with Mac, and we had our hustle that made us some good money. Doing hits for people who had the right bread. No set price we had, the dollars just had to sound right, and we'd take the job. For you slow muthafuckas, hits means murdering people. You pay us right, we'd handle ya problem. No questions asked. We made some enemies along the way but ain't shit we can't handle. Chrysler pays me good, but the streets pay better. Enough to make a nigga hood rich and not starve. I pulled my 2018 Charger into my mama's drive-way. I could smell the food from outside plus Mac was meeting me here as well. I noticed a car was parked in front of her house.

"Hey pretty lady, it smells good as hell in here." I kissed my mama on her cheek and set down on the stool at her kitchen bar.

"Hey love, you know my mama just called me." She hit the back of my head laughing.

"Damn what was that for?" I rubbed the back of my head.

"I told you about keeping your dick in your pants. My mama said she can't even get any sleep because two nurses keep coming in her room bringing her shit. Do you have to fuck everything with a pulse boy?"

"If it was born with a pussy and fine as fuck then yea. Why not." I laughed and put some grapes in my mouth.

"You are your daddy's twin I swear. Where my big baby at?"

"He should be on his way." I heard movement in the back, and then his ass walked in the kitchen.

"How you doing today Sada? You still playing ball on Dexter." I side eyed the hell out of Reverend Jones when he walked in my mama kitchen. Ma Dukes was dating this nigga who owned a church on Greenfield and west six-mile. Nigga wife ain't been dead for two minutes, and he couldn't wait until he could stick his dick in her.

My mama was a beautiful full-figured woman. She could cook, worked hard every day and had her own everything. She ran a daycare on seven mile. Her ass loves kids and was always down me and Mac throat to make her a grandma. But she never likes none of the bitches we fucked with. Anyway, I didn't care for this nigga here, so I was dry as hell.

"Sup. *Reverend.*" I made sure to emphasize his status when I said that. Turning my nose up at him when he kissed my mama she gave him a plate and walked him to the door.

"Ah damn ma, why you keep slapping me?" I rubbed the back of my head from her heavy-handed ass.

"Because I raised yo' ass better than that. Being all rude and shit."

"Man ma I don't even get why the hell you into that fat ass sloppy nigga. You can do way better plus his wife only been dead for a few months." She went and stirred her pot of greens.

"First of all, his wife been dead for nine months and I only been messing with him for two weeks. Second, mama need love too and big niggas quick to throw that cash." She pointed to my muscles.

"You pretty, built muthafuckas always want a bitch to jump through hoops. Let me live and have my fun."

"I'm sayin' you can have yo' fun but get'chu a nigga on yo' level. His ass clappin', yo' ass clappin' when y'all fucking. Probably sound like a damn choir in yo' room." She picked up her oven mittens and threw them at me while laughing. My mama always had such a homie relationship with me and Mac. I don't know how she did it. But she raised us to know not to fuck with her and how to just kick it with her to. She didn't smoke or drink with us but talking to her made you forget sometimes she was our mother. But she'd fuck us up if we played around in school or disrespected her.

"I swear you did not come from me. You always got some smart shit to say." Me and her both laughed while she took some plates out. I peeped she made some collard greens, black-eyed peas, cornbread, and some barbeque neck bones. Oh, I was about to smash. The front door opened and her face lit up just like it did when she seen me. Mac walked in, and we gave each other a slap, and then he hugged our mama.

"Sup wit'chu pretty lady? What's on the menu today?"

"I'm ok just about to kick yo' rude ass brother out my house. And I made all the food that both of y'all eat." Mac nodded and set on the stool next to me.

"The fuck you do now?"

"I ain't do nothing. Ma messing with Reverend Johns." Mac made an ugly face and looked at mama.

"Why ma, that nigga's neck got mo' rolls then a buffet. You playin' ya self." Mama so silly she was laughing hard as hell.

"You and Sada are not about to come at my man like that. Plus, that neck roll nigga just paid my high ass water bill, and your grandma rent for three months." Me and Mac got mad as hell, but his hot-headed ass spoke up first.

"What the hell you think me and Sada here for? Don't give that flubber ass nigga a reason to feel needed. We make sure you and grandma good." I laughed because mama was about to go upside his head now.

"Boy, I don't know who the hell you think you talking to. I gave you and this thick-headed nigga life, and I'll take it back. The money you use on me and grandma bills now y'all can put it in a bank and save it for a rainy day." She smacked the back of his head again.

"Don't forget everything I do is for the two of y'all. You think I don't know Chrysler isn't the only way y'all make money. I know the shit you, him and Maine out here doing. Now, get the hell up so we can sit at the table and eat."

***

"You talked to that nigga Maine?" Mac asked me while we smoked in mama's backyard.

"Naw but I gotta meet up with him later." I passed him back the blunt.

"We got into it earlier. You seen the news right?"

"Aw fuck, that was his stupid ass?" Mac nodded his head.

"Let me guess, you met up with him and y'all got down like always. Now he heated and don't want shit to do with you." Since we been kids, Mac and Maine would go at it. Be mad for a few days and then get back cool.

"Look, we got other beef with them Schoolcraft niggas. I don't need Maine, P, and Spudz out here acting stupid. I'm trying to put heat into them niggas soon, and I need Maine head together. Talk to ya damn cousin before I fuck him up even more."

"Y'all act like an old married couple. I'll holla at him though. Check this out, that new fat booty nurse at grandma spot. I knocked that bitch down."

"Told yo' ass that hoe would let'chu hit. That shit she do with yo' balls feel good as fuck don't it?!" We both cracked jokes and talked about that bitch.

"I want the director hoe next." I turned my nose up when Mac said that.

"She fine and all but her titties to long."

"Long titties need love to and I ain't had no chocolate in a minute." This nigga had me choking on the weed because I was laughing.

"You a fuckin' fool bro." We chopped it up and hung out with mama for a few more minutes.

Then I hopped in my ride to go talk to Maine. He stayed on Cherrylawn street over on Puritan. Twe have done so many hits for muthafuckas who got beef all up down Fenkell, Putitan, Seven and Six mile. And of course, Dexter area by Central high school. The more deserted an area was. Mean the higher the crime and the more drugs being sold. Enemies were made every day from drug dealers fighting over territory, money, respect or a take-over. Because of that, we stayed employed. I got to Maine's crib and laughed because you'd never think a crazy ass street goon lived here. His house is in the hood no doubt but looking at the outside was just funny as hell.

"Hey Sada."

"What up doe Alyssa." I walked in the house, and she closed the door behind me.

"I see you been doing that gardening shit again?" She chuckled.

"Yea, he just got pissed and told me to get rid of it. I swear he gets on my nerves."

"Where that fool at?" She pointed down.

"In the basement playing the game," I told her thanks and walked towards the kitchen where the basement steps were.

"Nigga don't come creepin' down here. Get'cho ass popped." He stood up smiling and gave me a slap. I noticed his bottom lip was busted.

"I heard yo' ass been doing enough poppin' my nigga." I sat down on the couch next to the recliner he was sitting in. Mac basement looked like he was in a cell. He had an old ass couch and a recliner. Four milk crates next to each other he made into a table. The only valuable shit down here was his badass sixty-inch curve TV mounted on the wall with his PS4 and all his video games.

"I ain't in the mood to hear that shit."

"I'm not about to lecture you. You and that busted lip don' heard enough." I joked picking up the controller.

"Fuck you nigga."

"So what the hell happened?" I asked him while picking out my team on NFL Madden game.

"We were all outside shooting dice at P crib. Them lame ass Schoolcraft niggas came walking down the street. I was already on tip when I saw them approaching, but shit was good. They wasn't checking for nothing. I won three-hunnid from one of them, and it jumped off from there. Nigga started talking smack, so I told that fool I'd see his ass." Maine looked over at me.

"On some real shit, I didn't know kids were in that house. Y'all know when I'm on tip ain't no calming me down. Mac came to the trap pissed, and we got into it."

"I know. I told his ass y'all act like a married couple." We both chuckled.

"But for real Maine you, P and Spudz gotta chill. Yo' dumb ass shot up that crib and only one of them Schoolcraft niggas was in it. Now they about to be on full alert." Maine stood up pissed.

"And!! Fuck them pussy ass niggas. I fucked up, but bets believe I'm handling that shit next time."

"Naw nigga. *We* handling that shit next time. P and Spudz don't eat with us. Them yo' niggas. It's me, you and Mac like it's always been. Trust me cuz, I want them niggas dead to but we gotta do the shit right. Ain't none of us tryna get locked up or buried." He tried to act like he wasn't hearing me.

"A'ight. A'ight, I'll chill." We both sat back down.

"Did you see that bullshit Alyssa put in the yard? I told her ass to go get that gay ass stuff up." We both laughed.

"When I pulled up I was cracking up. Grown ass nigga got lilies in his yard. Garden gnomes and shit." I clowned his ass for a minute then played him in two games of football before I left. I didn't have to work today, so I texted redbone thick nurse from earlier. I wanted to give that pussy a deep physical with this big ass dick.

Maine

After I let my cousin out the side door of my crib. I played another game, and then I called it a night. It had been a long ass day after last night. Before y'all think I'm this heartless nigga let me hip ya to some shit. I'm a cool as hell until I'm fucked with. I ain't walking around just killing innocent kids and shit. But, part of the game was killing muthafuckas who are in my way. Yea me and my niggas were a little sloppy with our shit sometimes. But a child has never died on my hands. Last night shooting was the first time one of my bullets ever struck a child. I didn't like the shit, but the niggas that were in that house asked for it.

I'm Maine for the streets and Jermaine for my family and my girl. I was an only child to my mama Pebbles and Malcom White. As Mac told y'all my pops had us close especially after my uncle Randall was killed in jail. My two cousins were like my brothers even when one of them were getting on my damn nerves. I would never take that fight I had earlier with my cousin from anybody else. Hell naw, by the time you got'cha sentence out I was killing yo' ass. Don't let Mac twist with y'all head. I could fight, but shooting was much easier. I grew up on the west side of Detroit in the Fenkell area. I'm twenty-years-old and went to Mumford High School where I met my boo, Alyssa. I'll talk about her in a second.

Me and my mama had an ok relationship. I was closer to my Auntie Joy, Mac, and Sada mama. I don't know what the fuck is my mama problem, but the way I deal with her is I don't. Just that simple, I don't fuck with her. Me and my pops were mad close though, that's my nigga. In fact, I had my own crib because of him. He has some properties all through Detroit, so he let me rent this house. I made money and hell naw it wasn't from a nine to five. I don't see how the hell my cousins did that shit. Even though Chrysler paid them good, I just couldn't get down. So why they worked there. I took care of our street business twenty-four-seven.

This was Detroit so if you think you the shit. There were ten other niggas who thought they were better, so we watched our backs a lot. With the new police chief in Detroit, shit was a little harder to move without a slip up. Mac was known for doing all our hits clean and smooth which is why he didn't like when I was messy. After coming upstairs, I locked up the house and looked outside to see if Alyssa ass got them damn flowers out my yard. Damn woman had the outside of my crib looking like an old lady house. I saw she did so I went to the back so I could shower.

"You happy now? Excuse me for trying to make your house more welcoming." Alyssa sat up in my bed rolling her eyes.

"You better get rid of that attitude by the time I come out the shower."

I walked in my bathroom and closed the door. I loved having my own crib because my girl could come over and spend the night. Living at home, my mama didn't play that shit. Plus she couldn't stand Alyssa. Who the fuck knows why but she just couldn't. She was always calling her a hoe which was false as hell. Alyssa wasn't the scary type so she would get back at my mama. Nothing too disrespectful but she would defend herself. That's mainly what gave him the idea of giving me my own crib. Alyssa and I met our junior year of high school. She was chocolate and a little on the fat side, but her face was lit as fuck.

I wanted her and locked that shit down. We were on and off because it was high school. Who the hell is faithful in during that time? I'd fuck up, and she would beat bitches asses. Then she'd fuck up, and I'd rearrange some niggas faces. Our thang was messy, but it was us. Once we graduated, Alyssa went to The Art Institute of Michigan for Interior design, and I hit the streets. She was into decorating all kinds of shit. Parties, homes anything she could get her hands on her ass was always trying to decorate it. I was glad Alyssa had a passion. We were strong now for two-years straight, and it was good. I was ready for her to move in but I knew her mama wouldn't have that shit.

Me and Ms. Neil got along but Alyssa was her baby, and she wasn't letting her move in with me. She already hated that her daughter spent the night with me. My thing is, Alyssa was grown, and I wasn't going anywhere. I loved my girl, and as soon as I got done with these streets, we were getting married, and she was giving me some babies. I was supposed to be Alyssa first, but we broke up one summer, and some other nigga slid in. I fucked his ass up so bad he still eating through a straw. Niggas knew not to fuck with my chocolate boo unless they wanted problems with me.

"What's the matter?" I asked her when I walked out the bathroom. She was sitting up in my bed looking like some heavy shit was on her mind. I peeped she had on my over-sized t-shirt and no bra. Alyssa was so sexy. Chocolate, some Chinese shape eyes, and full lips. Almost like a Blasian (black and Chinese mixed) type of female. She lost a little weight from high school and started working out. Her shape was thick as hell now, big thighs, flat stomach and a fat ass booty that was ridiculous. Her girly self-kept her nails, feet, and hair always done.

"I need to talk to you."

"Aw shit. What the hell did I do now? Do I need to fuck anybody up? Do I need to fuck you up?" She giggled.

"No silly, I just need to talk to you." I dried my long dreads off and threw the towel on top of my hamper. Turning around I grabbed my Old Spice deodorant and put some on. I was planning on getting some pussy but depending on what Alyssa was about to say. I decided not to get in the bed naked. I grabbed some boxer briefs out my drawer and put them on. I could feel her watching me like she always did. I was 6'2, brown skin and had a hard ass body. I was handsome as hell, long black dreads and a ten-inch thick dick that Alyssa couldn't get enough of. I climbed in my bed grabbing her and putting her on my lap.

"What's up boo?"

"How long do you plan on being in the streets Jermaine?" I threw my head back when she asked that. Alyssa hated me out there risking my life.

"Come on boo don't start this shit. You know I'm tryna make sure we good for a while. I can't punch no damn clock." I hated having this conversation with her because it always resulted to us arguing. For real I just wanted to fuck her good and go to sleep.

"Jermaine I'm starting to get scared. It's bad enough you, Mac and Sada be out here heartless as hell. But P and Spudz are just stupid. They always coming over getting you hyped up, and then you act just as stupid as them. What if you get locked up or worse?" She started looking sad, and I couldn't have that. I lifted her face and kissed her soft lips.

"I'm good Alyssa. I ain't saying I'm invisible to none of the stuff you just said. But I promise to be more careful and to stop letting my homies hype me up. I don't need you sitting here sad and thinking the worst." She seemed to be staring off like she wasn't listening to nothing I was saying.

"Alyssa you sure----"

"Jermaine I'm pregnant."

"Say what?"

"I said I'm pregnant. I found out this morning when I went to my doctor's appointment. I'm eight weeks." I heard her talking, but I was still stuck on her saying she was pregnant.

"Jermaine." I looked at her, and she had watery eyes.

"You don't want me to keep it do you?"

"What? Hell yea I want you to keep my baby. Tha fuck you talking crazy for? I'm just shocked as hell that's all. Shit, I didn't think this was what you were about to say." I wiped her tears and kissed her lips.

"I'm so scared boo, like are we ready for this?" She confessed, and I hugged her.

"You ain't never got to be scared, Alyssa. I got us, and I got our baby. You ain't got to go through anything by yourself. Damn. So you're about to have my baby?" I asked her smiling making her pretty self-smile.

"I guess so." We kissed again.

"I don't want you scared and worried about me boo. This changes a lot of shit about how I'm living. Not saying you are not worth changing for but a piece of me inside of you has me feeling a way. Not saying I'm about to quit tomorrow but I'll move differently. I promise." Alyssa straddled my lap and kissed me. I can't believe I was going to be a father. I wanted her to move in with me right away. I didn't want to miss any doctor appointments, and I imagined us having a chocolate little boy. His daddy looks and his mama skin and good ass hair.

"You know I love you, Alyssa. You and my lil man." She gave me a sweet giggle.

"I love you too Jermaine but how do you know it's a boy already?"

"I can feel it. I'm gon' take good care of you and our son." I kissed her again and pulled my over-sized shit over her head. Them C-cup full titties popped out, and I went straight for them dark nipples. That was Alyssa spot, and she moaned so loud when I sucked and pulled on her nipples.

"Ahhhhh shit." I grabbed her neck and flipped her over on her back. Pulling my boxers down while I kissed my way down her body. Alyssa had a fat ass pussy that would get so wet her thighs would glisten with her juices. She kept it bald, and that soft clit was my favorite. I opened her lips and put that clit in my mouth. Swirling my tongue and tongue kissing that thang was making my dick so hard.

"Uhhhh…..Mmmm. Shit mmmhpmh." Alyssa was moaning and gripping my dreads tight while she came all in my mouth. After her second time coming, I kissed the inner of them thick thighs and showed some love to them titties again. Alyssa grabbed my hard dick and started rubbing in all in her wetness. Her other hand was all in my wet beard as I kissed her getting her juices on her face too.

"Put that dick in boo." She positioned it at her hole and was slowly putting my dick in. Her pussy was so tight, and the thickness of my shit was always a struggle to get in. I started kissing and licking on her neck while I slid my dick all the way in. Alyssa was squeezing my biceps hard and moaning like crazy. I grabbed her hands and put them over her head while I fucked her so good. Stroke after stroke her pussy was gripping my dick like a never-ending goodbye.

"Listen to the sound of that pussy. You hear her boo?"

"Sssss yes Jermaine I hear her. Oh, God!" I was tongue kissing her cheek then her neck and back to her lips while talking so nasty to her. Between my strokes and my voice, Alyssa was cummin' over and over.

"Nobody does this pussy like big daddy right?"

"Right boo. Oh my goodness that's right." I kept them hands above her head and her legs were spread eagle.

"When I pull this wet dick out you gon' lick it clean ok?" I licked and pulled that bottom lip.

"You hear me ma?"

"Y-y-yea ooooo."

"Yea what?" I licked and bit on her ear.

"Yea what Alyssa."

"Sssss yea big daddyyy. Oh yessssss!" She came so hard, and I pulled my dripping wet dick out and got on my back. Alyssa did like I said and started sucking my dick so good. I had her riding me and then I gave her some back shots before we passed out in each other's sweat.

***

"Damn so I'm about to be a grandfather?" My pops looked at me smiling. I stopped by his house to talk to him really quick.

"Yea, Alyssa told me last night. Says she's eight weeks." He gave me some dab and then went in his drawer and pulled out two Cuban cigars.

"Here, we are about to spark these up and celebrate. You know I love Alyssa like a daughter. You ain't that much older than me when me and your mother had you. You got yo' own spot, car and you out here getting money." I accepted the cigar, but something was bothering me.

"Alyssa telling me she's pregnant got me thinking. I don't want nothing to happen to me out here mixed in some bullshit. Leaving her and our child alone because I couldn't slow down."

"I hear you son. But you also have to feed your family. I'm getting some new weight coming in and the money gone start pouring in. You need to leave this hit shit alone and come eat with your pops. You, Mac and Sada." I can't even lie and say I wasn't interested. I could buy me and Alyssa a new house. One outside the hood, good school for our child and safe areas for him to play in. I could do it without hit money we made but the type of cash my pops was talking. That was mansion type of money. The thing is, drug dealing wasn't my shit. Hell, killing wasn't either. But selling drugs, paying a connect, fighting over corners. Naw, I'll pass.

"That sounds good and all but that ain't for me or my cousins. It's all too much drama, and I want no parts. I eat good as fuck now. Pressin' for more is how a nigga gets clipped." He did a hard chuckle and said.

"You young muthafuckas just don't listen. Drugs is more money than killing. I'll be ya supplier, so it's a win-win."

You see my pops is in the drug game. Well, he was trying to get into the game. He found a supplier and wanted me and my cousins to get down with him. But we wasn't into working for my pops. No beef or anything it's just like I said, we didn't want no parts.

"It ain't about not listening. It's more so about everybody grown and can make their own choices. I'on think that's a good choice for me."

"You gone have to think different now nigga. You have a family to take care of. I love both my nephews, but Mac has so much of my brother in him. Once his mind is made up there is no changing it and Sada will follow. You just gon' follow to? All I'm trying to do is lead y'all so one day you can run ya own. It's better to have family in charge then a stranger who gon' eat for themselves." I downed the rest of my beer. I was listening to my pops, and he was speaking facts. I just did everything with my cousins. Even though me and Mac go at it, him and Sada are still my family. As me and my pops talked the front door opened and my mood changed.

"Sup mama." I stood up when she came in the house with some shopping bags.

"Hey, Jermaine." She didn't even look at me. I stood up and followed her to the kitchen.

"Mama, can I get some eye contact?" She put her food in the fridge and looked at me.

"What is it you want Jermaine?" My mama was a beautiful woman on the outside but a bitch on the inside.

"Look I don't want shit. I just wanted to tell you Alyssa is pregnant." She chuckled and put her hand on her hip.

"Is it yours? You know that black bitch is a hoe."

"You got problems lady. Hell yea that child is mine and if you want to be around him. You gon' have to respect his mother." She slammed the refrigerator door.

"I don't have to respect shit. I keep telling you that damn girl a hoe and you turn around and knock her ass up."

"I ain't about to deal with this bullshit. You trippin' for no reason. Keep that shit away from my child." My pops walked in the kitchen.

"The both of y'all need to chill the fuck out—"

"Naw that's where you wrong. I ain't chillin' on shit. Alyssa has never done nothing to this woman, but she keeps disrespecting her." My pops stepped in my face. See this is what he does. Me and him will get along fine but the minute me and my mama get into it he jumps on her side.

"This lady is my wife and your fucking mother. Show her some respect or dats yo'ass."

"Man fuck this shit and fuck y'all." I grabbed my keys off the table and walked towards the door.

"So you gone walk away like we weren't talking about some business."

"Nigga fuck all that business talk. My cousins not down and neither am I." I said while I kept walking. Then my bitch of a mama had to open her mouth.

"Let his dumb ass leave. I don't need to see him, that hoe or that bastard child." I could have turned around and lit into her. But at this point, I'm not about to argue anymore. For right now, it was fuck the both of them. I got in my car, and my phone went off. I assumed it was Alyssa, but it was a text from Mac.

Mac: We square nigga?

We never apologize or say we were wrong. It just wasn't me, him or Sada's thing. I responded then put my phone on the seat and pulled off.

Me: We square bitch ass nigga

I knew he was laughing because I always had to respond with a smart remark. I was getting up with him and Sada later. I wanted to talk to them about Alyssa and shit with my pops. I think it was time to get our bread up but not with my dad's help. We needed to do things ourselves and the way my pops would switch up. I didn't trust it. I headed to Coney Island on Lyndon street. This was me, P and Spudz spot. My cousins couldn't stand my niggas since we started hanging in high school. P was yo average airhead ass nigga with a dumb ass laugh. Spudz was always high off that purple drank, but the fool was funny as hell. We were cool because the two of them were down for whatever and they didn't switch up. Plus these niggas funny as hell.

"Niggas be out here thinking because I got a daughter I'm soft as fuck! Like I won't fuck they ass up after *Peppa Pig* goes off." Me and Spudz fell out laughing at P retarded ass. We were outside of the Coney about to walk in.

"You a straight fool nigga. Let me find out yo' ass having tea parties." I said still cracking up.

"Why y'all always gotta come in here being all loud?" Natasha rolled her eyes as soon as we walked in the Coney Island. She was this slim bitch with a fat ass. I knocked her down a while back when me and Alyssa were going through our shit. She missed the dick so bad that she pushed up on P. I told his ass to shoot his shot. I'm thinking this fool was gone fuck and dip. He ended up catching feelings and knocked the hoe up. They have a one-year-old daughter together, and his baby mama still wants my ass. I told him to cut the bitch loose but he in love. He ain't have shit to worry about my way, I don't want that hoe.

"Close that damn mouth girl and get our order ready? And where the hell is my daughter at?" P asked her through the glass she was standing behind.

"She with my mama nigga and I need some money for her some shoes." P chuckled and pulled a knot out. Her eyes got a glow when she saw them hundreds and fifties.

"I wouldn't have gave that bitch shit. Y'all daughter only one and she act like she go through shoes like a grown person." Spudz said when P came and set down with us. I don't speak on shit that ain't got to do with me, so I stayed quiet.

"Man I don't be wanting to hear her mouth. And I wanna stop by her crib and get some pussy tonight."

"Too much info my nigga." I turned my nose up pulling my phone out.

"Aye when we taking that trip to Cedar Point?" P asked.

"Shit whenever is cool with me after next weekend. I'm taking my daughter to the Universal Soul Circus." P said just as his baby mama came and brought our food out. I got my usual, chili cheese fries. I fucked with squeezed cheese, you sliced cheese people a freak of damn nature. I had some fried wing dings and onion rings. I felt Natasha stare at me when she gave us our food, but I ignored her ass.

"Me and Alyssa gon' have to sit this trip out."

"Why?" I shrugged my shoulders.

"Ma pregnant with my son and she ain't about to do no rollercoasters or walking around all day." P and Spudz looked shocked.

"Well damn homie throw some news at us like that?! Congratulations my nigga." They both gave me some dab.

"I just saw Alyssa at the barbeque, and she didn't look pregnant at all."

"She only eight-weeks my nigga. She told me last night."

"Well, then how the hell you know it's a boy?" P joked.

"Cuz all this dick right here can produce is boys." We laughed and my phone rung.

"Here go my boo right here." I picked my phone up walking away to the other end of the restaurant so I could talk.

"Sup boo? Y'all good?" I stood in front of the big ass glass looking outside.

"Yea we're good. Can you bring me some food after your done handling your business?"

"I'm at the Coney now with P and Spudz I was going to my cousins after here. But---"

"Why you at that damn Coney Island Jermaine? That hoe Natasha up there and I know she was all in your face." I laughed because Alyssa was jealous as hell but that's my fault. I made her this way. I worked at it all the time, so she didn't have to be.

"Chill that shit out girl, ain't nobody checking for her ass. I came up here to eat and to chill with my niggas. Who in my crib, in my bed with my son inside of them?" She blew out a long breath but didn't answer me.

"Open yo' fuckin' mouth when I'm talking to you, Alyssa."

"I am Jermaine, but that doesn't----"

"Ain't no damn buts. That's all it is, period. Now when I leave here, I'll bring you some *Uptown Barbeque.* I can get at my cousin's tomorrow."

"No go ahead I know you want to tell them about the baby. I want you with me tomorrow when I tell my mama and grandma. We can go to Grand Rapids this weekend and tell my daddy." I wasn't in the mood to deal with her mama. Alyssa grandma and pops loved me, and her mama did to she just was overprotective of Alyssa, so I knew she was about to have some shit to say.

"A'ight boo look, I'll drop yo' food off and then head to my cousins. Tomorrow and this weekend I'm all yours."

"You all mine anyway." Her smart ass said making me chuckle.

"Remember that shit when you start trippin'. I love you and our son. I'll see you in a minute."

"Ok, we love you more Jermaine." I hung up looking down at me and her as my wallpaper on my phone. We were about to go from just the two of us to the three of us. I was nervous but anxious as hell too. I was about to go back and eat, but I noticed a black Impala pulled in the parking lot so damn fast. Everything happened so quick after, I couldn't even reach for my heat and warn my niggas at the same time. I did, however, see three niggas with guns point at the window I was standing in.

TAT! TAT! TAT! TAT! TAT!

The bullets were flying, and all I could hear was screaming and my niggas cussing loud as hell. I was able to get to my heat, and so did Spudz and P. We started shooting back but there bullets were coming in fast as fuck.

"MUTHAFUCKAS!" I yelled out still shooting. I pulled my other clip out my back, and that's when I saw Spudz on the floor dead. P looked at me and pulled his other clip out to. He nodded his head at me, and we both went back to shooting. The door to the restaurant opened, and one of the niggas stood there with his gun pointed.

"LOOK OUT!!" Bullets and screams were all I heard. This shit could not be happening right now. Not when I just found out I was about to be a father. I promised Alyssa I would always be good. Naw, shit can't go down like this.

Hazel

(The Present-7 Months Later)

"Mama will you stop being dramatic, please. You act like I'm moving out of the country. It's Detroit, you know where you and I were born and raised." I packed my last bag and zipped it up. My mama was being extra because today I was moving to the city. I don't even think the problem was because I am moving. It's more because my older sister moved last year to Houston, Texas because her career took her in that direction. Goldie was single no children so why not travel and get it out your system.

My parents, Carla and Martin Monroe have two daughters. Goldie Monroe who is twenty-six-years old and instead of being in a doctor's office she needs to be on a runway. Myself, Hazel Monroe who is twenty years old and has a deep passion for cooking. My family used to live in Detroit, but when I was nine, we moved to Grand Rapids, MI. My dad and mom are both surgical dentists and opened up their practice here. Me and my sister grew up not wanting for anything. With our father being white and our mother being black we both have light skin, full lips, hazel eyes and a nice grade of hair. Goldie was shaped just like our mother. Thick with a flat stomach and big booty.

I was more on the slim side, but for some reason, I got the round ass like them. A swimsuit body, my mama, called it. Anyway, we were fortunate and had great parents who have been together since they were thirteen-years-old. No outside children and from what I know there has been no affairs. But get this, they have never been married. My mama just legally changed her last name to Monroe like my father when she was eighteen. Don't ask me why they have it this way because I have no answers for you. All I know is my mama always tells me sometimes a man and woman have an understanding that ain't nobody else's business.

I got my passion for cooking from my mama, and my sister inherited the medical background from the both of them. I graduated from Byron Center High School where all the bougie snobs went to. I'd be lying if I said I didn't have a little bit of the bougie in me. But I can turn it on and off, meaning I know how to adapt to my surroundings. Which is the reason me moving out of our mini mansion and going to the city was not a problem for me. I found out Oakland Community College has one of the best culinary programs, so I was all good. I had a great job as a junior chef at The Chop House which is a five-star restaurant. Me, the manager, and head chef were cool so they assured me that whenever I wanted to come back, I could.

"I'm not being dramatic I just want you to be careful down there. Them damn niggas will have yo' ass gone and then back up here crying. Don't go down there and get caught up."

"I'm not ma so stop worrying. After Khalil shenanigans I'm good on any male correspondence." My mama looked at me like I was lying. I couldn't do anything but laugh because she looked just like myself.

"I birthed you Hazel. All I'm saying is don't go down there and get in no bullshit. I love Alyssa but don't wrap yourself too much in her drama. Oh, and I want pictures of the baby when she delivers."

"Ok, ma. Can I finish packing please?" She kissed my cheek and left out my room. Speak of the devil. As soon as my mama closed the door my phone rung showing Khalil's name.

"What do you want Khalil?" I answered my phone rolling my eyes hard as hell.

"You already know what I want. Come on Hazel I'm tired of this beef." I smacked my lips.

"We are not beefing Kahlil, we are over. So go call Sani and bug her ass."

"You on some other shit. I don't want her and never have. All she been doing since me and you started was tear us apart, and you are letting her. I work with that damn girl, and that's it."

This liar on the phone was my now ex Kahlil. His dad owns the restaurant I was junior chef at. The slut Sani was a waitress there who has been wanting my man's dick in her mouth for a while now. Khalil grew up fortunate like me except he has some streets in him from his brothers. His mom owns a restaurant, and his dad is a divorce lawyer. Kahlil has two older brothers who are in the streets heavy. One lives in Tennessee and the other lives here. Kahili was sexy, light skin, clean cut, tall and a thin beard. I would be lying if I said Kahlil wasn't fine as fuck with some good dick and a sexy voice.

We were together for eight months and broken up for a month. My homegirl who worked with me recorded Sani coming out of Lil's office fixing her shirt. I went nuts and made a scene. I loved this jackass a lot, but you only get one time to play me. My mama didn't raise weak daughters, and our father told us how we should be treated. I cried and was heartbroken but now I'm over him and his bullshit. At least that's what I have to keep reminding my heart and body. My mind was on board, but Lil still had a small hold on my heart and my kitty kat.

"I'm not letting her do shit. You did, Sani owed me no loyalty, but you did Kahlil."

"I'm about to come see you before you leave." See this is what I didn't need. I could be strong as long as he wasn't in my face.

"No, I'm already on my way out." I hurried up and thought of a lie.

"Oh really?"

"Yea I'm putting my last suitcase in my car now." I stepped inside my walk-in closet and grabbed my make-up bag.

"So you just gone lie like that?" I turned around quick as hell when I heard his voice behind me.

"Your mama let me in after I promised I wasn't here to upset you. Your dad threatened me before I made it up the stairs." He looked around my closet.

"This don't look like your car to me." I rolled my eyes again and tried to ignore how good he looked. He had on a white Moschino t-shirt, matching jeans and some Balenciaga gym-shoes. Looking and smelling so good.

"What are you doing here? I'm leaving in a few minutes so whatever you have to say just save it Kahlil." He put his hands in his jeans and leaned against my closet door.

"I want us to fix this relationship. I don't know what the hell your friends told you, but I have never fucked Sani. That day or the present. I'm still about you Hazel even though you can't see that."

"Lil please stop ok. Nobody told me shit. I saw the video of her coming out of your office fixing her shirt. Why do you keep acting stupid?!" I was getting so mad because he has the nerve to look at me like a lost puppy. Fuck that. Kahlil fucked Sani that day, probably before and after. And watch I prove it.

"You know what. Me and you can be saved if you just stop lying. How can you say you want to start over of you won't be honest." I walked up to him with the same expression as his.

"Lil, just be honest with me. I don't want her to have one over me, but if you can promise that it won't happen again, then we can work on us." I turned it up even more and rubbed the side of his face.

"Hazel if we can start over I swear I'll fire that bitch." I nodded my head yes.

"I didn't fuck her Hazel I just played with her titties and let her suck my dick. But that shit is dead. I didn't fuck her until after you broke up with me, but like I said. I'll dead all that shit."

Now had I heard this a month ago. I would have been with the shits and went nuts. But having time away from him, I didn't even need to react. I was just happy to be done with this little boy.

"Kahlil get'cho lying ass out my fucking room and don't ever contact me again." He had the nerve to look at me like he was pissed and hurt.

"So you'll just play me like that Hazel."

"Naw, you played yaself Kahlil. I knew you and that nasty ass Sani were fucking. Not only am I moving out of Grand Rapids. But I am moving on from you. Now, get the fuck out." I pointed towards the door. He sucked on his teeth and did a sarcastic chuckle.

"I'll leave, but just so you know. We're not over Hazel" I put my middle finger in his face. He turned around and walked out my room. Hopefully, he was walking out of my life for good because I would never ever be with Khalil again. Hearing his confession now had my heart and my kitty kat completely immune to him.

***

"Ok, daddy's baby girl. That's the last of your suitcase." My dad closed the trunk to my 2018 Tesla Model S. I got the car for my twenty-first birthday in January.

"Yea that's it." I looked at my mama, and she was crying. Me and my dad just laughed, and I hugged her.

"Mama will you please stop. I am only a two-hour drive in the same state." She pulled away fixing my hair, and I wiped her face.

"You've never not lived at home Hazel. You and Goldie both leaving me in the house with this crazy fool." She joked.

"Yea whatever lady. You won't be saying all of that shit when we walking around the house naked----"

"Ooooook I'm out for real now." I was grossed out and didn't want to think of my old ass parents in that light. I hugged and kissed them some more, got in my car and pulled off. My phone chimed, and I saw it was my dad sending me five hundred dollars on cash app. I just shook my head laughing.

It was only ten o'clock in the morning, so I was making good timing. I had until two p.m. to make it to my destination, and I was so damn excited. I couldn't wait to see the look on my best friends face when she sees me and what I've done. Well, I had a little help from some people. But with the magic of FaceTime, I was able to be included in everything. I couldn't wait to see Alyssa's face.

***

"Hazel!!" I just got out my car in front of Alyssa's mama house, and she came out the side door.

"Don't run girl!" I joked as I ran to her leaving my front door open. I hugged her tight, and we were stuck together for a while.

I missed and loved this girl so much. Me and Alyssa met in the weirdest way. We are only a year apart so one summer when we both were twelve-years-old. My parents made me and Goldie go to this stupid ass girls retreat in Ypsilanti. Remember that bougie side I said I had. Well, it was in full effect for the first two weeks. Alyssa and her little crew enjoyed pulling pranks on me, and because Goldie was older, she was in a different bunk then me. Her fast ass had met a guy the first day, so her concern wasn't about her little sister.

Anyway, me and Alyssa used to go at it and the second week we both got in trouble for fighting. Instead of kicking us out they made us become bunk roommates. Living in the same space, no TV and one radio. You're bound to talk and share a few laughs. By the time camp was over, I had made a best friend. I would see Alyssa every summer and holiday when she came to visit her dad in Grand Rapids. Now, eight years later we are still going strong, and she was about to make me a God mommy.

"Oh my goodness look at your belly." I rubbed it smiling so big. I was so happy for her, and the glow her chocolate skin had was just gorgeous.

"I know girl I'm so ready to evict this baby. He sleeps all day, kicks all night, and I pee so much its crazy." I rubbed her stomach again, and my phone chimed. I saw the text I was looking for and smiled.

"Well let's go miss wobbles. We need to leave now to make our viewing appointment." Alyssa ran in the house to grab her purse and locked the door. I opened my car door and let her in.

"Don't put the seatbelt on to tight over my God baby." I closed the door and got in on the driver's side.

"You know you are a worser baby daddy than Jermaine. I'm not disabled just pregnant." Alyssa joked as I pulled out the parking lot.

"You know that fool didn't even let me go to Cedar Point, and I was only eight weeks then." Me and her laughed while I caught her up on my ending drama with Kahlil.

"I told you from day one that I didn't like Khalil. He is fine as hell and has money, but he wasn't shit. He gave me a nasty feeling when you showed me his pictures. Like slick but sneaky in the same breath. And that bitch Sani got some shits coming her way whenever I see her."

"Well just make sure my God baby is out your belly before you deliver the shits to bitches. Maine would never forgive me." The rest of the ride we talked and enjoyed each other's company. It was so good to be back with Alyssa again, and this time it was permeant.

"Um Haz why the hell are we in Warren? Since when are you an east side bitch?"

"I know and trust me I'm not. But I took the virtual tour online and this place is spacious, close to the malls and the rent was too good to pass up." I pulled in the complex of Parkview Towers, and we both got out after I parked.

"So do you think the baby will be a Memorial Day baby?" Alyssa smiled and rubbed her stomach over her long maxi dress.

"Please don't say that because that means I'll be three days past my due date." We both giggled as we got close to the clubhouse.

"I think the leasing office is around front Haz."

"I know, but the landlord told me to meet her in the clubhouse." I was so anxious as I opened the door stepped in first and then her behind me.

"SURPRISE!!" I stood in front of Alyssa and shouted with the rest of the room. Her face was priceless, and I was so happy I snapped the perfect picture.

I saw her mama was recording with her camera. I hugged my friend tight, and she kept asking me 'how' over and over in my ear. The room looked exactly how I knew she dreamed it to be. There were clear and yellow balloons all over the floor. Inside the clear ones were yellow and blue baby footprints and pacifiers. The tables had white linen cloths over them. There were white wooden chairs with yellow and blue ribbons tied on the back of them. The long table had chocolate cupcake tiers and balloons tied around the table.

Alyssa always wanted satin drapes covering the walls. I was able to find some beautiful baby blue and white drapes to cover the walls with yellow streaks across them. The room was gorgeous, and the food table looked amazing with every kind of pasta dish you can think of. Everyone wore baby blue and white like I requested.

"Is this why you asked me to wear a yellow maxi dress?" She asked through her tears.

"Yes ma'am it is. Listen before the crowd gathers I want you to have a good time. And girl you know I ain't no east side bitch." We giggled, and I hugged her again before she was stolen from me by her other baby daddy.

Alyssa

Getting one last look at all the gifts my son got at my baby shower. I smiled big and closed the door. I didn't have to buy anything, and I do mean anything unless I wanted to. Everything from bathtubs, toys, a bouncer, a walker. So many blankets, baby socks, baby wipes, diapers. My baby boy had more clothes than me already. I had two big baskets of *Johnson & Johnson* products. My mama and daddy got him a crib, car seat and a stroller. I feel so overwhelmed with love, and so does my baby boy. I stood in front of my mirror and got a good look at myself. I couldn't believe in just a few weeks I was going to be a mother. This little person was coming out my stomach and changing my life for the better. I smiled looking down and rubbing my stomach. Tears fell from my eyes.

"You ok?" I looked up in the doorway and saw Hazel standing there with a look of concern.

"I can't believe Jermaine will never meet his son. I'll never get to see him hold him or smile at him." I couldn't stop myself from breaking down.

Hazel closed the door and let me break down in her arms. I was crying so hard, something I haven't done since that day seven months ago. The day that changed my life in the worst way. That phone call I got from Mac telling me the worst possible thing. My other best friend, my man, my happiness when all else didn't work was gone. Him, Spudz and P were shot dead in Coney Island. When Mac said those words I couldn't and didn't process it. It was like my mind just couldn't believe. I remember hanging up on him and going back to what I was doing. Sitting on Jermaine bed watching TV waiting for him to come bring me something to eat.

I did that for about an hour when I heard the front door open. I jumped up smiling so big because I already knew who it was. It was Jermaine with my food laughing and telling me Mac plays too much. When I saw it was his dad and my mama I lost all feeling in my legs. I cried and screamed so hard that I passed out and had to go to the hospital. I kept waking up screaming Jermaine's name. I didn't want to eat or drink anything. The baby was at risk, and I had to stay in the hospital for a few days. I just knew the baby wasn't going to make it because I couldn't eat. I was living in a daze for weeks.

By the grace of God, my child made it, and I slowly started eating again. My heart was and still is broken and every day I wake up I just knew I was having a nightmare. Things would go back to normal. Me and Jermaine would be waiting for the birth of our baby. I would have moved in with him, and we would be happy. I never stepped foot back in Jermaine's house again. I asked my mama to bring me all of him and I's pictures, two of his hoodies and a bottle of his favorite *Perry Ellis Red* cologne. That's all I wanted and didn't care about anything else.

At Jermaine's funeral, I was so numb, quiet and I wouldn't go in until they closed the casket. I didn't want to remember my boo in any other way but the memories I have. Once I turned five months pregnant, I went to my ultra-sound appointment alone and found out I was having a boy. From then on, I lived for him. I was so happy because Jermaine said I was having a boy the day I told him I was pregnant. My heart hurts every day for Jermaine. But I will make sure our son knows him and knows how much his dad loved and wanted him.

"I miss him so much Hazel even when I try not to." Hazel rubbed my back and wiped my face.

"You'll always miss him Alyssa, and that's fine. It's ok to still love him and grieve." I sniffed and grabbed a tissue on the nightstand.

"Thank you so much for everything Hazel. You moved your life here for me, and I am so grateful. I don't know how I would have gotten through these months without you." I looked around my bedroom at my mama's house.

"I am so ready for us to go house shopping and move." Me and her laughed. Hazel and I were going to rent a house and move together. We both agreed to stay in the city, and I couldn't wait.

"Me neither girl. You know I love your mama, but she is a tad bit overprotective. I barely saw you at the baby shower because she made you sit under her the whole time." Hazel was right. My mama was extra and controlling at that.

"I know and believe me I was so annoyed. But let's not let that distract us from the fact that you threw me the most fabulous baby shower ever. Thank you again best friend, I loved every part of it." She hugged me again.

"So I did notice something else," I smirked at her.

"What?"

"I noticed Mac kept looking at you." A look of dismayed came on her face.

"Who the hell is Mac and when was he looking at me?" That was when I remembered she never met Mac or Sada before. Hazel always was in Grand Rapids and never in the city. I saw her every summer and holidays. She met Jermaine a few times, but it was when we visited my dad on Christmas. My mama took over the baby shower as host, so I didn't get to formally introduce my best friend.

"He's Jermaine's older cousin. Sada is Mac's younger brother. Don't even worry about it y'all will meet eventually. But he was staring at you, and I mean a gawk type of stare." I was smiling big.

"Get under some new dick to get over some old." Hazel rolled her eyes.

"Girl Bye. I'm not fucking with no men unless it's this widdle cutie when he gets here." She bent down smiling talking in a baby voice.

"Yea ok we'll see once Mac stakes his claim." She looked up at me and turned her nose up.

"You're delusional."

"Alyssa it's time to lay back and elevate your feet. Hazel, it's time to let her rest." I looked at my mama like she was crazy.

"Mama I'm fine, and Hazel is not bothering me. We're about to watch some movies and eat." My mama had the nerve to put her hands on her hips with an attitude.

"You don't ever want to listen to me. I tell you this though when my grandson gets here I'm not dealing with two fussy people." She turned and walked out my room closing the door.

"Alyssa I know damn well you told your mama that you were moving out?"

"I'm going to Hazel I promise." She got up and shook her head.

"Girl you have got to stop acting like a baby. We all know Hattie loves the hell out of you, but you're an adult boo. Trust me, she will be annoyed at first, but she'll accept it."

"I know and your right. I promise I will tell her and it would be so dope if you would be there with me." I poked my bottom lip out, and Hazel laughed.

"You look ugly." I gave her the middle finger.

"But you know I got'cho back." I hugged her, and we started our movie night.

***

"Why the fuck you sittin' outside in the heat?" My other pain in the ass walked on my mama's porch talking shit. It was a new day, hot as hell in Detroit and I wanted to go to the mall and get me some more maxi dresses. I was shopping for my after-birth body, not this wally the whale figure I was rocking.

"You act like I'm sitting in the sun sizzling. You can't even speak first without being a smart ass?" I wobbled off my porch with the help of Sada's mean butt.

"It don't matter. It's too hot to be sitting out here. Bring yo' fat as on." I laughed and hit him in his back.

"I swear I can't stand you." He chuckled and opened the door for me. Sada has shocked the hell out of me these past few months.

I never had any beef with Jermaine's two cousins. We just never really had a friendship outside of us loving Jermaine. Anytime I was around Mac or Sada we would do small talk, and I'd let them have their time with their cousin. When Jermaine died, I wasn't the only one who took it bad. Mac was a complete loose cannon. Any wrong look, bass in your voice or even if you made a mistake and bumped him. He was flying off. You were either going to get beat the fuck up. Or he was going to do worse. Sada was no different but what surprised me was how protective he came over me.

Mac always drops money or food off to me, but Sada turned it up a notch and came to doctor's appointments with me. He would take me to run any errands, any late night or early morning cravings I had he would handle. I wasn't comfortable with it at first because I felt like I was taking advantage or going to become annoying to him. But he shut that shit down and told me if I called someone else other than him or Mac, we would have a problem. I believe taking care of me was their way of showing love to Jermaine.

"So what all you getting' at the mall?"

"Just some maxi dresses and some sandals. One of my baby shower gifts was a gift card to Forever 21." He looked over at me and shook his head.

"Keep that shit for another day, I got'chu."

"Sada you don't have to do that. Really you and Mac do enough alre---" As I was talking this rude ass nigga turned the radio up loud as hell on me. I punched him in his arm, and he started laughing. Such a jackass.

We arrived at Fairlane mall, and I was so happy we found a parking space close to Macy's entrance. I looked around at all the cars, and I noticed the mall was going to have a small crowd. I didn't care I just hated to see people I knew because I always got that sympathetic look or that feeling sorry for me speech. I knew people meant well but the one thing I noticed when Jermaine died. A lot of fake muthafuckas came out of nowhere claiming they had love for him. How they was his friend, and they always talked. Straight bullshit.

People wait until a person gets in the ground to show them some love. Like Jermaine's mama. Oh, that bitch fell out all on the casket, crying and screaming. Cursing God and asking why him and not her. I was so mad because I felt like where was this love when he was alive? She hasn't even checked on me or her grandchild. I wanna see how she will act when I give birth. Malcom has been amazing. He was so hurt over losing his son, and he always told me he couldn't wait until his grandson gets here.

"Do you have any stores you need to go in?" I looked up at Sada and asked him. We were leaving Express and walking to the elevator. Forever 21 was on the third floor, and his ass wasn't about to let me take the stairs.

"Yea I'mma shoot by Jimmy Jazz since it's next to your store." We walked on the elevator, and like always he was a gentleman and let me get on first. Sada dreads had gotten longer, he had them all down a black bandana tied around them. He had on a green and black Jordan tracksuit with the jacket open and no shirt under it. His two long chains completed his fresh look along with his green Retro 12's on.

"Ok, I'll just call your phone when I'm ready." He turned his nose up when I said that.

"Get in the damn store fatty. I'm going wherever you go."

"Stop calling me fat Sada," I whined, and he just laughed.

"You a cute fat though so it's all good." I nudged him with my elbow and blushed.

"How the hell can you find anything in this store? It's to damn big." I chuckled at him.

"You ain't never been in here?"

"Why would I be in here? I ain't no fag." I cracked up and looked around hoping nobody heard him and got offended.

"I know that Sada. I just thought one of your little chicks would have dragged you in here."

"Fuck no. I don't take bitches shopping. They shop for deez nuts, and that's it." I fell out laughing while picking out some dresses.

"I swear you need some help." We were laughing, and I saw two girls staring at us out the corner of my eye. I pretended like I was looking at some clothes in their direction and I was able to get a good look at them. I didn't recognize them at all, but clearly, they knew me. I promise if these were some bitches that used to fuck with Jermaine and they were on some bullshit I was about to flip.

"You good?" Sada asked me, and I looked at him, but he looked in the direction where I was looking at.

"You looking at them hoes?"

"You know them?" I asked, and he raised his eyebrow.

"I know the back of their throat. Come on." He pulled my arm, and we started to walk towards the two girls.

"Tha fuck y'all lookin' in our direction so hard for?" The brown skin one with the braids rolled her eyes and flipped them.

"I'm confused on how you have a pregnant girlfriend but we both was sucking yo' dick last night at Keg's party." I was so disgusted mainly because these hoes faces were so busted. The only thing nice on them was their bodies.

"I don't owe you hoes shit especially an explanation. But check it, stop staring at this one right here. Either shop or get the fuck on." The two girls looked at me and then walked off mad as hell.

"Sada you look too good to be messing with hoes who look like that." I turned my nose up and walked towards the check-out counter with him following me.

"Good head don't have a face fatty. As long as it was born with a pussy and a nice body it's all good." I just laughed and shook my head.

"Why the hell you got these two small dresses in ya hand. You know damn well you can't fit these." I smacked my lips and he, of course, was laughing.

"These are for after I have the baby jackass of spades."

"How you gon' be fat and rude. You gotta pick a struggle." I couldn't even hold my laugh in because this fool was crazy.

"You gon' make my water break," I said between laughing so damn hard. My total came up to seventy dollars, and Sada paid it without a problem. We went to Jimmy Jazz. He got him some stuff and even let me get two FILA bodysuits. We went to the food court and got our grub on. I wanted some Panda Express and a six-inch meatball sub from Subway. After eating I felt so good. We stopped at Payless so I could get some sandals and Sada went to the jewelry store to get his battery changed in his Movado Bold watch.

"Thanks so much for today Sada. You can just sit the bags over there." I pointed to my tall bean bag chair. We were done shopping, and now he was bringing my bags in my mama house. I was glad she was in the basement because I didn't feel like dealing with her or her smart mouth. She didn't care for the way Mac or Sada had been helping me. Well not so much Mac more of Sada.

"No problem ma you know I got'chu. You good on food and money right." I smirked and looked at him.

"Yes, Sada, between you and Mac I promise I'm good. The both of you do more than enough. I'm just ready to get this little nigga out of me and get my body back to normal." We both chuckled, and he looked around my bedroom.

"This room is to damn girly for a boy."

"Me and the baby will not be staying in this room. We won't even be in this house." He looked at me dismayed.

"Word? How Pattie feel about that shit? I know she pulled that ashy ass wig off when you told her." Now I love my mama, but I hated her wigs because they were synthetic and just bad. I couldn't stop myself from laughing.

"You betta stop talking about my mama punk." I pushed his arm, and just like me, he was laughing.

"I haven't told her yet but me, and Hazel will soon."

"Who is Hazel?" I keep forgetting they didn't meet yet.

"She's my best friend from Grand Rapids. She just moved up here for good. That's who planned my baby shower. Right now she's on her interview for a job. It was so much going on at the baby shower you didn't get a chance to see her. Mac did though, he kept being a creep and watching her." He went to my tall dresser and started messing with my perfume bottles.

"That nigga weird. Well anyway, I'm bout to bounce on outta here." He turned around and walked up on me.

"Call me if you need me a'ight? Don't act like you bothering me because you're not." I nodded my head in agreement. He hugged me and kissed the top of my head. For the first time, I inhaled his cologne. He pulled away and smirked at me.

"Later fat ass."

"You're such a punk." I said as he walked out my room laughing. I started putting my clothes away and the shoes in my closet.

"You know that boy has a motive." I turned around and saw my mama standing in the doorway.

"What are you talking about ma?" I rolled my eyes and let out a long sigh. I just wasn't in the mood for this shit.

"You know what I'm talking about and you need to stop. Do you know how crazy you will look messing with your dead baby daddy's cousin?" I got mad as hell when she said that.

"Mama nothing is going on between me and Sada. Him and Mac loved Jermaine and helping me is them respecting him. Please just chill out." She shook her head at me.

"Ok, I'll stop but just don't be a fool. Now, lay down and elevate them damn feet. I made a healthy dinner for you later and no movie night with you and Hazel. You need to get a full eight hours of sleep." She left out, and I just went back to putting up my clothes.

I loved my mama , but her mouth was so annoying. Nothing was happening between me and Sada. We have never and will never look at each other like that. Hazel called me and asked if I wanted something from Krispy Kreme Donuts before she comes back here. I told her to get me some jelly filled and chocolate cream filled donuts. I put my pajamas on and put my straight bundles in a ponytail.

Climbing in bed, I propped my feet up, turned my TV on and grabbed my phone, so I can scroll Facebook. I saw a funny ass meme on there saying 'how you can tell if a nigga ain't shit.' Under the caption, it had the word 'light skin' written out. I laughed and shared it with the caption 'Facts.' A few minutes later my cell phone alerted me that I had a text message. Actually it was a picture message from Sada. This fool sent me a screenshot of the meme I shared.

Sada: *That's how you feel Alyssa?*

I laughed and texted back.

Me: Get off my page homie. But naw you know that's not how I feel. It's just funny as hell.

Sada: Yea a'ight. I'ma share a fat bitches ain't shit meme and see how you like it.

Once again I was cracking up at his dumb ass. Before I knew it, we had been texting for about thirty minutes when Hazel came back. I told Sada I would talk to him later and he said ok. Me and Hazel hung out, and she told me about her job interview. She also told me that she thinks she found a good house on six-mile. I was excited and couldn't wait to see it. Every so often while me and Hazel talked Sada face kept popping in my head. I kept finding myself laughing at his stupid ass calling me fat ass or fatty. Swear he is such a jackass.

Mac

I don't know what was up with Michigan this summer. We had some old southern type of heat this summer. That crack uh egg on a rock and watch it fry type of shit. I wasn't in the mood to be in this sun, but duties call. Sada called me and told me some shit went down with two of our guys. I was on my way to one of our spots we would meet up at. Me and Sada rented random homes under aliases throughout the hood.

Spots we could change clothes at and lay low in. We made sure to never keep personal shit in them and no bitches allowed. The heat plus my already high annoyance wasn't a good mix. Shit changed when Maine died. I started to see if never before that these streets gave no fucks about anybody. No matter how you stay loyal to the hood or call yourself moving smart. I didn't move the way Maine did.

If it wasn't him or my brother, I didn't hang with muthafuckas. I wasn't the smile in ya face type nor was I the hang with big crowds' kind of nigga. I tried to stay on top of all beef me, Sada or Maine had. I blamed myself for his death every day. I became just as heartless as these streets. If you even said me or Sada name in the wrong tone it was lights out for dat ass. Any gossip or rumors that a muthafucka said shit or even thought shit about me or mine. I was coming for you. My cousin was gone and that shit fucked with me.

Our last time together we got into a fight. That's how me and him always did even when we were kids. I still have my old phone from the last text we sent. No doubt in my mind it was them Schoolcraft niggas we been beefing with who did that shit. I just knew it was but most importantly they asses disappeared. I knew they were laying low and the minute I catch wind, it was lights fucking out. I missed my cousin and that shit hurt not having him, but life goes on. My job now was to make sure me and my brother weren't caught up like Maine.

Me and Sada's money flow hadn't slowed down. If anything, it picked up because I just didn't give a fuck anymore. Pay me, and I'll deliver the bodies. We still had yet to be caught, and fear started to be on these niggas faces when they saw us now. Money was different in a good way. I still stayed in the hood and wasn't shit chasing me out of it. My mama and grandma were still good, and I had no plans on slowing down. I was almost to the spot when my phone rung. I looked at it and saw it was Quinn.

"Yo."

"Am I seeing you soon?" I could tell already she was about to irk my damn nerves.

"Why you asking dumb shit Quinn. You know I'm picking you up Thursday for your doctor's appointment." Fuck yea, I slipped in her pussy one night on some drunk horny shit and got her ass pregnant. She was six-months pregnant with a boy, my boy let her tell it. I ain't no heartless nigga especially if I fucked you raw. My mama wanted no parts until the baby was born and I had a DNA test done. I already knew Quinn was fucking other niggas just like I fuck other bitches. But if this child was mines, I was stepping up and taking care of him. Me and her, however, we were done. I didn't fuck or touch her, but I did respect her. I made sure she didn't want for nothing, and I kept all her bills paid. She wanted more, and that's where our problem kicked in.

"Since my appointment is in the morning you should just let me stay the night Mac." See what I mean? She was always trying to pull this shit.

"Naw, that's not a good idea. I'll be on time don't even trip. I gotta go though, I just pulled up to my stop."

"Your stop? You mean at a bitch house? I hope she knows I'm pregnant and we don't do that step parent shit over here." I looked at the phone and turned my nose up.

"You always spreadin' that hot ass breath. I'll be there Thursday at 10." I hung up not even giving her a chance to say shit.

Quinn knew not to come my way with too much drama. My respect was everything no matter who you were. She felt because she could possibly be my baby mama that I was soft for her. Naw, if you wasn't my mama or grandma, I wasn't soft for shit. She would cry, pout and give me all them sad faces. I never was and never will be moved buy that bullshit. I still fucked with bitches and that's just how it was.

That's why Quinn made so much noise on social media about being pregnant by me. From the time she found out all the way until now, she been on social media going crazy. Quinn was trying to mark her territory, but all she was doing was looking stupid. Any bitch I wanted to smash I did, and they'd go running back to her with receipts telling her. I didn't care because Quinn shouldn't be trying to live a lie for the Gram. A chunk of me hopes this baby isn't mine so I could be rid of her for good.

"So what happened?" I stood in front of Black and Anthony with my arms folded waiting for them to talk. Sada was already there, and we had two guys on the porch who watches our spot.

"We went to---" I cut Anthony of mid-sentence.

"Were you driving?" I asked him.

"Naw he---"

"Then shut the fuck up." I looked at Black.

"Now, what happened." Black cleared his throat and started talking.

"I went and did the drop like you said in Northville. We checked the duffle bags and made sure the money was in there. Shit was good, so we loaded up and left. On our way to the city, we were pulled over. Police searched the car because they saw two black men. When they unzipped both duffle bags full of money, they laughed. Me and Anthony didn't say a word, Mac. On God, we didn't. So, they said they'd let us go if we give them a bag. If not, they were going to take us in. We would be looking at a shit load of questions and eyes would start watching us. I thought of our operation, so I told them to take the bag." I stood still as hell and looked at him and Anthony the entire time Black was talking. Arms still folded and face stern I said.

"Clip, go grab that tracker from under Black's car?" When I said that Black looked shocked.

"Damn nigga, you put a tracker on my shit? Like I'm some bitch you fuckin'?" I looked at him and chuckled.

"Naw, I put a tracker on your car because you had my green bitch in ya car and I like to make sure she's good." Clip came back in with the tracking device and he attached the end to his phone. I gave him a while to look at it while I kept my eyes on Black and Anthony. Something was fishy as fuck, and little do these two idiots know. I already knew what was up.

"Black that big booty bitch you sprung over name is Na'tisa that lives on Puritan right?"

"Yea, why what's up?" I ignored him when Clip walked up to me showing me his phone and whispered in my ear. Chuckling and shaking my head I put my attention back on Black and Anthony.

"Black you didn't go do the drop in Grand Rapids. Anthony did. And I know I'm right because Na'tisa drains my balls whenever I call. At her job, in my car, at her mama house. The only time she don't come through is when you're with her. So, my question is, why would you think I wouldn't find out and why would you go against my instructions." I waited for him to answer.

"Damn G you been fucking my bitch?" When he said that Sada laughed, and so did I.

"I was just trying to give my little brother some responsibilities. I figured if he did it right then maybe you'd give him a bigger position."

"Nigga shut'cho lying ass up. You didn't want to climb out some pussy, and now I'm short ten-grand." I looked at Anthony and pointed to Sada.

"This my baby brother. Love the nigga like he came from my nuts. But I'm so glad he ain't a fuck up like you. Police never stopped you. You did however go to the race track in Northville. Just like you lost two-thousand gambling at Greektown last week. And in February you lost five-thousand betting on the Superbowl." Anthony didn't say shit, but Black dropped his head.

"You got a problem, my nigga," I pulled my pistol out and pointed the handle at Black.

"Shoot him in the head." When I said that Black eyes bucked. He looked from me and then to Sada. Laughing he said.

"Stop playing man. You know I can't do that."

"DO IT LOOK LIKE I'M FUCKING PLAYING!" I stood there now heated and ready to get out this hot ass house.

"This lil nigga cost me money then he lied about it! Shoot his ass so I can go get my dick sucked by yo' bitch and have her feed me!"

"C'mon Mac please man, this my baby brother."

"Mac I swear I had a sure bet. I thought I could double the money on the horse I picked. I would never steal from you." Anthony looked at me and confessed. He was scared as hell, but I wasn't fazed.

"Shut the fuck up lil nigga. Rather you doubled my money or not. I still would fuck you up."

"It wasn't on him man. You asked me to do the drop and pick-up. He's just a kid." I looked at Sada, and he shrugged his shoulders. Our three men behind us were looking to see what I was going to do next.

"You right. He's just a kid who fucked up. I told you to do something and had you climbed out that Puritan hoe then we wouldn't be here." I took the gun from Black and gave it to Anthony.

"Shoot him." I tilted my head at Black and looked back at Anthony who was shaking.

"It's either him or you." Anthony pointed the gun at Black who stood there like he knew this was coming.

POW!

POW!

"Damn Mac you didn't even give Black body a chance to hit the floor," Sada said when Anthony body dropped the same time as his brother. He pulled the trigger, and so did I.

"These niggas was getting on my nerves." I put my gun up, and my niggas started getting rid of the bodies.

"Malcolm called today again. Said he wants to talk to both of us." Me and Sada walked out the house and the heat. Our uncle Malcolm had been trying to get me and Sada to do business with him for a few months now. If you wanna be dead on it's been before Maine was killed. I had love for my uncle and all, but I wasn't about to do business with him.

"That nigga act worse than my baby mama. Maine didn't want to do business with him, so neither are we." Sada nodded his head.

"I agree. But I still wanna meet with him to see what the fuck he keep pressin' for. He consistent for a reason and I wanna know."

"Yea I agree. You know grandma asked about you yesterday. She said she was fucking you up because she ain't seen you in two days."

"Aw shit. I gotta go see her now before she comes to me. You got Alyssa today?" I dabbed him up.

"Fa sho I got'chu bro." He hopped in his whip, and I got in mine.

I wasn't in the mood to deal with Alyssa mama today. Her pops was mad cool, but Hattie was a different story. She's never been rude with me because like I say, I don't play that shit. But she blunt as hell and overprotective of Alyssa. Me and Sada promised each other that we would always be there for her and the baby. We said she would never need or want for anything and we would make sure lil nigga know his uncles love him. Maine was gone because of me, so the least I can do is be there for his son.

I had yet to shed a tear over my cousin, but I did hurt for him. He'd never get to meet his son and be there for him. He loved Alyssa, and I know he loved their unborn, so it was only right to be there. I got to Alyssa mama's house and parked in front of it. It was so damn hot I was getting some of that good ass lemonade Alyssa be making. Walking up to the front door, I opened the screen and knocked. It took three knocks before the door opened.

"Can I help you?" Damn. Angel face from Alyssa's baby shower was standing at the door. I peeped her that day and was stuck stealing glances at her the entire shower. This bitch was so damn fine but not in an overly sexy way. She was a redbone slim type. Not even usually what I go for. I fucks with thick women or an occasional BBW when I want the extra fluff. But this girl was slim and had a round ass booty. Didn't even know skinny bitches could have that. Her face, gone and call a nigga corny but her face was that of an angel. Almond shaped eyes, clear skin, and some pouty ass lips. Ma was bad but looking at her and how she was dressed at the shower and even now. I could tell she was the saditty bougie type. The kind who had a smart-ass mouth and thought little of people who don't meet their standards. Also, the kind that I will slap the shit out of if need be. Still, though, angel face was fucking gorgeous.

"Yea I'm here to see Alyssa." She gave me that 'who the fuck are you look.'

"And you are?"

"Mac, her baby daddy cousin." She put her hand on the back of her hips.

"Is that supposed to mean something to me?" See this shit right here I was not about. But I kept my cool and chuckled.

"It don't gotta mean shit to you, but it means a lot to her. So, for the last time is she here?" When this rude sadity attempted to close the door. That's when I was done being calm. I stopped the door with my arm and pushed that muthafucka open hard as hell almost slinging her little ass. I helped myself in and closed the door.

"What the fuck nigga! GET OUT!" She yelled, and I just shook my head and made my way to the kitchen. I opened the fridge and grabbed the picture of lemonade. Helping myself to a glass, I poured me some and downed it in a second. I caught my breath and poured me another one.

"You know I could call the police on you?" With the glass to my lips I looked at her. She had on some spandex type of shorts and a little shirt that was tight and had her stomach showing. Mean ass had to be about 5'5 130lbs. But her thighs were a little meaty, that ass was round, and I bet soft.

"You ain't about to do shit." I put the glass down and turned completely towards her. She tried her best to keep an angry face as she picked her phone up.

"You don't know that. Yo' ass comes barging in like you pay the mortgage here." I just laughed and licked my lips.

"Look at'chu. You so busy lookin' at how fine a nigga is to even dial." Her cheeks flushed when I said that. It was true though. Her eyes went from my face, lips then to my arms, chest and my dick and finally my shoes. Saditty ass. Even on my bum day, I grabbed bitches attention. I was fresh today though in some black and mustard colored Jordan's Retro 13's. I had on some faded True Religion jean shorts on with a black and gold Kobe Bryant Lakers jersey. My tattooed covered toned arms were out. I bet if I go put my finger in her mouth, she'd be drooling.

"A-Ain't nobody looking at you and you bet not rape me." I laughed hard as fuck when she said that stupid.

"I'mma a lot of shit but a rapist will never be one of them." I put the glass in the sink and leaned against the counter looking at her.

"I told you my name, what's yours?" She put her phone down and folded her arm across her chest, and the other one held her elbow.

"Hazel. Hazel Monroe." I nodded my head, and she went back to checking me out. I laughed on the inside because not only did angel face want me. But just that quick that hot ass attitude was gone. Yea, she was used to fucking with lame ass soft niggas.

"Nice to meet you, Hazel. So how do you know Alyssa?"

"I met her a long time ago at a girls summer camp. I'm from Grand Rapids, and I didn't come to the city until now." I nodded, and she cocked her head to the side.

"You said Maine was your cousin."

"Yea, why?" She gave me a soft expression. Her hair was jet black and stopped at her shoulders. I bet all of it was real too.

"I'm sorry for your loss. I didn't see you at the funeral, but then again it was so packed---

"I didn't go. Don't do funerals." I didn't mean to cut her off, but I didn't like talking about this.

"So how long are you in the city for?" Her stare was strong on a brotha, and I wanted to wave my hand to snap her out of it.

"Oh um, I'm here for good. Me and Alyssa are going to rent a house and live together. I figured her, and my God baby need me more than ever." I was impressed as hell.

"Damn ma. That's what's up?" She squinted her arms and put her hands on the back of her hips.

"Why do you say it like that? Like I'm not capable of doing something selfless."

"Because you not that type. I bet Alyssa ya only 'hood friend'." I struck a nerve because she popped off from there.

"Fuck you, ok. Fuck you. For you to stand there, a judge me like you know me or even have the privilege to know me is disgusting." I had to laugh while she flapped them dick suckers because she was big mad. Ma was rolling that neck and turning her nose up.

"And I bet when Alyssa told you her baby daddy was dead you were more hurt for her than shocked." My nose flared then, and in a low tone, she said.

"That's not true."

"You too fine to be a liar. Look---" I pulled out a knot and counted some hundreds off.

"Tell Alyssa she knows she can call me or Sada if she needs anything." I put the money on the kitchen counter and walked passed her.

"Fuck outta my way." I made sure to look her ass dead in her eyes. She had mixed emotions I could tell. Ma didn't know if she wanted to cry, go off on me or run and hide in shame. I didn't give a fuck either way. Ma was just something to look at. I wouldn't even throw this dick her way. Saditty ass.

I made it outside to my car and pulled off. I didn't have to work tomorrow morning, so I had the floor free. I would have chilled at Alyssa's crib getting to know Hazel but everything I needed to know I did. I normally can fuck with any type of bitch. Hood-rats, hoes, the quiet type, the nerd and my favorite, the innocent girl.

But stuck-up and bougie wasn't my favorite. Now don't get shit twisted, a nigga had game without even trying. But my low tolerance for disrespect and attitude was set up for me not to fuck with that type. I'd smack a bitch or do like I did to Hazel. Read her ass and fuck her whole head up. As I drove home my phone went off.

Puritan Pussy: Can I get some of you right now daddy?

That was Na'tisa hoe ass begging for this dick. Little did she know I just clipped her meal ticket. Black sprung ass was paying all this bitch bills and taking care of her three kids. I started fucking with her almost two weeks ago. One night everybody decided to hang at Adam Butzel parking lot. For those who not from my city. Butzels is a big ass recreation center that has all kinds activities for kids to do all day. It banged in the summer because parents would drop their kids off and be gone all day. It was some of everything to do from swimming, a gym with basketball rims, arts and craft shit, game rooms and a big ass park behind the building.

When the building is closed the park, and the lot was free for the public. Niggas would park their cars, play loud music, drink, talk shit. Hoes would be clicked up watching for the next dick they wanted to fuck. It was like Belle Isle before the punk ass rules were reinforced. I was with my brother and our crew having a nice time. We had our cars parked, music blasting, drinks in the cup and weed going around. Every now and then I would show my face in a crowd and have some fun. Anyway, Na'tisa was there looking good as hell with these other two bitches. Sada fucked one in his car, and my nigga Clip took the other one home.

Na'tisa was in my ear talking shit and rubbing that big ass booty on my dick. Bitch was so fucking thick, and that was a nigga weakness. I got a room that night and fucked that bitch silly. A few days later I saw her out with Black. I was like 'damn I hit ol' dudes bitch'. But I didn't give a fuck and when she saw I was his boy. Neither did she. Her ass always wanted the dick unless she had to play nice to Black ugly ass, so he could pay her bills. She knew I wasn't the nigga to do that, so she made sure she did her thang.

＊

I ain't in the process of fucking my homie's girl. But if you tryna lock down a hoe, then you should expect this. The only bitches who were off limits was one that my brother was feeling. Other than that, keep ya' bitch from around me because even if I don't check for her. Believe me, her ass will check for me. I guess I took to long to respond because Na'tisa sent a video of her playing with that wet pussy. My dick took noticed, and I opened my glove compartment grabbing three Magnum condoms. I came up on Wyoming from the freeway and headed her way.

Me: Be there in ten.

"You lookin' at my dick like its gone suck itself." I sat on Na'tisa leather recliner with my hard eleven-inch out. Na'tisa opened her robe, and she had on my favorite, nothing. Her hips were wide, stomach had a little meat on it but still sexy. That pussy had a thin strip of hair going down the middle. Them big ass titties and brown nipples looked good on her caramel skin. She dropped to her knees while licking her lips and put my dick in her mouth. This bitch was always nasty when it came to sucking my dick. Her mouth stayed wet, and that spit would drip all down on my balls. I put her weave in a ponytail in my hand and fucked her face.

"Yea bitch. Just like that." She opened her mouth wide while I hit the back of that throat. Them gagging sounds and them eyes started to water letting me know I was fucking that throat right.

"Ughhh!" I came so good in her mouth. I still had a hold on her hair as I started fucking her throat nice and slow now. Na'tisa cleaned me up and then cleaned her face up. When she came back, I pulled a condom out my jean shorts. This bitch started smiling big as hell.

"Put it on." My deep low voice made her nipples get hard. On her knees again she sucked me up a little more then put the condom on. Straddling my lap, she eased that pussy on my dick. Natisa didn't have the tightest pussy, but it was decent. This bitch was so hooked on my dick she threw her head back and paused a little. I could see her grin as she started grinding slowly. I took them titties in my mouth while squeezing that big ass booty.

"Oh my God Mac. You have the best dick everrrr. Sssss mm." I bit my bottom lip and when her head went in my neck. I closed my eyes, and Hazel's face popped in my head. I don't know why but it did. That angel face, them pouty ass lips, long hair and that clear ass skin. I squeezed Na'tisa ass harder and imagined it was Hazel's ass. Na'tisa came twice, and now she was picking up speed. She got in a squat position while my dick was still in her and started bouncing up and down. I had put both my hands behind my head and watched her do her thing. Her big ass titties were going, and she was cummin' like crazy on my dick.

"Ooooo shit daddy! Ooo shit. Shit. Shit!!" I bit down on my bottom lip and squeezed one of her titties as I came for the first time and her for the sixth.

"And you see why I crave this dick." She came back and cleaned me up. I snatched the condom off myself and tied it up. I didn't need another Quinn on my hands, so I disposed of my own shit. Getting dressed Na'tisa had her short robe on and her phone in her hand.

"I keep calling this fat nigga and he not answering." She smacked her lips with an attitude. I knew she was talking about Black ass. I just chuckled and put my shoes on. Truthfully, I could go more rounds. But I never met a bitch that after the first time fucking over and over. I wanted to go rounds with after. I got bored easily, so one nut was good. I went to Na'tisa and kissed her forehead.

"I'm out." I jogged down her porch and hopped in my car. I didn't smell food in her house, so I knew she didn't cook. My mama was out of town with her friends so tonight I was the chef. I'll probably make a steak, mash potatoes, and some string beans. That shit gone slap after I smoke and shower.

Sada

BOOM!

"What the fuck!!" One of the niggas yelled when me, Mac and Clip kicked the door down to this crib on Dexter. They had three guys on the porch I guess they was supposed to be the watch crew. With our silencers on and the block being deserted with no street lights. We were able to sneak up on them and put two to the dome. We knew it was five niggas in the house so when Mac kicked the door down. We had the bodies in front of us as shields. They filled their own men bodies up with led, and we put holes between their eyes. I popped two, and so did Clip. One was left, and Mac walked up to him.

"Don't do this shit Mac man. Whatever they payin' I'll double that shit!! Triple!!" I could hear the nigga begging for his life while me and Clip gathered the drugs and money.

"Just tell me where yo stash is at and we're even." I chuckled and shook my head because Mac loved giving niggas false hope knowing he was going to kill them anyway.

"I-I-It's in the safe under my bed. Combination 2950, that's my age and my mama age." Clip took off to the back, and I finished bagging the rest of the stuff up.

"Good lookin' homie."

PHEW!

"You enjoy doing that shit?" I asked, and he shrugged his shoulders.

"Let's roll." We left out the house and got in the black Navigator with tinted windows. Mac pulled off, and we headed to our next stop in Farmington Hills. A nigga named Zeke paid us to take care of these fools on the Southside. Our no questions policy money up front was making our clientele rise. Me and Mac still were at Chrysler because I fucked out shift supervisor good. That bitch had us on overtime every day even when we weren't scheduled.

"Aye you ever met Alyssa friend from Grand Rapids" My forehead formed wrinkles when he asked that.

"What damn friend from Grand Rapids?" I heard Clip snort out a laugh and Mac looked at me laughing.

"Easy killa, I'm talking about her friend Hazel."

"Oh. Uh, naw I ain't met her." These two fools were still laughing.

"You got a thing for Alyssa bro?"

"Hell naw, I just didn't know who you were talking about." I lit my blunt hoping these fools would let this shit go.

Truth be told, I never looked at Alyssa as nothing but my cousin woman. Not one time did I think about her in any way except Maine's. When he died, I surprised myself at how I stepped up and started looking out for her. At first, I thought it was because I felt bad. You know how someone loses a person and the hype last for about a week or two. Then muthafuckas go back to their lives. I don't know what it was, but I just made sure I was always looking out for Alyssa. Making sure she was good and she didn't want for shit.

I was up late getting her weird ass pregnant food, taking her to run errands and taking her to doctor's appointments. In the process of doing that. I got to know Alyssa and her personality. Her goofy side, that bitchy side, how spoiled she was, but sweet at the same time. I never knew how pretty her smile was. That's why I called her fat ass or fatty all the time. I loved to see her laugh or smile big. But then I remembered who she was. What kind of nigga would I be if I go for my dead cousin baby mama? So naw, I wasn't and couldn't be feelin' Alyssa that way.

"Yea a'ight. But her friend Hazel is from Grand Rapids. When I went over Alyssa house to drop her off some money, I met her. I almost fucked her little ass up to. She one of them bougie bitches with her nose in the air." I passed him the blunt.

"You mean the kind you like?" I said and now me, and Clip laughed.

"I'on fuck with that type bro. Don't do me." His ass was bothered as hell.

"Nigga, what the fuck you think Shlaya type was? That bitch was a bank manager and stuck up as hell."

"Fuck you, no she wasn't. That was what she showed y'all. With me, she was soft as shit and did whatever I said." He gave me back the blunt. Clip didn't smoke.

"Same thing to me bro. I ain't even met this Hazel bitch yet, and I can tell she got'cha thong all in a bunch." Me and Clip were cracking up. Mac turned his nose up getting pissed.

"Y'all some fag ass niggas." That fool turned the radio up while we still were laughing. Brat ass nigga. We got to our destination, and all three of us got out.

"Is it done?" Zeke asked us when we got to the front of his porch.

Mac showed him the video on his phone and Zeke looked pleased. He gave us each a duffle bag with the rest of our money, six grand a-piece. Mac gave him a card with a number to reach us on. Every time we do a job, we give a card with a number to a burner phone on it. That's how we stayed in business. Word of mouth and recommendation was a blessing. The risk was always there. Would it be a set-up to kill us, a set-up from the cops or just some bullshit all around. But that was part of the gamble and part of the thrill being in this business.

We had our money so wasn't nothing else for us to do here. Getting back in the truck we dropped Clip off then me and Mac decided to go to Coney Island and grab some food. Our spot used to be the one on Lyndon, but we don't even fuck with that one anymore for obvious reasons. We got to the crib, and I headed upstairs to my half of the house. I was happy as fuck grandma left us this house. When you opened the door upstairs, you walked into my living room and my first closet where I kept all my summer clothes and gym-shoes. Then my kitchen was basic with the stainless-steel stove, refrigerator, and microwave.

I went to Art Van and grabbed the first kitchen table I saw. Blackwood with matching chairs. Two bedrooms were up here, the big one was mine, and the other one was my smoke room I called it. I had a 40-inch curve TV in there with my PlayStation 4 game system and games. A recliner chair and loveseat, I had my bitches on my walls too. Masika and Miss Nikki Baby fine asses from *Love and Hip-Hop*. I locked the upstairs door and went into my bedroom to get naked. I don't know why but since I was a kid, I love to eat and watching TV naked.

Dick and balls all out with a good movie or show on. My bedroom was my favorite spot. Wasn't shit special I had army green and black walls, a king size soft ass bed, a 50-inch TV and my two black dressers. I put my food in the microwave and decided to shower before I eat. I went in my standard bathroom and turned the shower on. Stepping in I took my dreads out the ponytail so I could wash them. My beard and dreads were longer, but the bitches loved it, so I kept both of them up. My stomach was doing flips, so I got clean fast and dried off even quicker.

I put my dreads up high and went to microwave my food. I was on some fat boy shit tonight. I ordered a double bacon cheeseburger, some chili cheese fries, and some onion rings. I had my Faygo Moon Mist pop and was ready to smash. I didn't see the *Bobby Brown* story, so I went to my DVR and decided to watch that. I was givin' my food the best head ever when my phone rung. I picked it up off my nightstand and looked at it.

"Fuck this nigga want?" I said out loud when I saw it was Maclom.

"What up doe," I answered.

"Sup nephew. I need to meet with you and Mac tomorrow if that's possible."

"If this is about the same shit it's a waste of time." I wiped my mouth and took a swig of my drink.

"What it's about is me not seeing my nephews since I buried my son. Me and Shauney done and I just need to be around some family." I felt bad that I wasn't close to my uncle like I used to. Hell, it was before Maine died. Me and Mac just started noticing how he kept pushing for us to work for him. That shit was annoying as hell, so we stop fucking with him.

"I'll let'chu know tomorrow around three."

"That's straight with me." I hung up and called Mac.

"Yo."

"Uncle Malcolm called. He wants to meet with us tomorrow around four." I know I said three but the asshole in me told Mac four.

"We ain't fucking working for him." Mac was obviously eating to because he was smacking loud as hell in my ear.

"I told him that shit. He said he wanted some family around." Mac paused then he said.

"A'ight, four it is." We both hung up, and I finished my food. Now full and ready to smoke I grabbed some boxer briefs from my drawer and went in my smoke room. My phone went off in my hand, and I saw it was Alyssa.

"Fat-Fat, what's goody?" She smacked her lips, but I knew she was smiling.

"So, you're having a kickback at your house for your 22nd birthday, and I wasn't invited."

"Did you forget your due in six days? You need to be at home with yo' phone in ya hand ready to call me when you piss on ya'self." She was laughing, but I was being real. I was having a kickback here at the house. Close friends, drinks, good food, and a D.J. I didn't need someone bumping into Alyssa stomach or worse. I would fuck somebody up, and that's not my mood right now.

"Come on Sada. My mama makes me sit in the house all damn day, and I'm going crazy. Plus, I need to slap Mac for pissing my friend off."

"That nigga mean as fuck I'on even know why she tried to talk to him. I swear you ain't staying long, and I'mma be watching yo' ass." She giggled and agreed.

"Ok well, I'm about to eat and then go to bed. Talk to you later."

"Bye fat ass." She cussed at me laughing before we hung up. I lit my blunt and as much as I didn't want to. I thought about Alyssa.

***

"Thanks for coming nephews. How y'all like my new spot?" Me and Mac finally came over to pay Malcolm a visit. It was weird as fuck being around him and the fact that he had me and Mac in the same room. Who knew what the outcome of this would be.

"This a nice crib. Shauney been over our mama house talking about you hiding money from her and shit. I mean from the looks of this place I see why she thinks that." I said as we set down at the kitchen table.

"Fuck that hoe. Ain't none of her business what I got. I'm eating good because of how hard I work."

It was crazy to hear him talk about Shauney the way he did. The two of them had a strong marriage, or so I thought. Maine died, and I guess their shit went with him. Now she is living in a condo in Oak Park, and he is living in this nice ass five-bedroom house in Orchard Lake.

"Y'all want something to drink or eat?" We both said naw. Malcolm looked at both of us and laughed.

"Well damn, the two of you act like I didn't help to raise you. I had to practically beg y'all to come over. What's up with the funny actin' shit?" I knew Mac was going to jump at the chance to speak first.

"Ain't no funny acting this way. When we see you, it's always about the same shit. Even before Maine died. Selling drugs rather it for you or God, ain't something we want to be a part of. Maine gone and that's even more of a reason we good on that. What it look like us switchin' up just because of the situation? Naw, we good." Malcolm chuckled and shook his head.

"Hard headed lil niggas. Look around and look how good I'm livin'----"

"And we livin' just as good my nigga. You see us still in the hood but understand that's by choice. You ain't on top of the drug game. You got hood dollars just like we do. The fact that you had to lie talkin' about I need family around me just to get us over here is yet another reason. You press too much." I stood up as I spoke because he did to and wasn't no man about to stand over me.

"Why you on this subject so tuff? If you at the table eating filet mignon, then let it be that. Leave us the fuck alone about it." He held his hands up.

"Look, I don't have no family, and I don't want to push the little I have away. You got my word, I won't say shit else to y'all about working for me. The two of you have your hustle and getting' down with Zeke. Like you said, I need to let it go. My intentions were always good, but I'll leave it be. Deal?" I nodded, and Mac folded his arms and did the same. We stayed for about twenty minutes and then we bounced.

"You been quiet as hell. You good?" I set on the passenger side of Mac's Magnum and asked him. He was about to drop me off at the crib, so I can get in my ride. I had to go see grandma, Alyssa, and then head to work. I get Mac wasn't feeling our uncle at the moment, but this was unlike him to be this quiet.

"Naw I'm not good. I didn't tell Malcolm about Zeke. As a matter of fact, I never talked to him about our business since we first started. And that's when we were seventeen.

"I didn't tell him shit either." We were quiet for a minute.

"You think maybe Zeke knows him and said something. Knowing we his nephews maybe he volunteered the information." I was trying to look at the shit from all sides. Mac furrowed his eyebrows, and I could tell he was in deep thought.

"I hope that's the case but until we find out. Eyes and ears open and keep that muthafucka far from our business. But close to us. If anything is off on any level." He looked over at me, and I already knew.

"Fa sho bro." We rode in silence with the radio on, but we both were thinking about the same thing. If Malcolm was on some funny shit or in any way trying to make it, so we had to work with him by fucking up our business. Then he gotta go. No way around it.

Quinn

"It's only nine o'clock and you already sitting by the window waiting?" I rolled my eyes before I looked at my older sister.

"I woke up early and got ready. No big deal." She snickered and said.

"Girl that yellow nigga got'chu so gone. All I know is he betta do what he needs to do to support that baby. That is *if* it's his." She laughed and continued to the kitchen to finish cooking. I swear she gets on my nerves. We got along, but she was always having some smart shit to say. She low key was just mad because she wanted Mac and he would never touch her.

"Mama getting off work late today too so you gotta pick her up."

"I know that Starrenna damn." She had the nerve to smack her lips and give me the finger.

I already had talked to my mama before she went to work, and I told her I was picking her up. Me and my mama had a good relationship. She was shocked that I was pregnant because I was only twenty-three and she knew I didn't have a boyfriend. But she had Starrenna at fourteen and me at seventeen, so she didn't judge. Me and my sister stayed with my mama on Sussex and Fenkell. The house was a two-story with all the rooms upstairs and the living room and kitchen downstairs. My sister had two kids, so I gave all of them the upstairs and my room was in the basement.

I loved my room because it was spacious, and my mama let me set it up anyway I wanted. Starrenna worked at Walmart, and I worked at Footlocker in Fairlane mall. We paid my mama rent and helped her keep the house up. My sister was always a little jealous of me because she was tied down with two kids. Also, she was around 230lbs, and for some reason, she thought that was my fault. Like Bitch I didn't stuff cookies down your throat. And no one told her to keep poppin' that pussy for her baby daddy ugly broke ass. While she talking about me, she sprung off her baby daddy just like I was. At least mine has money and look good. Her nigga looked like a bucket of what the fuck and he was broke. He worked but he didn't have money like Mac so to me he was broke in my opinion.

Mac was someone I wanted when I saw him at Clip's party at Club Truth in Detroit. He was so fine and throwin' money at strippers like it was endless for him. His clothes, his beard, those thick jet-black waves, even the way he was sipping on his liquor was so fucking sexy. He was light skin to which shocked me because I fucked with dark skin guys. But I wanted him, and I played my shit cool about it. I made my move when Mac went to the bar. I knew he was going to fuck with me because I was fine as fuck. Caramel with some slant eyes, thick body, and honey blonde hair.

We spoke a few words, and I gave him my number. The nigga didn't hit me up for almost two weeks. I was mad as hell but answered as soon as a number I didn't have saved called me. He invited me to a barbeque, and I went back to his place. We fucked all night, and a bitch was hooked. It was our thing for a hot second then he started falling back. We fucked, but I just couldn't get him to make me his. I been in his bed, made him breakfast, been in his car and I would suck his dick so good. But he made shit clear we were nothing more. So, I did me, and he did him.

Then he stopped letting me spend the night, and I saw less and less of him. We were at a block party, and both were drunk. I let him fuck me in my car, and now I'm pregnant with our son. I was having the baby at Sinai-Grace Hospital since it's up the street from me. Mac only came to one appointment, and that's when the doctor confirmed I was pregnant. He would drop me off and pick me up. Even though I worked, he made sure I was good. He told me his focus was finding out if this baby was his or not. But I knew this was his son, it had to be.

"I'm gone, Renna!" I yelled, and I was out the door before she could respond. Mac got out when he saw my front door open. He walked around to the passenger door and opened it for me. He looked so good in some basic blue basketball shorts. He had a white V-neck t-shirt on with some blue FILA slides and navy-blue ankle socks. Them jet black thick waves made me want some seafood and that beard made those sexy pink lips look so good. Can you believe me and Mac have never kissed. He has never even eaten my pussy. But it's all good because we were about to get as intimate as two people can get.

"What up doe Quinn. You good?" He gave me a bullshit church hug and kissed my cheek like I was his grandma. His cologne smelled so good, and I can't lie, I was happy to be close to him.

"Hey, I'm good just ready to get to this appointment. You good?"

"I'm smooth ma." He closed the door and walked to the driver's side. His phone was in his cup holder and it rung. The name Shanay popped up, and I got mad.

"Who is Shanay?" I started as soon as he got in.

"What?" He looked confused but saw his phone ringing and looked at it.

"None of yo' business Quinn. Don't start that shit like we together." He started driving while sending a text to the bitch. I don't know what he said, but I could see her name at the top. I was so damn mad. I started pouting and folding my arms. He didn't even show a concern and the fool turned the radio up. I just had to keep reminding myself that I was the baby mama. No matter what I was having his baby, so I was going to be number one.

"Good morning. What can I do for you today?" The nurse asked us as we walked into the specialty building of the hospital.

"My name is Quinn Griffin, and I have a ten o'clock appointment." She typed my name in the computer.

"Ok you can have a seat, and Dr. Nijai will be right with you." She smiled at us, and we both went to go sit down. I was twenty-four weeks, so it was time for my sugar test. This was the only reason why Mac was here. I made him think it was more to it because I just wanted him with me today. I didn't give a fuck. He was my baby daddy, and he needed to start acting like it.

"Can you attempt to act interested in me and your child?" I looked at him with an attitude.

"Be quiet." He didn't even take his eyes off his phone when he said that. That's the kind of attitude Mac had. The less words you got, the more he really didn't give a fuck which was making my attitude grow. He took a phone call from Sada, his mama and then his grandma. I pulled my phone out and went on Facebook. I made a status with my location and tried to tag Mac, but his name didn't come up.

"Did you block me?"

"Yea." I smacked my lips and turned my body towards him.

"What the hell did you block me for?"

"Cuz you always doing the most."

"So, you ashamed of the baby?" He finally looked at me, but his expression was making me wish he wasn't.

"Why tha fuck you be on me so tuff? We not together and if this baby is mines, we never will be. Ain't shit shameful about my child no matter who I make it with. You can continue to make yo'self-look stupid for Facebook. Tryna make bitches think we more. Naw ma, we fucked and now we here. That's it. Nothing more, nothing less." I wanted to cry but then again, I thought about the months I had ahead. He was right, I needed to chill and stop doing the most. Mac is not a 'gotta be seen' type of nigga. As long as he wasn't in a relationship, then I always had a shot to make us a family.

"I apologize Mac. You're right, I've been being extra and calling stuff what it's not."

"It's cool ma, just chill the fuck out." The door opened, and the lady called my name. We both went back there, and she told us to go to room three. She came in and checked my weight and blood pressure. We heard the baby's heartbeat, and everything was fine. Then the actual glucose test started. I had to drink this nasty ass shit that taste like flat orange pop. Then I had to get my blood drawn which I hated. I almost threw up, and to my surprise, Mac was asking was I ok. This test took almost two hours. I already couldn't eat eight to fourteen hours before the test.

"I'm so damn hungry." We walked out the office. I was glad my son was fine, and I didn't have diabetes. Now I was ready to eat some food.

"What'chu got a taste for?"

"Honestly it's these pinwheels that Kroger's sells. Can we swing by there and I can get me some stuff to make a salad?" He nodded his head and drove in the direction towards the store. His phone rung again, and I saw it was Alyssa. I didn't give a damn about that. I knew how close Mac was with his brother and his cousin. I had seen Mac and Alyssa together, and she didn't look at him as anything but a brother. Sada on the other hand, that was a different story. One I don't give a fuck about as long as she wasn't coming for Mac.

"You good Lyssa, you need something?" I don't know what she said, but he looked confused then he laughed.

"Man, I didn't do shit to that damn girl. I called her on some bullshit, and she couldn't handle it." Who the hell was he talking about and what shit did he call them out on? It was a bitch I knew that much.

"A'ight, I swear I'll chill." They talked for like a minute, and then he hung up.

"Who were you rude to Mac?" I asked that way instead of my normal rude way.

"That don't even concern you." See, that's that rude ass attitude he always gives. I didn't even say shit else. We got to Kroger, and like always he let me get what I wanted and paid for the food. Mac never gave me money in my hand. He paid my mama her rent to her, and he told me until he gets a DNA test, he wasn't buying nothing for the baby. My mama was throwing me a baby shower at home, and I wish Mac would come, but he already told me hell no.

"So, we going back to your crib? I don't have to work today." I asked as he pulled out the parking lot.

"We don't do that shit, Quinn." I sat back and folded my arms. I pouted the whole drive until we got to my house. He opened my door and brought my three bags in the house.

"Later ma." He kissed my cheek and walked out the front door. I just had to keep telling myself that I was the baby mama. I was number one, and I had to switch shit up. Fall back and let Mac fall in my lap. I was fixing my salad when my phone rung. Looking down at the name I rolled my eyes, but I answered it because after I ate. I knew I was going to be horny.

Hazel

I was so excited nothing could bring me down. I got the job I went on my interview for a few days ago at *Motor City Casino*. The restaurant was called *Iridescence,* and they serve five-star food. Both of the head chefs made me feel comfortable and were impressed with my resume. I cooked my salmon on top of sweet corn and seasoned tomatoes. They loved it and called me yesterday to tell me that I was hired. I just left from downtown where the casino was; filling out paperwork and getting my uniform. I ordered two pairs of non-slip shoes, and I couldn't wait to start in two weeks. I have some training to go to, but it's paid training. Speaking of paid, my hourly pay was more than exceptional.

"I am so proud of you boo. I swear you make me can't wait until I return to work." Alyssa and I were at *Outback Steakhouse* having lunch. I told her I wanted to go eat and even though her mama wanted her in the house all day we left anyways.

"Thank you so much, Lyssa. Girl, before you know it six weeks, will be up, and you'll be back at the boutique." Alyssa was manager of a nice Boutique called *Dollz* in Oakpark. She had sent me some pieces I seen on their website when I was in Grand Rapids. That was another thing about moving to Detroit that was beneficial. I was closer to her job so I'm sure she would be getting half of my paycheck every week.

"So, speaking of our new house." I threw in there laughing, and she did to. Me and her went to see a house the other day and fell in love. The city was the goal, but it wasn't working out for us. Finally, the perfect house for our budget and what we were looking for was in Southfield. Which isn't far from the westside at all. A twenty-minute drive was what we were looking at and the hospital Alyssa was delivering at was in Southfield.

"I know Haz. I'm talking to my mama today. I mean I kind of have no choice, everything went through, and we can move in whenever. With us decorating the house from scratch is making our move easy so I'm getting the talk out the way today. I promise." I smiled, and the waiter brought our food. I ordered a steak with some fried shrimp and loaded potato. Alyssa had ribs, macaroni, and some French fries.

"That's what we could do when we leave. Go to Gardner White Furniture and pick some stuff out. We can do the living room and our bedroom since your leaving your bed at your mama's house. If you're up to it. I don't want you to overdo it." I laughed because Alyssa had a mouth full of food.

"Girl don't listen to my mama. My doctor told me moving around will speed up the labor. I'm up for it. My daddy sent me some money, so I got it. But I kind of gotta talk to you about something." I nodded while I took a bite of my shrimp.

"Sada's birthday is tomorrow, and he's having a kickback at his house." She smirked, and I arched my eyebrow.

"I thought it would be fun if we go. I promise Mac will not bother you." I smacked my lips.

"Girl I am not thinking about his rude, judgmental ass. Of course, we can go. I feel like I need something new to look at. Kahlil blows me up all the damn time, and I feel like I'll fall back into his lies if I'm bored long enough. But I swear I will slap Mac if he says anything to me." Alyssa laughed.

"I know he pissed you off. Trust me Haz I know you're not snobbish or self-involved. But it's because I know you. You have to let people know you and see that you're not that person. Me and you talked a lot about Jermaine in the streets. Rather I wanted to accept it or not we knew his path would lead in one or two directions." As she talked her eyes got watery, and I gave her a sympathetic expression and squeezed her hand.

"Shit. I can't even say his name without crying." Alyssa picked up her napkin and wiped her eyes.

"I know boo, and it probably will always hurt. But you're doing so good living your life, making sure you and my God son are healthy. You'll always miss and love Jermaine. You get to tell the baby all about his dad and how he loved him before he even knew what he was." She smiled at me, and I smiled back.

"Mood change. I think you and Mac like each other but y'all had a rocky start."

"Bitch bye. I do not like that man at all." She called my bluff.

"You've talked about him every day since. You call him every name in the book which means you're trying to convince yourself that he's not all that. You like him, Hazel. That mean attitude he has does something to you."

"I'm not about to even give you the energy bitch."
She laughed her ass off at me, and I just kept eating. I
seriously wasn't going to respond because it was pointless.
Yea Mac was fine as hell. When I say fine, I mean ship all
the niggas away because he would be all you need. His lips
and them pretty white teeth I couldn't keep my eyes off of.
Then he had all these tattoos on both his muscular arms. He
had the veins in his hand that let me know he works hard.
Then his voice, oh my goodness I have never heard a voice
that sexy. He could get into details and explain how bowel
movement looks and I'd be turned on. But my point is, I
don't like him. The way he judged me just made me so mad,
I couldn't get it off my mind.

"You good over there?" I snapped out my thoughts
and Alyssa was smiling so hard in my face I wanted to smack
her.

"Yea, you like him." When she laughed and said that
I just ignored her.

We finished eating and did like we planned. Gardner White was so fun. I swear I almost emptied my bank account being in there. Alyssa was just as bad. But I found a mirror and diamond bedroom set and a good king size bed. All that room just for me I didn't mind because I loved a lot of pillows on my bed. Alyssa found this nice ass chocolate brown and cream bedroom set, and she got a king size bed as well. It just made more sense because you get the free delivery and no tax if you get king size.

Plus, they were having that get a set and get a free 40-inch flat screen TV, so that saved us money on buying them. Our dads called and surprised us with them paying for our living room furniture. We got a fluffy grey long sectional with two ottomans and two glass end tables. Today was such a good day, and we both were feeling really good. I was driving us back to her mama house, so Alyssa could talk to her about us moving. I wasn't looking forward to it, but I was here to support my friend. We walked in the house all smiles and talking random.

"You gone learn to stay off your feet." Hattie came on us as soon as we walked in the door.

"Ma, I feel fine, and the baby is fine." Alyssa always remained respectful even when her mama was just a lot.

"Why y'all go to Gardner White?" Oh shit. Me and Alyssa special needs asses didn't even realize we were holding the folder they give you with your receipt and delivery information on it. We both were stuck looking stupid. Alyssa looked at me and let out a long sigh.

"I been meaning to talk to you about this. So, you know the reason Hazel moved back to Detroit was to help me with the baby. She found her an amazing job cooking at Motor City Casino. You know I have my job. And, well we uh." She was so nervous, so I figured I should step in.

"We found a good house for rent in Southfield. We tried to stay in the city, but the houses were all wrong. This house is amazing. Three-bedrooms fenced backyard new kitchen appliances, and we got approved for it. The rent is affordable, and if you want, we can all go see it now." Shit now I was nervous. Hattie looked at me while holding her oven mitten in one hand and her other hand on her hip.

"And the people y'all are renting from are legit? You checked them out? Is the area safe and a good area? Now you know you not putting my grandbaby in no daycare right." When she smiled at us, me and Alyssa were both relieved.

"Oh, my goodness mama I thought you were going to flip," Alyssa said as she hugged her mama. I hugged her too and was so happy this didn't come out bad.

"I mean I don't like it, but I trust you and Hazel. But I want to see this house. Give me all the landlord's information, and I want to drive around the area. Did you check the area for pedophiles?"

"Ma it couldn't be no worse than living here in the city." I let them talk for a minute, and I went to my room. Kicking off my shoes I hopped on the bed and got comfortable. I saw Goldie texted me, so I texted her for a minute. I showed her the pictures of the house, and she was so excited. We talked about my new job and how she was doing. After we were done, I turned the TV on and put it on Nicktoons so I could watch my favorite cartoon, *Fairly Odd Parents*. I let it play while I picked my phone back up and went on Instagram. I smacked my lips when I saw I had a follow request. It was either a hair page or them scammers telling me I can flip three-hundred dollars into three-thousand.

"Holy shit," I said out loud but low. The follow was thuga$MAC313. It was no way this could be him.

He didn't even like me, and I didn't like him. I clicked his name, and his account was private. I wasn't adding him, so he can check my page out first. I hit the request to follow button and waited. I bet he was about to be petty and not accept until I did. In the next three minutes, I saw that red dot above the heart. I clicked on it, and sure enough, he accepted my request. I started going through his page with a fine-tooth comb. As I said before, this man was so fine. The videos he had when he was rapping to some lyrics, smoking or when he would brush his waves.

I watched those more than once. I don't know why but I went to a few of the comments. These bitches were so fucking thirsty, and I couldn't help but turn my nose up. He didn't pay not one comment any attention which I was glad. The more he licked his lips or showed a fresh outfit and shoes he had on the more aggressive comments were. One girl said she bet she could lock him down with her pussy. My petty ass reported the comment because she was doing a lot and pissing me off. This was like her third comment under the same video. Just a starving hoe. That red dot was back under the heart on my page, and I clicked on it. He commented on one of my pictures 'Yo' head big as hell.' with the laughing emoji.

"I swear I hate this little ass boy." I got mad and went to his page. 'Yo' lips crusty as hell nigga.' I put that under one of his pictures when he was brushing his hair. He commented back fast. 'Bet you'd kiss me though.'

"Ugh!" I exited out my Instagram app and threw my phone on the bed. I hated that I let him get to me, but he did.

***

I brought my niggas to the bank, then we cashed out

I brought my bitch to the bank, then she passed out (Bitch)

Woo, woo, woo, yes sir

Woo (Hey!), woo (That's hard), yes sir

I do not talk about niggas out my damn mouth (No)

I pull up on you, pull the trigger, then I air it out (Uh)

Woo, woo, woo, yes sir

Woo (Hey!), woo, woo, woo, yes sir

Me and Alyssa walked on the porch of Sada's and Mac's house. It was a few people here but not as many as I would have thought. The music was loud, and as soon as you opened the front door, you could smell the good food. I kept it simple in some black biker shorts, black and white Pumas and a crop top that said 1-800-FUCK-YOUR-FEELINGS. I wore that shirt for Mac stupid ass. I decided to wear my real hair down and curly with a side part. I put on my belly button ring Alyssa bought me with my August birthstone hanging from it. Alyssa was so pretty in her short skater dress, and I wand curled her long bundles, and she wore her Gucci slides I bought her.

"I am so hungry." She flew to the kitchen to make her a plate. I looked around, and the crowd seemed pretty chill. There was some girls dancing and niggas playing cards, domino's and smoking. Speaking of men, damn these niggas looked good. You had some that were busted, but for the majority, they all looked good.

"Ok do you want to go outside?" I told Alyssa, yes, and we headed to the back room where the backyard door was.

"Yo!" Me and Alyssa both looked to the side at who was yelling, and she smiled big, so I assumed this was Sada. I loved how he looked out for her and as much as I hate to admit it. Mac looked out too, and I respected that. Me and Alyssa talked about if she was feeling Sada and she told me she wasn't. I personally think because of the situation she didn't want to admit it. But it's not like she's cheating or anything. And I think Sada has a thing for her too. Like how he is hugging her now. They hugged like a couple who have been through some shit. He looked over at me and smirked.

"What up doe ma, you must be Hazel." He gave me a one arm hug, and I couldn't help but laugh at the difference.

"Yup that's me. Nice to finally meet you face to face Sada. Thanks for taking care of my love."

"No doubt. So, fat-fat and you under me tonight because I didn't want her ass to come any dam ways because of this." He pointed to her stomach.

"You cool with that? I mean you can mingle and shit, but her ass can't." Alyssa shook her head while she stuffed her face.

"I'm good. It's not like I know anybody here." I shrugged my shoulders.

"Yea you do. My big brother Mac in the yard. You can hang with him if you want." I could tell he was trying to be funny because he was laughing, and so was Alyssa.

"Fuck the both of y'all. I'm about to go fix me a plate." I went back in the house, and they followed me because he kicked everybody out and told them to move everything outside. The kitchen, living room and dining room was now empty. *Meek Mill Fall Thru* song came on which was my shit. I started rapping and swaying my hips while I fixed my plate.

Yeah

Sad to say it but I love you

Don't take no offense but you're my bitch

Yeah, you gone fall through every time a nigga call you

That's why I ball how I ball when I spoil you

We was in Miami, first time I saw you

I was in a Phantom when I pulled up on you

It was late nights, late nights in the bando

Fucking on you good got you bustin' like you Rambo

If you keep it hood so you really understand though

You was there through my ups and downs like a camel

I was back outside on the porch sitting next to Sada and Alyssa. I'm telling y'all he wasn't playing. This nigga wouldn't even let anybody stand near Alyssa. He kept saying he didn't want to fuck nobody up. I thought it was so cute and Alyssa was so busy eating she didn't even pay attention. Sada would get up and mingle and put his gifts in the house but only for a second. I went half with Alyssa on a gift card to Footlocker and Macy's. Even though I didn't know Sada that well. Alyssa liked him, so he was cool in my book. I was done eating and was now sipping on a wine cooler.

Some people started moving towards the front of the house, and that's when I saw Mac. This shit was annoying because he looked so damn good. I never paid attention how thick and full his beard was. It probably was so soft, and I imagined running my nails through it. Them lips oh my muthafuckin' gosh! He had on a navy blue and tan Salvatore Ferragamo t-shirt, matching belt and some dark denim jeans. His all tan J's looked to be fresh out the box. He had a diamond in each ear and a nice watch on.

"Earth to Hazel." Alyssa waved her thick ass hand again.

"Uh." I know I looked so damn stupid.

"Damn ma, that ugly nigga got'chu like that?" I rolled my eyes.

"I'm sick of y'all, he ain't got me like shit." I took a sip of my wine cooler again while these two fruitcakes laughed. I saw two bitches go over there towards Mac. They were cute and all, but they didn't have shit on me. Anyway, one of them was all on his dick. I promise I didn't even feel my face form, but obviously, two people didn't miss it.

"All you gotta do is go over there and break that shit up. He ain't gone do nothing but let'chu cuz he feelin' you to." I looked at Sada.

"I. Do. Not. Like. Your. Brother. I was just embarrassed at how those hoes are making a fool of themselves." I looked back over there and oh shit. Mac was coming our way. Why is my heart speeding up, hands clammy and my mouth felt wetter.

"Heyyy Mac." Alyssa had to be extra when she spoke to him as he walked on the porch. Her and Sada were sitting on the bench which was at the start of the porch. I was sitting in the chair on the side of the bench.

"What up doe ma. Look at'chu ready to pop." He walked over to her and hugged her. I smelled him before he even reached her.

"What up Hazel." Maybe I was a little much when I looked up at him from my phone slow and all mean, but I didn't care.

"Mac." He chuckled and said.

"Big head ass girl." He shook his head and walked in the house. Sada laughed and looked at me.

"Y'all need to just fuck and get it over with." I was so damn mad. More so because he always pushed my buttons.

"Let it go ma. I see that look in your eyes." I looked at Sada and gave him the middle finger before I jumped up and went in the house after Mac. I heard Sada say 'shit' and I didn't know if him or Alyssa followed me or not.

"What the fuck is your problem? I've done nothing to you yet, and still, you judge me and then you're rude as fuck." He was standing in what I guess was his bedroom which was so neat and nice.

"I know you betta get the hell outta my room talking crazy and you see me on the phone." I put my hands on my hip pissed the hell off. Then I saw Alyssa and Mac standing in the doorway.

"I don't give a fuck what you're doing or who you're on the phone with. You're rude to me, so I'm gonna be rude to you!" He told whoever he was on the phone with to let him hit them back. When he put his phone back on the charger, he looked at me and folded his arms. His stance was so hard and serious. But I still didn't give a fuck. Like my shirt said, fuck his feelings.

"Alyssa I advise you to get'cho little friend before I fuck her up."

"Come on Hazel boo." I turned and looked at Alyssa then back at Mac.

"No! Fuck him and how mad he call his self-being. He a little ass boy who likes fucking with people and now I gotta chill because he getting mad. Naw, I don't give a fuck about his feelings." He unfolded his arms, and his nostrils flared. Suddenly he rushed in my direction, pushed Sada out the doorway who pulled Alyssa back at the same time. When he slammed his door so hard the mirror on his wall shook, and he locked it. I almost disappeared. He slammed me against the door hard, and he was all in my face looking corrupt. Through his tight mouth and gritted teeth he said.

"I don't fucking take kindly to disrespect. You are a stuck-up spoiled brat who probably only dates niggas as soft as yo' ass; who don't ever tell you about yo'self. If I tell you to get the fuck outta my room as a matter of fact if I tell you anything. You betta fuckin' do it and not make me say the shit twice." I didn't want to, but I couldn't stop tears from falling. He was so mean, and I promise I really don't know why.

"Them tears don't come anywhere near to making me feel shit," Mac said and I believed him. But I wasn't crying to get him to sympathize with me.

"I just don't get why you don't like me. I'm not who you think I am." I wiped my tears and then looked at him. He still was close to my face and still looking so vicious.

"Apologize," Mac said and I knew he wasn't asking.

"I apologize Mac. I don't look at you, Sada or Maine like y'all are beneath me. I can be in my ways at times, but I am not so stuck on myself that I mistreat people. I moved here to be with Alyssa and my God son. She didn't ask me or even hint that she needed me here. I did this move because I wanted to." I sniffed and wiped another falling tear. He looked in my eyes and then he stood up straight because he had to bend over to get in my face.

"I apologize to then. I did judge you, and I shouldn't have. But yo' ass bet not disrespect me again." I nodded my head fast as hell agreeing with him. He was still so close to me and when I looked in his eyes. My heart started speeding up again. When he bit his bottom lip, I did the same thing on queue. Suddenly he lifted me up with my legs straddling him and my back against the door. When our lips crashed my arms went around his neck, and I let it happen. Our tongues were like Siamese twins. It was like kissing expensive material or a sip of a delicate wine. Those lips were soft like I knew, and he was squeezing my booty just like I like. While we continued kissing two light knocks came to the door.

"Mac, please don't kill my friend. I don't have anymore." Alyssa said and I covered my mouth trying not to laugh. She sounded so sad and serious.

"She good ma." He said, and then he looked back at me biting that damn bottom lip again. I was still straddling him, and he started massaging my ass.

"So where do we go from here?" I asked and he looked at my lips and then at me.

"I'm gon' take you out, fuck yo' mind then I'm gon' fuck you." I honestly didn't know what the hell to say. I never had a guy talk to me that way without me wanting to slap him. But with Mac, I was so turned on. Still, though I had to play it cool.

"I don't wanna fuck you, Mac. I don't even know you. Hell, what is your real name because I know it's not Mac."

"I'll tell you my real name once you let me hit." My mouth dropped.

"I'll let you hit if you can promise me that we'll be a couple or moving in that direction." He shook his head, and I arched my eyebrows.

"I been doing me out here for a while angel face. Tried that relationship and every bitch been on some corny shit. I'on even know if I want another one." I understood where he was coming form, but that wasn't fair.

"You want something from me, and I want two things from you. Your real name and if I like you then I want more. If you can't do those, then I can't give you what you want." I wiggled my way down and fixed my clothes.

"But'chu get two things, and I get one. How is *that* shit fair?" I smirked and pecked his soft lips.

"My pussy is worth both of those things plus more." He bit his bottom lip and hit my ass while I unlocked the door and tried to walk out, but he grabbed my arm before I opened it.

"You don't run shit angel face." Then he pulled his phone out.

"Now, put your number in my phone." I would be lying if I said I didn't listen which wasn't even like me. I keyed it in, and I gave his phone back to him.

"Y'all fucked?" As soon as I opened the door, Sada and Alyssa were right there. She hugged me and looked me over like I was in danger. I mean I was but thank God it went in another direction.

"Man, shut'cho ass up. Naw I ain't fuck her. I got dat ass together though." Him and Sada laughed, and I shot him a nasty look. He arched his eyebrow, and I felt my cheeks flush as I put my hair behind my ear. Alyssa put her arm through mine, and we walked towards the backyard. It was crazy because the next string of events happened so damn fast. I thought it was a few people on the back porch talking which is why we still headed outside. Then in the blink of an eye we stepped outside, and one of the guys pushed the other. He fell on top Alyssa who then fell on top of me.

"Tha fuck!!" I heard Sada yell so damn loud my ears popped. He snatched the guy up so fast and started beating his ass. Then Mac punched the one who pushed the guy on us. I mean they were going in on those guys.

"Are you ok Alyssa?" I stood up on my knees about to help her up, but she wouldn't move. She held her stomach.

"No. Something's wrong." I panicked and grabbed my phone from the side of my shorts. My hands were shaking, but I realized where we were. I know enough to know I didn't need anything involved that might come with the police.

"SADA ALYSSA NEEDS TO GET TO THE HOSPITAL!!" I yelled so loud, and I went to look between her legs to make sure she wasn't bleeding.

"Ok boo, I don't see any blood so that should be a good thing."

"Ok. Ok. Ughhh! Something hurts!!" I went to look at her, and before I could call for help again, she was swooped up off the floor. Sada had her bridal style and carried her to the front. I looked at the guy who he had beaten up. There were some other dudes stomping him and a bunch of other guys started making a closed circle around him. Like they were hiding what was going on. The same thing with the one Mac hit.

"Come on angel face we gon' drive them to the hospital." Mac grabbed my hand, and we flew to the front. Some tall, dark skin guy threw Mac some keys, and we got into a dark green Ford Explorer. When he opened the front door for me, I saw Alyssa in the back and Sada was holding her. I hurried and got in the front seat and buckled up.

"Is she ok?" I looked in the back, and Alyssa looked to be in so much pain.

"Oh my God, this hurts!" She yelled as Mac took off down the street fast as hell.

"You gone be good fat-fat I promise. Just hold on." I nodded my head and started speaking positive stuff to her just like Sada was. Shit, I have never had a child or seen one born in person. But movies told me that her water was supposed to break, and I don't think that has happened yet, so maybe this was contractions. Mac was zooming because we arrived at Sani-Grace Hospital so fast. We all hopped out, and Sada carried her through the double doors.

"Hi, I think my friend is in labor," I said quickly to the ladies at the front desk. They wasted no time getting a wheelchair out for her and taking her out of Sada's arms.

"I have your purse boo I'll fill out your paperwork and call your parents," I yelled as they were about to roll her to the back.

"Ok. I don't want to go back there alone." Alyssa cried out, and she grabbed my hand.

"I got her ma, don't worry about it." Sada stepped in, and I was so shocked, and I believe Mac and Alyssa were too. They all rushed to the back, and I called her parents with her phone. I was so glad her dad wasn't home in Grand Rapids. He was downtown, and her mama was at home. The other front desk nurse gave me Alyssa paperwork, and I set down next to Mac and filled it out.

"Oh, my goodness I am so nervous." I looked over at Mac's hand and saw his knuckles red. I blew through Alyssa's paperwork and went up to the front desk to turn it in.

"Excuse me can I get a First-Aid kit, some ice and a clean rag." I smiled and asked the nurse. She said yes and went to the back. When she gave me the stuff, I walked back over to him and kneeled between his legs.

"Give me your hand champ." I joked, and he chuckled. I started cleaning his red bruised knuckles up.

"You know you do have a big ass head." I looked up at him with my nose turned up.

"Ah shit girl." He flinched and snatched his hand from mine.

"Stop being rude Mac."

"My bad angel face, you right that was rude as hell." He gave me back his hand.

"Why do you keep calling me angel face? Is that what you call all the bitches?"

"Typical female. Just ask the question without all the smart shit after." I started wrapping up his hand.

"Your face."

"What about my face?" I put his hand on his lap and looked up at him. He was so fine I just can't say that enough.

"It's fucking stunning ma. Call a nigga corny, but God put his best angels on the job to make your face." For the first time since I have met his rude ass. He made me smile hard, and when he smiled back, I melted.

"Hazel." I looked behind me and saw Alyssa's mama and dad. I hugged both of them and told them she was in labor. They ran back there to her room, me and Mac went back to sit down.

"Mac who knows how long this will take. You can leave if you want." I told him because who knew when this baby will come.

"Naw angel face I'm good. You gone keep me up, tell me about you." I smiled and sat next to him.

"Ok let's make it fun. You can ask me any question, and I have to answer. The same for you." I held my hand out.

"Deal?" He looked at my hand and then at me while shaking it.

"A'ight but I'm first." I agreed.

"Full name."

"Hazel Elise Monroe." He nodded his head. I knew he thought I was asking his first name but nope.

"Is Sada your only sibling?"

"Yup."

"How old are you?"

"I'm 20 my birthday is August 10th. How old are you Mac?"

"Twenty-Four and my birthday is November 1st"

Wow, I didn't think he was that old. I assumed my age.

"Are you single?" He nodded.

"That pussy tight?" My goodness, I could tell he was the type who was unpredictable. You never would know what he was going to say.

"Uh, I-I don't know I mean." He started laughing hard as hell.

"I'm fucking wit'chu baby. I'll find that out on my own."

"You're so cocky. I told you if we are not together or headed in that direction then you will get nowhere near me in that way." He grabbed under my arm and pulled me into his lap. His hand went between my thighs, but he didn't touch my pussy.

"Stop lying to yourself. Not only do you want me to fuck you, but you know I could get as close to you as I want. You give me what I want, and I'll give you what you want. Right now, I wanna keep talking to you while we wait. Then take you out after everything calms down then you gone let me in dem guts." He bit that bottom lip again, and I couldn't even press my legs together hard because I was on his lap.

"Let me get them lips again." I kissed him again as my fingers did what they wanted to do earlier. They went through his long beard. It was so soft and full. He set me back in the chair next to him, and we continued talking. I decided to save the name question for later.

Alyssa

"So what if you're right and it is a boy. Do you want a junior?" Maine had just put it down on me after I told him I was pregnant. I didn't know how he was going to take it. I thought he would flip out. Maybe want me to get rid of it or break up with me. But to my surprise, he was fine with it. More than fine. Like now he's rubbing my stomach gently as if I was far along.

"The junior shit don't bother me. I'm not a junior, so I want my son to have his own name." I had my hands going through his long dreads.

"What about Liam or Judah." He chuckled.

"That ain't no real nigga name bae."

"Jermaine we are not raising no 'real nigga' or 'goon'. We are raising a boy who will have street and book smarts." He kissed my stomach a few times making me giggle.

"You right Alyssa bae, I fucks with Liam though. It flows good with our three names. Liam Jermaine Smith."

"I love it." I smiled big with my eyes closed. I could feel him moving, and when I opened my eyes, he was in my face kissing my lips.

"Not like I love you." We started making out, and I just couldn't wait until I had our baby.

I opened my eyes a little and looked around the room. I forgot I was still in the hospital. My mama and daddy had left a few hours after I gave birth. That shit was a pain that is unspeakable. As a matter of fact, I don't even want to talk about it. Just know I pushed him out, he's healthy, I'm fine, and the process took six hours. My mama was laughing talking about how lucky I was because she was in labor with me for a whole day. I don't give a damn.

Six hours was long as hell to me. There was a little drama because my mama felt Sada shouldn't have been in the room. The thing is, she had no control over this. Those contractions gave me a big ass backbone. I told my mama with all due respect. Either shut up or get out. My daddy, the nurses, and Sada were cracking up. She didn't say another word about him being in here. Liam Jermaine Cooper was born May 27th at 7lbs and 12oz. Him and Sada shared a birthday which I thought was so funny.

"You sleep well fat-fat?" I turned over and saw Sada sitting in the chair holding Liam.

"I'm not pregnant anymore asshole." I joked.

"How long have I been sleep?"

"For about three hours. Hazel and Mac visited, and her ass took a million more pictures. He was sleep when you woke up. The nurse gave me a bottle and said when you wake up try to put him on them titties." I laughed because I know she didn't say it like that.

"Thank you so much, Sada. You have been so much help, you don't even know." I got out of bed, so I could get clean and brush my teeth. I also was hungry as hell. I couldn't believe how my body recovered from having a child. I could walk, and I felt good. My kitty was a little tender, and my titties felt like they weighed 50lbs each but other than that I felt fine.

"You don't have to keep thanking me girl. This lil homie right here." He stood up and gave him to me after I got back comfortable in the bed.

"I gotta call Hazel and tell her thanks for bringing my bags up here."

"Yo'ass would have a fashion show the day after having a baby." I laughed because I knew he was talking about my Adidas leggings I had on with a matching sports bra. My bundles were in a high ponytail with a black headband on.

"Shut up, I can't go long looking a mess." He turned around, so I could put Liam on my breast. I told him he was good after Liam was positioned right. I had my own nursing cover-up with me, so I had that on. Sada set next to me while Liam ate.

"You did good as hell Alyssa. The baby is healthy and beautiful, you held yo' shit together and really pushed lil man out. I never seen anything so dope before. Maine would be proud." I smiled and tried not to tear up, but I couldn't help it.

"Thanks, Sada. I swear I appreciate that so much. I don't know how I did it without him but now that Liam is here. I feel like I can do this and be ok with being alone." Sada wiped my face and then put his hand under my chin.

"You ain't gon' never be alone so chill on saying that." I smacked my lips, and kind of got annoyed.

"Sada let's be real for a minute. You're young just like I am. The only difference is I have a kid now. I appreciate you for everything you have been doing but the 'alone' I'm referring to is something no one can fill. I understand you'll always be there, but this is all new. In a while, it will wear off, and everyone will go their own directions. You, Mac even Hazel and I know it's not personal. It's just life and you all have a right to live it."

"Man, you talk to damn much. I get what'chu saying and all but for real. Shut up. I'll always be here, so will Mac and so will Hazel." He stood up and turned so I could take Liam off my breast. I took the cover off of me and put his throw-up towel over me, so I could burp him. Sada set back down and smiled looking at Liam.

"Lil homie cute as hell. He got'cho chocolate skin and all that long hair from you and Maine." His phone rung and I saw Clip name on it. He ignored it and then a text came through saying meet at the spot. I don't know why my stomach dropped and I just had to be real with him one more time. Liam burped, and I laid him down in the hospital bassinet.

"Please be careful out there Sada. I feel like déjà vu saying this to you but um." I started knotting my fingers together and looking down at my feet, but for some reason, I couldn't stop talking.

"It's different with you now and uh, I uh. I have never looked at you anyway. And it's not like I do now I just want you to be careful. I..... I can't take another one. You and Mac have become so much to me." It was quite for a second probably because I sounded like a stammering fool. Sada pulled me up by my hand and made me stand between his legs.

"You feeling me Alyssa?" Oh my God! I wasn't expecting him to put me on the spot like that. What the fuck should I say? Was this wrong? I thought of the best response.

"Are you feeling me?" I asked, and he smirked and did a light chuckle. The next thing I knew his hand went on the side of my face, and he pulled me in for a kiss. Lord, I was kissing Sada. What the fuck was life right now. I never thought twice about Jermaine cousins or his friends. Now, I'm making out with his cousin. I mean we were kissing, and I was getting wet. His lips were soft, and his tongue felt so good I started thinking how it would feel all over my body. Then the door opened, and we separated.

"Oops. I'm sorry mommy and daddy. I just have to take this little guy to get circumcised. Mommy, the doctor is going to do a check-up on you. If everything is fine, we can have you discharged this evening. We want to give Liam here a few hours here after his circumcision." She smiled at both of us while she rolled Liam out with her. I decided to have my baby circumcised because he wasn't having no smelly turtle dick. A bitch goes to give him some head, and it smell like hot Cheetos and peppers. Naw, not my son. They left, and me and Sada were so awkward when the door closed.

"Uh, I gotta make a run real quick." He picked his phone up and put it in his pocket. Before I could say anything, he was gone. No hug, he didn't look at me or even say bye. What the hell?

Liam had a successful surgery if you want to call it that. He came back sleep, but his eyes were puffy. I knew my little guy had been crying. I could tell he was going to be rotten and mainly by me. I held him so much even when he was sleep. I couldn't help it, I was in love. His head was so round and little. There was black hair all over it, and when he did open his eyes, they were chestnut brown like Jermaine's. He was a perfect mix, and from the moment I saw him my life changed. My doctor came in and checked me out.

She said everything was fine and at 6 pm I would be discharged. I was too excited. I hurried and called Hazel, and her loud ass screamed in my ear. Liam was coming home to me and Hazel new place. I couldn't wait to fix his room up and mine. I took a little nap with Liam after I had some Subway from downstairs. When I woke up, my nurse was coming in the room to give me my discharge papers. She also gave me instructions on how to care for his little wee-wee while it healed. My nurse taught me how to strap Liam in the car seat.

He was so little I thought I'd be scared to handle him, but surprisingly I did it good. I was now waiting on Hazel, and for some reason, Sada popped in my head. I looked at my phone, and something said don't call him, but I ignored the voice and dialed him anyway. I just wanted to make sure we were good. It rung twice and then he picked up.

"What up doe Alyssa?" I caught off guard because I was used to him calling me fat-fat or fatty. Even though I hated it, I still was used to it.

"Hey. I just wanted to tell you that I'm being discharged. Hazel is coming to pick me up." It got quite, and I don't know if I was being weird, but I was expecting him to say something. Anything. That's what's up. Glad to hear that. Whoop de-fucking-do. Something. But he was so quiet.

"Ok well, that's all I wanted to tell you. I'll talk to you later."

"A'ight I'm visiting my grandma. I'll hit'chu later." He hung up, and I felt a little better. Maybe that's why he was so quiet because he was with his grandma. My phone rung again, and it was him. I can't even lie and say I didn't smile as I answered it.

"Hello."

"Hellooo." It sound like some loud clapping.

"Mmmm shit Sada. Just like that daddy, fuck meeee."
My mouth dropped, and I hurried and hung up. I made a sour
ass face as I looked down at my phone. What the fuck was
the point of lying? If he was with a bitch why didn't he just
not answer? And why the hell are my eyes getting watery?!

"Hell naw, I'm not dealing with this shit again," I said
out loud to myself. I looked over at my beautiful sleeping son
in his car seat. Getting up, I went to the bathroom to fix my
face. After I got myself together, I looked in the mirror at my
reflection. I'm a mother now. I have a great job, just got a
good house with my best friend. My family has my back and
if I could just be conceited for one minute. I was fine as fuck.
Chocolate, thick as hell and a bitch wore bundles because she
wanted to. My only focus needs to be on my son, myself and
work. Jermaine was gone, and I'll always love and miss him.
But I had no business even thinking about a relationship now.
Especially with one who is just like him. Hell, to the
muthafucking naw. I flipped my hair and turned the
bathroom light off. The door opened, and Hazel walked in
smiling big, and I smiled back.

"You ready boo?" I put my feet in my Adidas slides.

"Let's do this." The guy behind Hazel came in with a
wheelchair for me, and Hazel picked up Liam's car seat. I set
our bags on my lap, and we headed downstairs. Fuck Sada
ass. It was all about me and Liam.

SHE GOT IT BAD FOR A DETROIT HITTA

Malcolm

(Two weeks later)

I got to my destination and parked my Lexus. I brought my new bitch a few weeks ago. Money was finally rolling in deep for me, and I was enjoying it. This is what I was trying to get those three empty-headed niggas to understand. Money was better and longer when you sold drugs. You make your own hours, and when you get really in the game, you have people selling for you. Although wasn't nobody above me but I let my boys have their own little crew. At the end of the day, I ate first. You see I'm trying to have all of Detroit on lock. East, west, and southside. Eventually, I'd run Michigan and can expand to other states.

I was looking at Minnesota as my first pick. You see I been trying to get on for some time now. I was in the game since I was ten years old. My older brother Randall was in charge. He had the fucking streets of Detroit on lock. I mean his shit even stretched to the suburbs. I don't know what it was about Randall, but since he was born, he just demanded control. He wasn't a bad big brother by far. Randall always had my back. We'd get in fights like brothers do but nothing too deep. Our mama didn't play that shit. We had different fathers, and for some reason, my father was a fucking rolling stone.

He wasn't in my life, but he spread kids all through this bitch. Babies used to be left on our doorstep because people knew my mama as his wife. Not knowing that nigga took off when I was eight. Randall's dad was in his life heavy. He'd get him all the time and have him spend weekends with him. He'd take my brother on trips, football games. Randall has been to so many Superbowl's I lost count. His dad didn't look at me like shit but his baby mama son. Every man doesn't have that decency to remember kids are innocent. My mama would try to do little shit to cheer me up.

She'd take me out to eat, to the drive-in or making my favorite food. She tried, and I appreciated it, but over time I developed a hate for my brother. Now, here is when shit gets deep. Joy Willis, Mac and Sada's mama, she was my fucking woman first. I met her when we both were sophomores in high school, and Randall was twenty already out of school. First off, the nigga sick because Joy was only sixteen. Yea she had a body better than most grown women. But she still was underage. Joy always had a crush on Randall, but he looked at her as jailbait. Because she wanted him so bad, it made me want her even more.

I became obsessed with her. She decided to make me her boyfriend, and I knew it was only, so she could get close to Randall. Still, I figured I'd make her love me anyway by showing her I was the better choice. Besides Randall was with Joy best friend at the time, Shauney. My hoe ass now ex-wife. She was head over heels for Randall, and he was into my woman. Eventually, they found each-other and Joy left me for him. We spent a whole two-years together, and the minute she turned eighteen she rushed to Randall.

Me and him got into the biggest fist fight we ever had. Don't get shit twisted, I got hits in and so did he. Anyway, we didn't talk for a few months but after some time. I stopped caring and was happy with Shauney. I went back to work for Randall and shit went back to normal. I was doing me in the streets but went home to my woman every night. Shit caught up to me, and some bitch claimed she was pregnant. She told Shauney which made her dump me. By then Randall and Joy were done, and she was pregnant with Mac. My brother wasn't the relationship type.

That nigga could never find pussy he wanted to be loyal to long enough. When he did have relationships, he picked some dumb bitches and either he cheated, or she did. Fast forward, and I faded more and more in the back. Randall wouldn't even give me my own crew, the nigga said I didn't do business right. Tal'embout my greed and the way I was loud with everything would be my demise. So I plotted to get rid of my brother. I was going to have him killed, but he lucked up and caught a body. The nigga was looking at life. But his crew was too loyal, and they paid a high-end attorney. I couldn't have that shit, so I knew people who knew people in the inside where he was locked up at.

I went completely broke paying to have my brother killed in jail. I even had to get a job which I just quit since money was back on top for me. All my problems were solved. I had my wife; my son and I was good on the street life. Until Mac grew up to be just like his fucking dad. That nigga got in the streets, and he was the lookout for this drug dealer named Mooch. Joy was fucking him, and she worked a lot, so Mac and Sada were with him a lot. He taught them a few things in the killing world. Mac and Sada took on easily, but Mac ass was a natural born shooter. I think it's because he always had a smooth plan first.

Sada wasn't like me, that nigga was in the limelight with his brother. The two of them just had it, and Jermaine was right along with them. But my stupid ass wife wasn't the model mother. So Jermaine gravitated to Joy more. Mac and Sada became like his brothers, and he started doing hits with them. It was then I wanted back in the game. I couldn't do it and not have Mac on my side. I could get up like I am, and someone could want Mac to take me out. Because we were family, I knew he'd do the shit when I least expected it. I couldn't have that, so I wanted him with me. Sada and Jermaine would come along too because Mac did.

But that muthafucka just wouldn't cooperate. He said no, and they said no. My own damn son didn't want part in the drug game. I told them we all could run Detroit and eventually the state. But these lil bastards just wouldn't see shit my way. Seems like since I was born things never went my way. Since Jermaine's death, I made a vow to change my life for the better. Success, money, and power by any means necessary.

"This is it?" I looked at one of my workers pissed off.

"What'chu mean boss? That's seventy-thousand right there." I threw the two duffle bags on the floor.

"That we have to split three ways!!"

"Boss that's over eleven G's apiece. Sounds like a good payday for me." I walked up to my other worker who said that and punched the shit out of him.

"That ain't no good payday nigga!! I said I wanted at least twenty!!! That means you muthafuckas is slackin'." I looked around at them and was disgusted. This little change wasn't about to get me no power anytime soon. I didn't want to be hood rich, I wanted to be wealthy. I'd been training these muthafuckas for a while now. This the crew that I was going to let Mac, Sada, and Jermaine run had they followed my lead. I found a seller of pure cocaine in Ohio a few months before Jermaine was killed. The nigga was as hard as they come but when I mentioned my brother's name, he showed respect.

He gave me a certain amount of product every two months, and he expected it all to be sold. Nothing left over and his exact amount every two months. I had no problem getting my supply from him because I still had Detroit. He didn't have any other sellers in Michigan, and he hadn't planned on getting any. The only thing he wanted was his money, or it was my head. Which is why eleven-grand ain't cuttin' shit. I had to give my supplier six of my eleven.

"Do better niggas. I'm doing y'all a favor, now I need you muthafuckas to step up." I picked up my half of the money and left out the spot.

I was mad as hell when I got back to my car. I was looking forward to at least eighteen to twenty-thousand. My boys sold all over, even in areas they weren't supposed to. They knew either sell anywhere or deal with me. As soon as I got in my ride, I opened my glove compartment and pulled out my mini black glass bottle. I poured a little bit of the white powder on top of my hand and sniffed it up my nose. Instantly I inhaled and closed my eyes. I sat back in my seat and let my body float. This was why I owed my supplier six G's. I had what most people thought was a problem.

But it's only a problem if you a broke ass nigga. I had money to supply my habit I was just breaking the cardinal rule. Don't use ya own shit. In my case, don't use ya supplier shit. I was good at paying for what I used, and I had no plan on slowing down. This powder heaven was almost better than pussy. As a matter of fact, if you mix the two, then shit really turned up. I was in Atlantic City last week with strippers, my powder bitch and stack on stacks of money. Shit got wild, and I planned on repeating that again soon in Miami. I poured a little more and sniffed it up. Putting the glass back in the glove compartment I wiped my nose and pulled off to go home.

"What did you ask me to come over for if you're in a bad mood?"

"Because I wanted to see you. You been dodging me ever since that mistake." I pointed to Quinn's round stomach.

I started fucking with her some months back. I was at Annex nightclub in downtown Detroit. She was there with her girls throwing back shots like they were tea. I went over making sure she was good. Mac had stopped fucking with her, and it had her in her feelings. Like father like son I thought when she told me. A few more drinks and I had her here in my spot bent over. I been hooked ever since. I wasn't in love, but Quinn had me stuck. She was fine as hell, didn't hound me, and she wasn't in my pocket for shit. When I found out, Mac slipped in her raw and she got pregnant I was pissed the fuck off.

I didn't say shit to her for a while, and her ass didn't even notice. Her focus was my nephew and being a family. His focus was the streets and his money. Wasn't long before she came running back. We fuck on the low, but I wanted her to leave Mac alone and be with me. The only way for her to see he wasn't shit. Was for him to drop her on her ass and I be right there to catch her. Mac was a product of my fucking brother, it wasn't in him to be shit when it comes to bitches.

"Don't call my son a mistake Malcolm or I'll leave." I walked over to her and looked down at her.

"You ain't going nowhere. You staying the night and I'm inside that pregnant pussy all night like I have been since day one." Quinn had some decent pussy, but it was even better now that she was pregnant. Just wet and she gripped my dick so good.

"Malcolm, we have to chill. I'm trying to make things work with Mac. I shouldn't have never gotten involved with you?"

"That nigga is never going to be what you want. You need to let that shit go Quinn." I was getting impatient with her high hopes in my nephew.

"You don't know that."

"I DO KNOW THAT!!" Quinn jumped when I yelled, but I didn't give a damn because she was talking stupid.

"Calm down with all the yelling." Her freak ass looked down at my hard dick.

"Why you lookin' at my dick if my nephew on ya brain?" She looked back up at me and pushed me against the wall.

"This is the last time."

"Shut the fuck up lying and suck this dick." She dropped to her knees and did what I said. Quinn's head game was sick. She got the balls good, and she'd slob on my eight-inch dick. My shit may have not been the longest, but I had girth. Quinn and any other bitch I fucked came good as hell from my shit. I held my head back and had a grip on her scalp.

"Shit Quinn." I was still high, and she was making me feel like I popped an E pill. I pulled her up and took her leggings, shirt, and sandals off. She had a thong and a strapless bra on, and I hurried up and took that off to. I undressed and pulled her to my bedroom. I was so horny, and the coke was making me feel like a wild animal. I sat her on the edge of my bed and got on my knees. Spreading her legs wide and leaving her sitting up I put my face in her wet pussy. I felt like I was in an illusion as my face swirled in her wetness. I was loud with it, and she was moaning making me go in more. I even sniffed her juices all in my nose while my tongue played with her clit and my fingers were in her hole. Spreading her legs wider I literally rubbed my entire face in her soaked pussy. My entire face was soaked. I put that clit back in my mouth and focused only on it. Quinn was scratching my head up, and the pain for some reason was turning me on. She came for a second time, and I stood up and laid her back. My dick was so hard as I stood between her legs and rubbed my dick on her clit. I went in and moaned so damn loud. I bent down and started sucking on her nipples. I pulled them so damn hard, and she was calling my name cumming on my dick. I felt me getting closer as I pumped hard as fuck. I fucked her like she wasn't pregnant hard and pounding. When I was seconds from cuming, I pulled out and came all on her stomach.

"FUCK!!"

"Really Malcolm?" I shook my dick and looked at Quinn sitting up pissed.

"Should've been my fucking baby." I shrugged and headed to the bathroom. I heard her cussing as I picked my phone up and closed the bathroom door. Quinn was bitching, but all she was about to do was clean up and lay in my bed for the rest of the day. I saw one of my boys called me twice. I sat down on the toilet and called him back.

"Shit good?" I asked when he picked up.

"Naw boss. I'm on the eastside, and we got a problem." Aw shit. As he talked, I went in my medicine cabinet and grabbed my mini glass bottle. I felt my stress level go up and shit was gonna be different from here on out.

Mac

"A'ight so what's up Mac. You said you wanted to meet with us." Sada and Clip walked in the basement of one of our spots. I asked them to meet me here because it was payday and I had some shit to tell them. I stood up and gave both of them two stacks with the currency band that had $10,000 on both of them. We did a job in Pontiac, and our hired was satisfied at how neat shit went down, so he gave us an extra band.

"I found out some shit about Malcolm." We sat down in some folded chairs that were down there. We had two of our guys upstairs keeping an eye on shit.

"An informant told me, Malcom, been sneaking and selling his drugs on the eastside." I looked at Sada.

"The respect pops left behind was the only reason I was informed this. Malcolm is being disrespectful and if we can't get him to stop. He's our next hit." Clip and Sada looked at each other and then at me.

"That's y'all family, so I'll roll with whatever." I nodded at Clip then looked at Sada.

"He family Mac, we just can't kill him. What about Maine bro? Shit seems foul."

"I feel you, bro. That ain't what I wanna do either. Especially if he ain't harming us. But let's just be real. Them niggas ain't looking out twice. He'd get clipped by us or by them." Sada started massaging his temple.

"I mean the shit ends bad either way. He been trying to get you, him and Maine to work for him for a while. Nigga on a power trip. Y'all talk to him about this shit he ain't go' chill. He either gone try to go for the east side niggas or come for us." Sada set up then, and I think we all knew what Clip said was facts. I stood up started pacing.

"Fuck man. Why the fuck he even in the game?! Nigga over forty-five and just lost his son. This shit gon' get worse. I can feel it."

"We could set him up to be robbed. Them niggas in Inkster always looking for a lick. We don't know who his crew is and clearly, the east side niggas don't either. But they must know it's him somehow." When Sada said that I remembered something.

"He's putting the same logo that pops used to put on his product."

"Ok well let's set Malcolm up to get robbed. We can tell the Inkster boys no killing just take his product." I ran my hand over my face as Sada talked. Clip was shaking his head, and I knew he was thinking like me.

"That's stupid as fuck Sada. Look, I say we talk to him. Actually, let me do it."

"Hell naw, he say one thing wrong and yo' ass will be ready to clip. I'm coming with you and shit will go good. Come on Mac we just buried his son." I heard what Sada was saying, and I wasn't trying to be negative. I was being a realist, Malcolm wasn't going to fall back, and shit was going to pop off. I didn't plan on me, Sada or Clip being the ones on the fucked end of this.

***

My dog just caught the bag, I ain't runnin' from the grams

You got that internet beef, you run straight to the 'Gram

Pussy nigga got shot and he ran to the Gram

If I get shot I'ma shoot 'til it jam in my hand

You in your phone all day, ain't makin' no bands

I told my lil dog count it as fast as he can

Soon as he run, it's off with his head

I need that bag and your life like fuck is you sayin'?

We were all back at Butzles chillin'. It was hot outside but not the sticky hot that we been getting lately. A few niggas were barbequing, and the usual cars parked with music playing. Thick west side bitches walking around looking good as fuck. I was posted on the wall with my brother and Clip. We had some Patron in our cup and weed going. I wasn't in a smoking mood, just tequila right now. I had on some red Puma basketball shorts, white and red matching shirt. I wore my Citizen white diamond watch and Air Jordan One red and white Retro's. Niggas were walking by nodding in my direction as a form of speaking, and the bitches were doing everything to get me to notice them.

Even call my damn name like I'm supposed to answer. I saw a Tesla S Model pull up and park. I wasn't about to give it a second look until the driver's door opened and Hazel stepped out. Alyssa opened the passenger's side and got out. They both looked good, but my eyes were on Hazel. Angel face was looking so sexy in these tight black leggings that were ripped from the bottom all the way up the middle of her legs and thighs. She had this black tube top on, and that long black hair was touching her shoulders curled. That face was flawless as usual, and I was glad she didn't have on make-up. She seriously didn't need that shit at all even on them soft full lips.

When she turned and closed the door, I saw that round fat ass. How the fuck a slim girl get a fat ass fucked with me every day. I watched her step up, and she had on some black NIKE Airforce One's on with the white NIKE sign. Her feet were little as hell like a damn kid. The way I was looking at Hazel, Sada was looking at Alyssa. Ma had on some dress that looked like a ripped bleached t-shirt, and it was off the shoulders. She had these long ass black heels on that stopped at her thighs. Alyssa was thick, so her thighs were jiggling, and I could have sworn I heard this nigga cuss under his breath. She had some long corn rolls in her head and neither one of them seen us yet.

Alyssa knew some of the girls here, and you could see her introducing them to Hazel. I could have went over there, but I fell back. I haven't took Hazel on that date yet, but we did text a lot. Nothing happened I just haven't gotten around to it. Me leaving the doors for communication to her open was my way of showing her I was feelin' her. Hazel was a dope girl, I got to know a lot more about her and her family. Angel face is spoiled and privileged, but she has a really good heart. Her drive in making her dreams come true with owning her own restaurant was admirable. I talked a little about myself but not much because part of me felt my hood ways would be too much for her.

"What's up wit'chu and Lyssa? You ain't been around her that much, and you only see the baby when I have him." I asked Sada while I took a swig of the Patron.

"We good she just a mama now, and I have a life nosey nigga." I laughed because clearly shit went sour with them, but I wasn't about to press. He'd tell me eventually. Alyssa son was cute as hell. He had Maine eyes and his mama everything else. She let me take him to see my mama twice, and her ass fell in love. I told her to chill out because I wasn't giving her no grandkids anytime soon. I couldn't speak for Sada loose dick ass. I went to my car, so I could pour another drink. If you keep ya liquor out in the open muthafuckas thought it was a pass to ask for some. I'on share shit so to keep down confusion I kept my shit in the car.

"Hey, Mac boo. You coming to my party?" I looked out the side of my eye and saw this bitch named Amelia came over and asked me. I fucked her last year and she been wanting me to do it again, but I was good on that.

"I might swing by. When is it?" She reached in her purse and pulled out a flyer. I looked it over and saw it was this weekend at *Jeans&Moet* downtown.

"I hope I see you there." She winked at me and walked away passing out more flyers. I went back over and chilled with my brother and crew for about twenty minutes. The girls still didn't see me and Sada unless they were playing that shit good. I had a nice buzz and was high now because I decided to smoke.

"I'm about to take a piss," I said to Sada, and he nodded. I went to the back of the building and took a piss. Damn liquor was going through me. Putting my dick back up I walked back to the front and saw Hazel a little further in the park. Some nigga was all in her face, and she was smiling. He put his arm around her neck and pulled his phone out. Naw, this ain't even about to happen. I looked over at my brother and Clip, and they saw what I saw. We signaled each other so they'd be on the watch if shit went south. I walked over there, and Hazel had yet to see me.

"Aye, my nigga you need to create some space." Hazel stopped smiling, and dude looked at me like he wanted some.

"Mac you can't have every fucking female. I know for a fact this ain't yo' woman because she just told me she was single."

"I'on give a fuck what her big head ass told you. It's about what I say, now get the fuck back." He took his arm from around Hazel then got in my face.

"Fuck you, Mac, you put fear in the rest of these pussies but you'on put shit in me." Respect was free and easy to give. This nigga was on one talking to me that way. I chuckled and head-butted him twice in his nose breaking that muthafucka. He was about to fall, but I helped him out by hitting him in his jaw. Hazel pushed me in my chest all the way until we got behind the building. I saw some dudes come and help ol'boy up. Sada and Clip gave me the signal that them and our crew had eyes open. Me and Hazel got behind the building, and she lit into me.

"What the hell are you doing Mac? You can't walk around acting like a fucking wrestler head butting people."

"Naw ma that's where you're wrong. I do what the fuck I want." I leaned back against the wall and looked at her. I was good and high plus I was ready to beat the fuck out ol'boy. Hazel put her hands on the back of her hips looking fed up with me.

"I'm not yours. Let's just get that shit clear. We text and that's it. You haven't even taken me on a date yet." My eyes were on her lips and then her sexy face.

"I'on move when you want me to." She folded her arms and arched her eyebrows.

"Then I don't behave the way you *want me to*."

"And I'mma react the way you just saw but only worse." I put my hand under my shirt around my stomach. Her eyes followed my hand, and I smiled.

"Why you lookin' at me like that?" She looked at me and rolled her eyes.

"I'm not looking at you like nothing. If anything, I think you're crazy as fuck Mac." I poked my lips out and nodded over and over.

"I am Hazel. Ain't shit about me sane. You still want that date?" I wanted to see with her seeing a light version of me snappin' would she still wanna fuck with me.

"I do, but I'm not about to wait on you." I took her hand, and we walked to the front of the building.

"Gimmie yo' keys," I told her, and she did. I looked around for Alyssa and found her with some girls.

"Lyssa." She looked up and smiled at us. I gave her a hug.

"You good taking Hazel's car? She leaving with me." Alyssa mouth dropped, and she looked from me to Hazel smiling like a child.

"I'm good. You crazy kids have fun." I still had Hazel hand as we walked to my car.

"Mac I'm not sleeping with you." I balled my face up.

"Ain't nobody about to fuck you. You said you wanted your date so tomorrow we are doing that." I opened my passenger door. Before she got in, she said.

"Then why do I need to leave with you now?"

"Because I want you to spend the night with me. I ain't no teenager Hazel I can keep my dick put up." She thought about it first but then smirked and got in. I closed the door and went over to my brother to holla at him. That nigga eyes were glued on Alyssa who I knew saw him because she knew I was here. I couldn't wait to find out what went down between them. After I chopped it up with Sada, a jogged back to my car, hopped in and pulled off.

"Ok baller, I like the new bedroom set." Hazel smiled when she walked in my room. I brought a new chocolate brown upholstered bedroom set and a new marble kitchen table with chairs. I was making more money, so I figured it was time for a change. I upgraded the kitchen appliances too. Nothing to crazy just some grown man shit.

"Thanks, ma I'm glad you like it. You can put your stuff anywhere you want." I took her home, so she could get her a bag together. Then we went to Rite-Aid on Livernois and Oakman street, so she could get all her girly shit.

"Oooo I like this." Hazel kicked her gym-shoes off and laid on my leather chaise lounge chair.

"It came with the set. The sales lady was talking to me like I wasn't a hood nigga. I told her I didn't care as long as my shit wasn't gay lookin'." Hazel laughed as I took my jewelry off.

"I'll let you shower first then go after. I'm bout' to order our food."

"Ok." She got up and took her bag into my bathroom and closed the door. I went to my DoorDash app and ordered us some food from *Taylor Made Burgers* on seven-mile. I got the shrimp, steak and rice bowl with a grilled chicken corn beef sandwich. I got up and went to the bathroom and opened the door.

"Angel face what'chu want from Taylor Made Burgers." I talked to her through the shower curtain.

"I can get anything?" I laughed when she asked that.

"You ain't got no broke nigga Hazel." I already knew she was rolling her eyes and about to say some smart shit.

"I don't have a nigga at all." Told you. I ignored it but made a note to come back to it later.

"Can I get the loaded potato bowl with shrimp and lamb chops. Oh and ooo they have a banana pudding cheesecake. Can I get two slices."

"You uh inner fat bitch ma." She laughed hard as hell and stuck her middle finger out to me. I laughed and closed the door. She could have ordered the whole menu, and it was cool with me. I wanted her comfortable and women are easier to deal with when you feed them. I ordered our food, and I jumped up grabbing my heat when I heard my front door open and slam.

"You good nigga?" I asked when I got to the front and saw Sada in the hallway.

"Hell naw, Alyssa gone have me catch a fuckin' case." I laughed because he was hot. The nigga's face was balled tight, and he had his fist balled up even tighter.

"What happened?"

"Man she at Butzels bein' a complete thot. All dancing and then on that clown ass nigga Mario. I should have fucked both of them up." I ran my hand over my face to keep from laughing hard.

"You sound bothered my nigga. You want Lyssa?" He turned his nose up.

"Naw I'on want her hoe ass."

"Don't talk about my best friend nigga." We both turned around, and Hazel was standing there brushing her hair looking at Sada like she was about to fight him. I looked at her tight shirt she had on that showed her hard nipples and these short ass pajama shorts showing her legs.

"Aye get'cho big head ass in the back dressed like that." She smacked her lips, but she did what I said showing that round ass. I know my brother, we don't go after each other's bitches. We'd pass a hoe along to one another but not our main.

"I'm 'bout to smoke and go to bed." Sada walked upstairs, and I closed the door. I put my heat in my back and went back to my room to get this damn girl together.

"You want me to fuck you up?"

"What'd I do?" I was up on her mad as hell. O'l big head ass was really confused.

"This shit'chu got on is for my eyes only. I can see ya hard nipples and yo' shorts to damn short. Had that been one of my niggas I'd uh had to fuck them up." Hazel saw how for real I was and she understood then.

"I apologize Mac. I wasn't trying to be disrespectful and just so you know. I'd never do anything with your brother or your friends. So you would never have to fuck anyone up."

"I know you not that type ma." I kissed her cheek and went to the bathroom to shower. Hazel had my bathroom smelling all sweet. I got cleaned and decided to put on some boxers and basketball shorts. I put my NIKE slides on and went to the dining room because I could smell our food.

"You know we are eating in the room right?"

"Oh, I didn't know if you wanted us eating in your bed. Let me grab us some more napkins and something to drink." I told her cool, and I picked up our food and took it in the room. Hazel came back in with two *Faygo Rock&Rye* pops and napkins. I left the covers pulled back on my bed, and we both set up with our back against the headboard. I don't know what it was about me and Hazel talks that I was into. I turned the TV on, but it was just for extra sound because we talked our entire meal.

"You know what I thought of?" I chuckled when I looked at her cleaning the hell out of her lamb chop bone.

"What's that?"

"You never ask me about my exes or anything about who I've had sex with. Why is that?" I finished chewing my steak and drunk some pop.

"Why the fuck I care about some past shit? Tha fuck that gotta do with me and you today?" She looked so confused.

"But I ask you about your past relationships and the bitches you've fucked. It's just a part of me wanting to know you." I laughed when she said that.

"Women do think that." I shook my head.

"When y'all ask any nigga y'all diggin' about exes and who they've fucked. It ain't to get closer to us. It's to be nosey and see if you will be the first anything for the nigga. For example, if I told you I have never came off of head. Yo' ass would get cocky as hell thinking you'll be the first. Off that alone in your head, you think you'll have a nigga sprung and chasing the pussy." She started laughing.

"That is not true Mac."

"You know that shit is straight facts. Then y'all be burning in the inside when we answer all the questions you ask about our past. Have you ever been in love? When was the last time you had sex? All the shit y'all know as we answer you be rolling ya eyes mad as hell. I'on need to know shit except is you clean and are you a virgin. I just don't give a fuck about past shit. That's what insecure bitch niggas do. Hold a female past over her head. Naw, that ain't me. Plus like I told you earlier. I'm crazy as fuck so any bitch I'm diggin', I've built up in my head that I'm ya first everything. I don't wanna know about a nigga touchin' mine rather before me or not." Because I feel like I got Hazel figured out. She was about to fuck with me and see my reaction.

"But you're not my first Mac, of anything." I put some rice and shrimp in my mouth and said.

"I bet I be ya last and I dare you to say some smart shit about that." I heard crickets after I spoke. Hazel wasn't running shit, and it was time she knew it. I was done with my food. I saved my cornbeef sandwich for tomorrow. I put my empty tray on my nightstand next to me. She finished her food and stood up with her boxes in her hand.

"You know you can leave that in the bag on the nightstand until the morning." Hazel picked my bag up with her face bunched.

"Naw I can't even function with all of this in here." Maybe that was a woman thang because my lazy ass would have kept that shit in here until the morning. I got up and pulled my covers back. My shit wasn't made up because I wasn't into all of that. I'd wake up and just pull my covers back. That was my version of making my bed. Hazel came back when I took my basketball shorts off leaving my boxers on. I turned to one of my favorite movies *Coming to America* and got in bed.

"Oh my goodness my mama used to watch this all the time." She giggled.

"Word? My mama did to, me and Sada used to know the whole movie word for word." I watched her sexy ass get in bed all the way on the fucking end. Ma was nervous being this close to me. All that slick ass mouth and poppin' off she does, and a nigga intimidates her. The movie started, and she was all in. I was too but I kept finding myself looking at her.

"What?" She finally caught me and asked. I was laying on my back with my hand on my chest.

"You just gorgeous as hell to me." She turned on her side with her hand propping that big ass head up.

"Thank you, Mac." I could feel her leg shaking, and I knew she was uneasy.

"Mackenzie. You can call me Mackenzie if you want." Her pretty ass smiled so damn big, and she bit her bottom lip.

"I love your name; it's so sexy and unique." I pulled her on my chest by her arm. Her entire body stiffed, and I could feel her heart speeding up.

"Why you so damn nervous? You know I'd never do shit to harm you or to make you uncomfortable." She relaxed a lot more and put her hands flat on my chest, and her chin was on top of them. Her soft ass legs were entangled in mine. She still was a little stiff, but her heart slowed down a little.

"Don't do that nigga, you don't make me nervous. I just never know your next move."

"You always tryna be hard when you know that ain't you." I moved some hair out her face, and she blushed.

"Why you don't want me to be your girlfriend?"

"I never said that. I said I tried the relationship thing and it just ain't for me. It always ends bad, and I don't need the drama. I cheat, you cheat. Or I get bored, and you start pressing too much. I don't want that with me and you. I want you around angel face." I ran my hand through her long ass hair.

"Ok, I understand. But when I talk to other guys, you can't get mad." I felt my self about to get annoyed because I knew she wasn't playing. Hazel is fucking breathtaking, smart, level-headed and she ain't a hoe. Hard shit to come by with some of these westside bitches. A nigga comes along with the right game, he'd have her, and that would fuck with me. But getting into a relationship would fuck our shit all up.

"You right I couldn't get mad. So it's best to make sure I'm in a good mood if I find out or see you talking to a nigga." She looked in my eyes with a sweet face.

"Why weren't you in a good mood today?"

"I saw a nigga touching you." I was speaking nothing but the truth, and I looked in her eyes without blinking so she knew I was serious.

"What sense does that make? You just said-----"

"I had to react the best way I know possible." Her mouth dropped.

"That was your best way possible? To head butt someone in the face?" I nodded.

"You really are crazy." I laughed a little because her voice was low as if she's just now believing me.

"And I have a bad temper but like I said. I'd never hurt you or make you uncomfortable." I saw her eyes glued to my lips.

"You wanna kiss me, Hazel?" She hurried and looked at me.

"No." She put her head down laughing, and I laughed.

"Come here." Her eyes met mine again, and she moved closer to my face. Our lips touched, and I wasted no time letting my tongue enter her mouth. Them lips wrapped around mine like butter and her soft hand was on my face. I flipped her over on her back without breaking our kiss.

"Wait, wait. We have to stop." I looked at her under me, and there was no way I could stop. Although I would because I don't rape bitches. But I wanted Hazel bad as fuck.

"Angel face I promise we will still go on a date tomorrow. I know what'chu want, and I'll try to be that. I won't fuck around with your feelings if you don't fuck around with mine." I waited on her to say something, but she smiled and kissed me. We made out for about five minutes. Her pussy was hot and wet, and my dick was so hard. I set up between her legs and pulled her top over her head. She had the perfect set of titties with some light caramel nipples. I took her shorts off, and her pussy was nice, bald and them lips were waiting for me to open them and expose that pink lil baby.

"You so fucking gorgeous Hazel." I got back on top of her licking and sucking on her neck. She was light skin so I know I gave her a hickey or two.

"I can't let anyone else have you," I said in between licks and sucking on her titties. I licked and kissed all down her body until I was face to face with her pretty pussy. I put her legs on my shoulders and kept my hands around her thighs. I wasn't using no hands on her pussy. All face, tongue, and lips. I licked my tongue nice and slow between her lips. I mean I took my sweet time working my way from the bottom to that pink pearl. Once I reached it, I added pressure and swirled my tongue all around it. I sucked on it gently and then went back to licking.

"Mmm shit Mackenzie." My name coming out her mouth was so sexy. I was hooked on it already and knew I only wanted her to call me that. The more she said it, the more I showed that pussy some love. My grip was so tight on her thighs all she could move was her head. I didn't want her to cheat me with this pussy. It was so sweet and savory.

"Uhhh, mmhmm." I felt her back arched as she came in my mouth for the second time. I eased up and started kissing her thighs. I bit down gently and kissed on them too. Once in her face, we kissed deep as hell. Both of us tasting her juices. I leaned to the side of my nightstand and opened the drawer to grab a condom. I slipped it on, and I saw how nervous she was when she saw my dick.

"I won't hurt you, Hazel. In any way." She nodded quickly, and I climbed back on top kissing her. Her legs were spread far, and I rubbed the head of my dick on her clit. Getting by her hole, I kissed her and slid in a little.

"Sssss." She moaned in my ear and bit my shoulder. Her pussy grip game was the best. It was so wet and snug with some soft ass walls. I got all the way in and started to stroke slowly.

"Shit Hazel." Her small hands were on my back, arms and then on my chest. Her faces were making my dick jump inside of her. She kept licking her lips and when she would open her eyes and they'd meet mine. I knew she had me. Damn.

"Ahhhh, uhhhh. Ahhhh, Mackenzie." I didn't want to come yet, so I had to think of other shit. That didn't work because her voice was pulling at me. I put my hand around her throat and kept my stroke up. Bringing my lips to hers, I kissed her and squeezed a little tighter. She loved it because she came but that pussy still had grip.

"Listen to that wet pussy. I need to taste her again." I pulled out and flipped her sexy ass over. She was weak, so I had to position her on all fours. That perfect arch and ass was looking up at me as I was eating her pussy from the back. Her hand went to the back of my head, and she was grinding in my face like I liked. Yea baby, fuck daddy face. Before she could cum, I stopped and slipped my dick in from the back.

"Throw that ass back angel face. Twerk that shit." I knew from the moment I saw her round ass booty it was soft, and I wanted it to twerk on my dick. I let her do her thang for a minute then I spread them ass cheeks apart and dug in. I got on my tip-toes and leaned forward while still killin' that pussy with this eleven-inches. I kissed her back and licked down the middle of it.

"I… I… Ohhhh.. shit I'm cumming again!" I pulled out, and she squirted a lot as I busted in the condom.

"Shit!" I fell on the side of her breathing hard. Hazel was all fucked up with that back still arched and her face in my bed. Her hair was pressed on her soaked back, and she looked so damn sexy. I got up and cleaned myself up. Coming back with a rag I cleaned her up from the back and slapped that ass a few times. I grabbed one of my large towels and came back in the room. She was on her back now smiling. I covered her wet spot up and got back in bed.

"You ain't been fucked right, Hazel." I was naked, and so was she. When she turned my way them small hips, and titties caught my attention.

"And you ain't had no good pussy to have you like you were." She started imitating my faces, and we both laughed.

"Shut the fuck up and get over here." She came and laid back on top of me.

"You may not be my woman but you gone have to act like it."

"What!?" I know I fucked her head up with that, but I was just being honest.

"You call me spoiled but look at you. You want me to act like I'm yours while you're out here being a hoe?" She laughed, but I didn't find shit funny.

"I said I'd try."

"Well, then that's all I got for you too." She pecked my lips and laid her naked ass on top of a pillow. I started to yank her ass up and get back in them guts. But naw it's cool, I'll show her better than I can tell her.

Alyssa

Don't touch my hair
When it's the feelings I wear
Don't touch my soul
When it's the rhythm I know
Don't touch my crown
They say the vision I've found
Don't touch what's there
When it's the feelings I wear

I sat on my stool in front of my full-length mirror. I had took my braids down yesterday and washed it. Needing a break from weave I was now flat ironing my hair while *Solange* played on my phone. Liam made my hair grow because it was at my bra strap. Speaking of my little chubs, he was just a blessing. I loved that little boy so much. He was almost a month, and in just that short time I was all about him. My body was snapping back, and I was feeling really good. Me and Hazel were in our house and had it all set up. I couldn't wait to go back to work soon, and my mama was even acting right. Well, she wasn't too overprotective with me more with Liam, but it was all out of love. The only thing missing was Sada.

I missed him so much that whenever I saw him, I wanted to smack him in his mouth. He had the nerve to act like he had an issue when he saw me talking to Mario at Butzels. I was being extra dancing on Mario but so what. I didn't and wasn't about to fuck, but I wanted Sada to hurt. Since he lied to me the day after I had Liam then hearing him fuck a bitch on his phone had me in my feelings. It also made me realize Sada was young in the mind still. He'd handle shit the wrong way. Still, I missed him calling and checking on me, riding in his car and him calling me fatty or fat-fat. I hated that I missed him, but it's just how I felt.

"I'm so in love with this little boy." Hazel walked in smiling so big holding Liam. I turned my music down even though it wasn't that loud.

"Don't let Mac here you say that." It was so cute when she blushed but tried to front.

"I ain't thinking about Mackenzie. According to him, I'm not single, but he is." I put my flat irons down and looked at her.

"What?"

"He's Mackenzie now?" Smirking and still looking at her blush so much I wanted to scream, but Liam was here.

"Hoe you fucked Mac?" I put my hand over my mouth laughing and swinging my legs.

"I knew it. I knew when you spent the night y'all were going to fuck."

"See you acting like ya daddy, inserting yourself in some shit. Just pull out bitch." Hazel laughed and kissed Liam chubby jaw.

"Don't kiss my baby slut. Where them lips been?" I teased but just playing with her.

"I didn't even give him any head. I will soon though because that thang is big and beautiful." She did the Cardi-B and stuck her tongue out. I laughed with her and gave her a high five.

"We had a breakfast date at Dime Store downtown. It was so fun then we went walking on the Riverwalk. He is the fuckin' deal, Alyssa. Kahlil didn't fuck me half as good as Mackenzie did. But he still wants to be a hoe that's the only thing. Like I swear the thought of him in a bitch face pisses me off."

"You got it bad bih. But I knew you did when you wouldn't stop talking about how he annoys you. I think you're what he needs and he's what you need."

"So are we gonna pretend that you're not what Sada needs?" I rolled my eyes and turned to finish my hair.

"So he flipped on you at Butzles. Him and his brother are too damn much. All these expectations they put on me and you while they act a fuckin' fool." I looked at her when she said that through the mirror and then I looked at myself.

"I don't know what to feel about Sada. Like I never ever thought about him in any way before. Now, he occupies my mind, but I don't want him to. Why do we get close to the things we should run from?" Hazel was quiet, and I looked at her and laughed. She was beaming at Liam and rubbing his back.

"You're not even listening!"

"I am I swear I was. He moved his head, and it threw me off." We both giggled, I finished my hair and got dressed.

I decided to wear my blue and white IVY PARK yoga shorts with the matching sports bra. My blue Huaraches looked good with it. Today was beyond hot outside but I still put Liam on a NIKE onesie, matching hat and his mittens so he wouldn't scratch is eyes. One of the many gifts my mama brought him was a crochet car seat cover, so I put that over it. He looked so handsome, and my breast milk was beefing him up a little.

Hazel went to work, and I was so proud of her for coming out here and doing her thing. Strapping Liam in my 2017 Impala I got in and put my purse on my passenger seat. I was so nervous about where we were going I was chewing on my bottom lip the entire time I drove. I thought the radio would distract me, but it failed. It was time for me to do this and I couldn't think of anyone I wanted with me more than my son.

"Hi, Jermaine." I gripped the handle on Liam stroller because I was so nervous. Even though I talked to Jermaine when I'm deep in thought or if I'm writing in my journal, I've still never been to his grave.

"I apologize for not coming sooner. It's just hard seeing your name on this tombstone." I tried not to look at it because his picture was on it, but it was hard to avoid it. The tears started before I could even talk. I cried for a minute and then pulled it together. I needed to do this and just be honest.

"I miss you, Jermaine. It's not fair that you're gone and Liam will never meet you." Saying my son's name made me smile.

"Jermaine he is so beautiful. Remember we used to talk about what our baby would look like? Well, we were way the fuck off. He is beyond perfection, and I know you would be just as obsessed as I am." I wiped my tears and continued.

"The labor was awful, and I have a feeling you would have annoyed the hell out of me. I pushed him out with no drugs. Which wasn't my choice but I was too far along to have any. Everyone says my labor was quick, but I beg to differ. I promise Jermaine Liam will know you, know all about you and what you look like. How goofy you were, how sweet you were and how much you loved me and him." I felt my tears start back up, but I stopped them.

"I know you saw what happened with me and Sada. You know I have never looked at him or anyone you even know in any way. That's not how me and you did each other. He snuck up on me when I was at my lowest. I apologize if you feel disrespected in any way." I got quite for a minute.

"As soon as Liam's a little older I'll take him out so I can show you what he looks like." I went to my phone and pulled one of the many pictures of Liam I had up. Smiling big I said.

"Here's a picture though, I told you he was beautiful." I put my phone back up.

"I will always love you, Jermaine Liam Smith." That was his middle name which is why I suggested it when we picked out names. I smiled while I left his grave site feeling better and I had more peace in me.

"DADDY!" I ran straight to him when I saw his car at my mama's house. I hadn't seen him since Liam's birth, and I missed him.

"Mini-me, how is my only baby doing?" He hugged me back and kissed the top of my forehead. My mama greeted me to and wasted no time getting Liam out his car seat.

"Alyssa, did you brush his hair and lotion his body up good?" Me and my daddy shook our head when she started with the questions.

"Naw ma, I decided to leave him nappy and ashy." She popped me on my arm laughing.

"Where are you and my grandson coming from?" My daddy asked. Domonic Collins, my dad, was the perfect father. I not only had everything I wanted when I was growing up. But I had his time as well. Him and my mama's relationship just didn't work out. Nothing more nothing less. I never questioned anything because I got the best of both of them. They got along, and they loved me, so I was fine with it.

Plus I knew from time to time they still fucked. It's gross as hell, but hey it ain't my business. My mama was gorgeous and chocolate just like me a little thicker than I am. My dad was tall as shit, slim built with waves. My dad favored NBA player Kevin Garnett so much that he doesn't like anything associated with that man anymore.

"Me and Liam went to Jermaine's grave site." I sat down at the kitchen table next to him. I told him about it and how I felt so much better. Of course, I got a little misty eyed, but I smiled a lot telling him about it.

"That's so good Alyssa. Nothing is better than getting some peace. That's how it was for me when granddad died. You ready to go back to work?"

"Oh my goodness daddy yes. Like I appreciate how you and mama have been helping me financially, but I miss work. I miss the store and going through all the new shipment." We both laughed, and my mama came in holding Liam. My daddy got up and washed his hands so he could hold him. I went to the kitchen see what my mama had because I was hungry. My phone went off. I was tagged on Facebook in an event to Amelia's party and *Jeans&Moet.* I sent the screenshot to Hazel, and she called me.

"How's it going Iron Chef?" That made her laugh.

"Shut up, and it's going good. I love it. But listen cause I only have a few minutes. I am so down to go to that party. I need to get sexy and go out."

"Ok cool well let's go get outfits for it today, and I'll ask my mama if she can keep Liam."

"Oh bitchhhh." I was scrolling through my Facebook while talking to Hazel on my Bluetooth.

"What's wrong?"

"Why this bitch tagged Sada in some pictures. One they in the car and he's driving not even paying attention. The other one, they at Burger King and she, captioned it 'time with bae'." Me and Hazel smacked our lips at the same time.

"Both of them are doing the most. We have to step out extra sexy tomorrow night, show him and that bitch up."

"Hell yea." Me and Hazel hung up, and my trolling ass went on the bitch page and looked at her pictures. She was basic looking. Caramel complexion, slim thick with some dry ass blonde tracks in her hair.

"Ugh." I got off Facebook and went to my parents and Liam. Sada can go suck a dick.

***

"Oh Lord, what did Mac do?" I plopped down on our couch in the living room next to Hazel. She was looking in her phone with her nose turned up.

"He didn't do anything, it's the bitches on his Instagram. I should just unfollow him."

"Girl Bye. Mac, Sada, and Jermaine always had bitches following behind them. Mac is older so he handles his more smooth. Sada and Jermaine, now that's another story." I took her phone because she was obsessing.

"How the fuck did you handle it?"

"Well first off Jermaine's hands ain't clean. You know how many times I called you because he was talking to another bitch. Or when we break up, he fucks whatever wasn't tied down. It took me a minute, but then I was like fuck that. I'm about to start doing me. His ass went crazy and didn't know what to do." We both started laughing.

"Remember he slept in your backyard on the swing!" We laughed so loud, and hard that I rolled on the floor.

"Bitch when you sent me those pictures I died over and over. Then yo' mama cut the sprinklers on him."

"Bitch stop I got tears coming out my eyes." I managed to get out between laughing hard as hell. We talked for a while about all the crazy ass shit me, and Jermaine used to go through. I called Hazel so much mad, crying, excited, and when I lost my virginity to Jermaine. We were an after-school special TV show.

"Show Mac ass that he ain't the only nigga in Detroit. Rather he gets mad or not, how the fuck does he expect you to behave when he isn't. His brother is the same damn way." An idea came to mind.

"Ooo bitch let's go to my job and get us some outfits for tonight." Hazel jumped up excited and ran to her room to grab her shoes. Tonight was Amelia's party, and we still didn't have anything to wear. I was dropping Liam off to my mama later, and I was having a true turn-up tonight.

Hi mamas! Look at the snap back on ya body." My boss came from behind the counter smiling and hugging me when we walked in the store.

"Thank you, oh my gosh I can't wait to get back to work. Let me see that handsome baby boy." I looked around the store and just missed it. The boutique I worked at was in Oak Park, and I loved everything about the store. My boss ran it with her two sisters, and they were the designers. They remind me of the Kardashian sisters, Kim, Kourtney, and Khloe. They were white mixed with black and had the plastic bodies but a heart of gold. Sybil was normally the one here with me and the other two girls that worked here.

"This is my best friend, Hazel. Hazel this is my boss Sybil." They shook hands smiling and speaking.

"Ok, so we have a party to go to tonight. We need club attire, no dresses or skirts. Shoes, accessories would be nice too."

"Girl you know your way around. Your discount still applies so have at it." She let us do our thing while she worked. Even though I have a passion for interior designing. Anything I can put together or make look amazing always grabs my attention. I already knew what I wanted both of us to wear. Liam was in his stroller knocked out as usual. My chubs only woke up to eat and shit. I loved the newborn stage but I was ready for like five or six months.

***

"I knew you'd slay the fuck out that outfit!" I smiled so big when Hazel walked in the kitchen. I was done getting dressed and waiting on her. I picked out some knee-length jeans that hugged my juicy ass tight. They had slashes through them with my thick thighs showing. I wore a dark peach bralette and some nude pumps I got from ALDO. I wasn't feeling the ones we had at the boutique. I used my deep wave curlers and put some waves in my real hair. I was looking so damn good, and so was my best friend. I picked out some white jeggings with the sexiest bodysuit in our store. It was sleeveless with mesh material, and it fitted her body like fine silk. I picked her out some red pumps, I wand curled her hair and gave her a side part. I knew for a fact Mac and Sada would be at the party tonight. I wanted them to be bothered as fuck especially Sada.

"Thank you boo, I feel sexy as hell. Alyssa for real I don't even swing that way but ummm." She bit her lip smirking at me, and I laughed.

"Come on let's get to it." Tonight was going to be so damn lit!!

We decided to take a Lyft to the party because neither one of us wanted to fuck with parking. We both wanted to drink and just didn't want the responsibility. It was packed as Amelia parties always are. She usually does a strip club, but I guess she wanted to do something different. The line wasn't long but I saw more cars coming so looks like we came just in time. Me and Hazel were meeting my two friends Raynor and Tory. They clicked so good with Hazel at Butzles so I figured we could get a section together. I grabbed Hazel's hand as we made our way in.

"Damn gorgeous, save me a dance." This tall light skin guy licked his lips at me and said. He was cute but nothing I would be dancing on. I gave him a light smile as we continued to walk.

"This my shit!" Hazel yelled in my ear when *Shardaysa Gimme My Gots* came on. This song banged and was the new twerking anthem. I saw my girls signal us to them, so that's where we headed.

"Hey ladies! Oooo look at the two of you!" Tory was geeking us up. She was a plus size beauty that did a lot of modeling for Fashion Nova. Raynor was pretty to just very slim. Her confidence and taste in fashion made niggas and bitches take notice.

"Has Amelia been extra on the mic yet? Y'all know she raps now."

"Girl hell yea, she was doing what she called rap a few minutes before you two came. It was awful." We all laughed, and I grabbed a glass of champagne. The club was two floors, and Amelia had the upstairs VIP. It was a first pay first get and Raynor reserved her section when Amelia first announced her party. She split it three ways, and we paid her out half through Cash App.

"So what the fuck does Mac think he's doing?" I stood next to Hazel looking at some bitch all in Mac face. He was leaning against the white leather couch with his Detroit Pistons fitted hat down low on his head. He had his head down while the hoe was on his arm whispering shit in his ear. Clip was there to and so where their other three niggas they hang with. Sada was sitting on the couch Mac was leaning on with the same bitch from Facebook sitting next to him. Her legs were crossed, and she was sipping on a drink.

"This is him showing me that he's trying to be with me." Hazel chuckled and just shook her head. Mac finally looked up and saw us, but he didn't act like a nigga who got caught. He said something to the girl, and then she smiled and went to sit down. Hazel been stopped looking and I saw him pull his phone out. I stole some more looks of Sada. Oh my goodness he looked so sexy in his Burberry jeans and fitted matching POLO. He had his dreads braided in corn rolls, his chain and watch was blinding. I just wanted to slap the bitch whose hand was on his thigh.

"This fool texting me talking about 'come here'. Naw nigga I'm good, you had a whole hoe in your face." I swallowed the rest of my champagne in the glass.

"We didn't come here to mope about them. Let's go dance." I shouted in Hazel ear. She smiled and agreed just as *Travis Porter Bring It Back* song came on.

Shawty goin hard, concrete
She can shake her ass, one cheek, two cheeks
Both cheeks, both cheeks
I got a white girl freak she got no cheeks
Got a police bitch on a short leash
Got good mouth like she got no teeth
She a slut, she a dog, she a bitch with it
Man you see the way she work she super thick with it

We were fuckin' it up on the dance floor. Hazel would twerk on me, and I'd twerk on her. It was fuck all niggas right now because we were having the best time. Tory and Raynor came over and danced with us too. The bartender came over with a thing of shots and said it was from some guys. My phone was vibrating, and I saw it was Mario.

Mario: You look good as hell. Enjoy the shots and when y'all done come to my section.

Me: Thank you boo and ok.

We danced to a few more songs and then we went to the bathroom. On the way, we stopped in Amelia's section and wished her a happy birthday. I knew her through friends, but I didn't want to be at her party and not even speak. After the bathroom, we went back upstairs, but me and Hazel went over to Mario's VIP. My girl was straight ignoring Mac, and I was glad. I didn't want her focusing on him at least not right now. Mario section was directly across from Mac and Sada.

"What's poppin' ma, you lookin' good as fuck." Mario gave me a hug and a kiss on the cheek. I introduced her to Mario, and I noticed his friend Rice was looking at Hazel hard. I met him at Butzel when I met Mario. I thought Haz was going to be a little shy, but she helped herself to a seat and picked up a champagne glass. Me and Mario sat down as well, and I grabbed a glass.

"Did I say you can have some of my champagne lil mama?" Rice played with Hazel and talked shit. She flipped her hair and drunk from the glass anyway. Me and Mario chuckled, and Rice licked his lips at her.

"I don't need permission nigga." She joked back, and they smiled at each other.

"So you been smooth Alyssa? How has motherhood been?"

"It's been good I love it. And I've been great about to return to work in another week." I gave him a half smile. He was looking at my mouth and body. I been knew one thing was on Mario mind but I wasn't ready for that yet. At least not with him.

"That's what's up. I gotta tell you some shit." He leaned over and whispered in my ear. I looked at Haz and Rice talking, and he got comfortable too when he moved some hair behind her ear. I don't know how Mac got over to us so damn fast, but it was like a tall as shadow hovering over us.

"My nigga this one is spoken for so bag the fuck up off mine." Rice put his champagne bottle down and stood up. At least he attempted to stand up.

"Lil nigga---"

WHAMP

Mac wasted no time knocking Rice out. I know he gon' look different when he wakes up. Mario jumped up, and I saw his hand go in his waist. Rice was doing the same with a bloody lip.

"You'll be dead before you pull that shit out, my nigga." Mac was so calm, and I looked at Mario and Rice chest. It was two red dots making circles on their chests. Me and Hazel looked back at Mac section, and his boys including Sada were facing us but the way they were sitting, I knew what was up.

"Hell naw, you muthafuckas can keep the drama. Come on Haz." I stood up and grabbed her hand, and we flew down the stairs. I already had my phone out ordering us a Lyft.

"I cannot believe them crazy ass niggas. We tried to go out and have a nice time but these fools gotta fuck everything up!" Hazel was just as mad as I was. Our Lyft came quick, and we both were in the back so damn amped up. Plus we were drunk, it didn't help that Hazel went Live on her Instagram while we were in the Lyft.

"This my best friendddd!" She put the camera on me, and I stuck my tongue out laughing. We both got in the camera.

"Bitch we fine as fuck right now!" I shouted and kissed her cheek.

"Hell yea we are, fuck these lame ass niggas." We started giggling and putting the middle finger up.

"Bitch I'm starting to think somebody dumb ass mama swallowed my soulmate or had an abortion!" Hazel drunk ass said in the Live. I fell out laughing especially when she zoomed in on her face and yelled.

"Thanks, bitch now I'll never be happy!" We laughed even our driver was cracking up.

"Look at your number of views! Bitch we poppin'!" I pointed out because we had over a hundred views already.

"Aye, we just left Jeans & Moet bar. Bitches in there looking like Leggings & Corona!" We both were just acting silly and talking shit.

"You got some fine ass followers boo. Hey, zaddy! I'm singleee! Come thru!" I said talking shit and Hazel agreeing.

"Oooh look bitch." She scrolled back up, and we both saw Sada and Mac were watching. We both looked at each other and laughed. It was hilarious because we both didn't even give them the satisfaction of saying their names. We just continued talking shit, and Hazel male followers were being thirsty as hell in the comments which we loved.

"Aye homie with the ginger beard. Slide in my DM baby boy." Hazel laughed, and I scrolled up on the comments to get the name of the dude I thought looked cute.

"Allen313 hit my DM up to zaddy, LovelyLissaKisses. We need to link up."

"The next nigga I fuck he bet not ask whose pussy this is!" Hazel said between laughing.

"Ima tell his ass 'pass me my panties G you doin' too much!"

"Bitch you so damn stupid. I hate niggas who have a good woman in they face! But would rather want a bitch whose pussy smell like house keys and vinegar!" We were on Live the entire ride until we got home. Our driver was cracking up at us. I gave him a cash tip because he was so cool and he had us some good music playing in the background.

"I'm hungry as hell. I'm about to warm up that food I cooked last night. You want me to make you a plate?" Hazel asked me.

"Yes, that sounds so good. Thanks, boo." She made some bomb ass ketchup meatloaf, corn on the cob, mash potatoes, and macaroni. I went to my room to wash my face, put my pajamas on, and I put my hair up. My room was downstairs, and Hazel room was upstairs. I wanted to call my mama but it was after one in the morning, so I knew they were knocked out. I missed Liam so much I couldn't wait to get my baby tomorrow. After I had my pajamas on, shorts and a sports bra, I went back in the kitchen. Hazel walked down the stairs with her pajamas on to and her hair in a ponytail. We both were so hungry and about to eat when someone was knocking on our door so damn hard that me and her jumped. We both grabbed the tasers we keep in high places throughout the house.

"OPEN THIS FUCKING DOOR OR I'MMA SHOOT THIS BITCH DOWN!!" We looked at each other.

"Oh my God," I said out loud, but I hurried and opened the door because I knew he was true to his word. I promise I barely unlocked it before he barged in with a gun in his hand. This fool went through the living room, dining room. We heard him go in our basement and then back upstairs where we were. The two bedrooms down here were mine and Liam. He went in both of them, and we heard him in our bathroom. Me and Hazel stood frozen with our mouths open and just stunned. Sada didn't even look at us as he walked passed us and went upstairs where Hazel's room was. We could hear him walking around and in her bathroom. He came back downstairs and looked at both of us looking like a psychopath.

"Where the fuck you hididn' that nigga at?"

"WHAT?!" Me and Hazel said in unison.

"Don't act fucking stupid. The nigga you was talking about DM'ing and telling him to come over. Where is he? Don't save his life and I got my man's outside so if the nigga think he can run then he dumb as fuck."

"Sada there is and never was anybody here. Have you completely lost your mind?"

"For real like this is crazy." Hazel chimed in walking to the kitchen.

"Yea whatever the only reason Mac ain't here is because I came. He talked shit about he wasn't about to chase you, but I wasn't trying to hear that shit. He knew if I saw a nigga here for you I would have called him." He looked at Hazel. She turned her nose up when she came back with her plate and pop in her hand.

"You a snitch."

"I'on give a fuck that's my brother and you his woman."

"I'm not his woman, and I never will be. Call his ass and tell him that." She walked upstairs, and I put my attention back on him. He put his gun in his waist and had the nerve to look at me like he wanted to rumble.

"Why are you here Sada? Do you understand that I have neighbors who could have called the police on you?"

"I don't give a fuck. Who the hell is this person in front of me, huh? You at Butzles actin' wild, on Live calling niggas daddy and shit. Tha fuck Alyssa."

"First of all, whatever I do has nothing to do with you. I'm home every damn day and night with my son, and I wouldn't have it any other way. When I want to hang with my girls and have fun when I want to talk to a good-looking guy and flirt. That's my damn business, and second, I'm fucking single!" His nostrils flared.

"All of that you sayin' don't mean shit. I'on like seeing you act that way. That nigga Mario ain't shit and you all in his damn face." I chuckled at the obvious.

"That sounds like a personal problem. Close your eyes the next time you see me or look the other way. And as far as Mario I'm not stupid nigga, I don't expect shit to come out of me and him."

"But'chu expect for him to put his dick in you right?!"

"Maybe." I arched my eyebrow and said that shit with confidence. I didn't want to fuck Mario at all, but Sada shouldn't be standing in my living room talking to me like he's my father.

"You fuck him, and I swear I'll kill his ass. On God Alyssa, that nigga will be my best kill."

"What right do you have?! Sada we kissed, you got weird then you lied and said you were with your grandma. Yo' stupid ass pocket dialed me, and I heard you fucking some bitch!" I said that and he looked like blood drained from his body.

"Yea nigga, you pushed me away. The thing that hurts the most is, you didn't have to do me that way. I wouldn't have put any pressure on you Sada." He didn't have anything to say, and I pretty much said all I had to.

"Good night Sada." I folded my arms and looked away from him. In my peripheral vision, I saw his hand go over his face.

"I apologize, Alyssa, that was some sucka ass shit. I just panicked man and I ran under some dry ass pussy trying to convince myself that I wasn't feeling you. I still look at'chu as if you're his." I looked at him when he said that.

"We have been around each other since 10th grade, and I never looked at you in any way since Maine claimed you. Me, him and Mac never got down like that. Me and you got so close when I started checking on you. I saw your personality, and we bonded on a level that I thought was the homie. That shit changed and I started feeling you. I fought it all the time and when we kissed I felt like shit. I apologize for treating you like that." His eyes looked so sad as he waited for me to say something.

"I accept your apology Sada, and I was battling the same thing too. You and Mac were just Jermaine cousins. I'm not that girl who looks at her man's friends or family any kind of way. I started feeling you towards the end of my pregnancy. I felt guilty to when we kissed, but I never would have done what you did. Still, though, I accept your apology." Looking at him and how good he looked I couldn't help but blush. Sada smile and bit his lip.

"I missed you, and I'm still feeling you heavy as hell Alyssa. I know my age and how I act throws you off but fuck all of that. I want you to quit this single shit and be mine."

"Would you be mine, like all the way mine?"

"Hell yea." My heart was beating so fast, and I had a stomach full of emotions. I wanted this so bad, but then I felt guilty. Now I feel like I have to move on, I need to move on, and I don't care who side eyes us. I thought about the shit people would think and maybe even say.

Was I ready for that? My name stayed in people mouths when Jermaine was alive. Bitches were thirsty in the comments under his pictures. Everybody and they mama was always talking about when we were broken up what he did. Who he talked to, what party he was at. When we were together it was all kinds of shit said trying to break us up. It's a never-ending thing with social media and people's opinions. It's no way to escape it, especially when people see you happy.

"If no matter what we can rock through the bullshit of people opinions and side-eyes then I'm in. Oh and I don't want to be like all them hoes calling after you." He laughed because he already knew.

"Why you gotta be difficult? Come here." I wasn't expecting him to pull me to him and lay a kiss on me. This wasn't like our first kiss. Sada hand his hand on my lower back and the other on the side of my face. My body just melted in his and then we were all into it. Before I knew it both his hands were on my lower back and then on my ass. His grip, soft lips and his scent was doing all the right things for me.

"Mm." I moaned in his mouth when he picked me up and put me against the wall. I couldn't believe I was kissing Sada. Like what the fuck, and I was loving it. We were so into our kissing that we didn't even hear Hazel come downstairs until she spoke.

"About time you idiots got the shit right." She said the shit so nonchalant then her ass hiccupped and burped so hard while walking to the kitchen. Me and Sada turned our noses up.

"O'l stank ass girl. And you betta call my fucking brother. I'm telling you, you don't want them problems on ya hands." Hazel came back in the living room with a bottle of water rolling her eyes. Sada still had my arms pinned against the wall.

"I don't care about your brother nigga, and he don't scare me. He has all them bitches to keep him busy. You just better take care of my best friend." He squeezed my ass cheeks as if she could see him.

"I got her don't worry about all of that. You got my brother in his feelings, yo ass need to run." He laughed, and I hit his arm. Hazel gave him the finger and ran upstairs.

"Leave her alone." I giggled to now that she was gone.

"I'm for real, that nigga flipped when he saw o'l boy touch her." He licked his lips and looked at mine.

"Just like I flipped when Mario touched you. Alyssa don't have me around here loose on them fools. You my woman now and against all the odds people will create. I want us to stay tight and unbreakable." I kissed him again.

"Ok, Casada I can do that." He laughed and kissed me again.

"I'm gone have to get used to that shit. My mama and grandma don't even call me Casada." We both laughed.

"I gotta ask you something."

"Ok."

"Has Malcolm or Shauney been to see Liam?" That caught me off guard.

"Malcolm hasn't since the day after he was born. Shauney won't until I have a DNA test. That bitch is really testing my patience."

"Malcolm been on some other shit lately, so I wanted to see if he at least been to see his grandson. Me and Mac are going to holla at him tomorrow."

"Well tell him Liam is always here when he's ready. But uh as much as it feels good grinding on you. I still have another week before I can have sex." I nibbled on my lip looking at him. He went back to rubbing and squeezing my booty.

"That's cool fat-fat I got plenty of time tuh dig in that pussy." He started sucking on my neck hard making me giggle.

"Mm. I'm gone kill that sweet pussy too." Oh my God, he went back to licking and tongue kissing my neck.

"I want you to ride my face and cum all in my mouth." *Kiss*.

"I want you to pull on my dreads while you cum over and over." *Kiss*.

"When I give you this dick I'on wanna hear shit unless it's you calling my name. I'mma kiss and lick all over this chocolate ass body."

"Sss Casada stop your making this so hard." He lightly bit my neck one more time then pulled away smiling.

"I need to chill before I get blue balls. Come on let's go to bed." He carried me to the back to my bedroom. I thought it would be so awkward with him in my bed. In nothing but boxers and his arms around me. But it felt so damn good even though his dick poked me in my ass all night. Ha!

Sada

It was another hot ass day, and for some reason, I wanted a cold beer. Hazel gave me a plate of her food she cooked yesterday, so I was heading to the crib to eat and then go with Mac to talk to Malcolm. Coming out of Jay's liquor store I walked to my car after looking around me and got in. I always made sure my surrounding was good because you never knew who wanted to try you. If muthafuckas thought yo' head was in the clouds for one second, then make their move on you. I wasn't the riches, and I wasn't flashy all the time. But I had money, and on my good days, you could tell. Detroit got some many broke, lazy niggas in it that if they thought you had even a dollar more than them.

"You ain't come home last night. I take you and Alyssa rockin?" Mac came from the basement of our crib. I had just got back home about ten minutes ago.

"Yea we rockin' and I told her ass to let them weak ass niggas know." Mac laughed.

"I'm glad for y'all bro. I get how shit is with Jermaine and all but you know I know you, and he ain't like that. Just fuck what anybody else got to say. Alyssa a good girl and I saw it about two months ago." I stood up and grabbed my plate out the microwave.

"Where the fuck you get that from?"

"Yo' woman, she made some food, and this was the rest of it. Alyssa keep me bustin' good, and Hazel keeps me fed. I'm living the American dream." I held my hands out laughing, and that nigga looked like he wanted to kill me.

"Fuck you, nigga, you ain't living shit with my woman."

"Oh yea that's right, she said she ain't yours." I fell out laughing putting some of Hazel good ass meatloaf in my mouth. Got damn girl can cook her ass off.

"Whateva' nigga, you saw how I was at the club when that fool touched her. She been ignoring my calls and that shit pissing me off. But it's all good though, I got something for her ass later."

"You uh sick ass nigga, if she doesn't want you just fall back. Hazel fine and all but it's plenty of bitches out here." He turned his nose up.

"Shut the fuck up bro, you know damn well you wouldn't have took no for an answer if Alyssa said no." He was right about that shit so I couldn't say nothing. I finished my food while Mac got his haircut in our basement. Swear since we were younger this fool always got what he wanted. He'd talk his way out of anything and always had shit his way. Blue had his own barbershop but here he was in our basement. One thing I appreciated about my brother when he ate he would always make sure I ate. Like our Chrysler job, he was hired in first, and within a week I was hired in even though they weren't looking for more employees. That's big bro for you though.

"Have you told Hazel about Quinn?" I asked because his phone went off three times with Quinn blowing him up.

"Naw I was thinking of not saying shit until I find out if the baby mine."

"Bad idea bro. Just get the shit out and tell her it's a possibility. That's what I'd do. She already gone talk shit about you not telling her in the beginning." We were sitting in his black Yukon truck. We kept this truck in the garage at our mama's crib because she lucked up and had a three-car garage. The owner of the house she stayed in before her built it. She let Mac keep his Yukon and me keep my Suburban truck in the second one. We were parked a few homes down from Malcolm's crib. He had three cars parked in front of his house. Mac thought it was best for us to stake it out and wait. This nigga Mac always moved like a natural hitman, but I followed because he was always smart about his shit.

"You might be right. She gone give me hell, either way, I was just tryna take the real road out."

"Well sense you taking my advice you might wanna hear me out one more time."

"Speak on it."

"I noticed with Alyssa no matter how much I jumped off when I saw her with niggas, or how much I threatened her ass. I had to show her that I was on some real shit. I ain't do no grand gesture I just was real and told her how I felt and what I wanted. You might wanna think about that with Hazel, You can't tell a bitch you want that she can't do shit, but you can do you. All I'm saying is if you want her then you might gotta switch ya shit up." He nodded his head and rubbed his chin with his hand.

"I hear you bro and you talking facts. Had I not been between Hazel's legs and known the feel and taste of it then shit would be good. But I did so here we are." I couldn't do shit but laugh and shake my head at this fool. We saw Malcolm door open, and three niggas came out.

"You seeing this shit," Mac asked while we both were staring at them with bookbags on. Clearly, they had product or money in it. That wasn't even the problem though.

"Yea I'm seeing it." Once they left, we got out and headed to his house. Me and Mac were strapped just in case. He knocked on his door, and some white bitch opened it. She looked at me and Mac, and I knew that hoe got wet. She was bad as fuck too, thick and had her nipples pierced. Bitch answered the door in this gown that left little to the imagination.

"Please tell me I can help both of y'all."

"Naw ma but you can go tell our uncle Malcolm that his nephews are here." Me and Mac stepped in the house like we brought it. O'l girl called Malcolm and we stood in the living room.

"I need you to keep yo' fucking cool baby bro," Mac whispered to me. If he had to tell me that, then shit was bad. I'm younger and make more noise when I'm heated, as you can see at Alyssa crib.

"You don't know how many bitches in his crib or what kind of bitches they are."

"I'm good. We walkin' outa here." As I said that Malcolm came downstairs with two more girls. They had on these little ass robes, and they were fine as fuck. Not fine enough to distract me but I'm still a nigga, and I noticed it. Malcolm was shocked to see us, and he was a little dismayed.

"Nephews, to what do I owe the pleasure?"

"We just stopped by to holla at'chu about something important." He sat down on the couch, and his girls did the same. The white bitch came back in the room and sat on the other side of the couch.

"Ok, what's up." Me and Mac sat down, and when I had to sit next to the white bitch, she sat back and crossed her legs. Malcolm smirked.

"Coca likes you, Sada. She good as fuck and loves black dick if you wanna take her to the back." I looked back at her, and she licked her lips. I was tempted but naw, shit was fucked up, and my situation hada changed.

"Naw I'm good. I got a girl now." Malcolm laughed.

"And she got a husband, who gives a fuck." I looked at Malcolm ready to let loose, but Mac stepped in.

"Listen that ain't why we here. So word on the street is you pushin' yo' weight on the eastside in a disrespectful way." I looked at him good, and he gave off a nervous, thrown off mood.

"Is that what'chu heard? Well, I didn't think the streets belonged to anybody. I thought it was a free country." He finally was still and looking dead in Mac's eyes. That nigga was trying to act like he was making a statement by looking hard. Shit me, and Mac didn't have to put on no punk ass look nor would we ever let another man intimidate us.

"You sound like a five-year-old, don't nobody give a fuck about that free country bullshit. The hood wild as fuck. The way we been minimizing a war is by staying in our own area. Being greedy and moving like you ain't got no damn sense. You got H.P, Pontiac and a few other areas that's free claim." The two of them didn't even blink. The two girls sitting next to Malcolm just kept rubbing his chest and kissing on his neck.

"How the fuck the two of you gone come in here and tell me anything about these streets? I was runnin' them before you bastards were born."

"Naw my nigga our pops was running shit. You was acting like you are now." I chimed in, and he looked at me like he wanted to jump.

"You talking about respect but you and him in here disrespecting me. I'm y'all damn uncle, I helped raised y'all when Randall died. So what, someone from the east side sent you to warn me?" Me and Mac were quite until we both stood up. It was funny how we moved the same without having to give a signal all the time.

"We ain't saying shit except it's not much you can do in these streets moving the way you move. Out of respect, this was brought to us to bring to you. Do with it what'chu will." Me and him walked away towards the door.

"I AIN'T STOPPING SHIT!! I DO THINGS MY FUCKING WAY!!" I slammed that nigga door and balled my fist up.

"I'on believe that muthafucka. I swear to God bro I wanna kill him. Fuck this east and west shit, we need to do it." Mac let me rant because I was ready. I wanted to storm in right now and fuck his ass up. That nigga wasn't shit to me now.

"I feel you trust me, I feel you. The one thing I know about Malcolm, he don't know what the fuck he's doing. I noticed some shit that I bet you didn't because you so mad."

"Like what?"

"That nigga snorting that shit. He couldn't sit still, he kept sniffing and wiping his nose. That means he always on one. Sloppiness is the only way he moves, and I bet he's snorting his own shit. It also means he'll be more paranoid and us coming in there just made it worse. He about to put all protection around him, but he'll still move his weight. No doubt we gotta kill that muthafucka and his crew."

"Bro but did you see who the fuck his crew is? His own son." Me and Mac were quite for a minute in his truck. Malcolm crew was them Schoolcraft niggas that Maine, P, and Spudz were beefing with. The one's that killed them, we knew because P baby mama told us before she moved to Arizona.

"I know, shit nasty as fuck, but I got a plan to make sure when we kill Malcolm, that nigga will suffer," Mac assured me.

"Meanwhile, he'll be watching us. We need to just act like shit good. I'ma holla at my eastside informant and let him know what's up. I'on want them to take Malcolm out." I nodded my head and gave Mac some dab. I couldn't wait until all this shit goes down. Sucka ass nigga.

***

"You see how he stopped crying once I came in and saved him." Alyssa smacked her lips at me. I just got to her crib to pick her and Liam up. He was crying loud as hell, and you could tell she was having a hard time getting him to stop. My mama used to keep kids as a side job. She told me if a baby is screaming crying after you've tried everything then it's probably gas. I came in, washed my hands and took my shirt off. Alyssa gave me a blanket to put over my chest, and I started walking her room and rubbing his back. I went from rubbing to patting and applying a little pressure. Lil homie burped twice and farted hard as hell. Now he was sleep on my chest.

"Shut up Casada. I would have thought of that, but the crying was clouding my brain."

"Girl shut'cho lying ass up. Just say thank you, daddy, and gimmie a kiss." She crawled her sexy ass on her bed and got in my face.

"Thank you, daddy." Her lips touched mine, and I made sure to bite on the bottom one before she pulled away. Alyssa was fine as hell and even though our thang became official only forty-eight hours ago. I was into it heavy, and I felt good as hell when I was around her and Liam.

"Can you stay the night with us?" She kissed me again after she asked.

"Yea, I got work tomorrow morning but you know I'll be back when I get off."

"Ok cool, I'm kind of nervous about today. Mostly because I don't know what will be thought about me." I strapped Liam in his car seat. He was knocked out which he probably would be the entire ride. I walked up on Alyssa and put my hands around her waist.

"Don't be nervous, my grandma will love you. She's the last person to judge you. Trust me she's not a typical grandma." Alyssa had these leggings on with black and white stripes on them. This white top that her back out was sexy on her chocolate skin. I cupped her pussy from the outside of her leggings. I felt that kitty purr as soon as I touched her.

"You look good as hell today Fat-Fat." I kissed her neck, and she giggled.

"I'm not pregnant anymore Casada." Her eyes were closed, and she spoke low.

"I know, but you got a fat ass and a fat pussy, so the name fits." Her phone rung as I was kissing on her neck. I saw it was Malcom. Alyssa looked at her phone shocked. I let her answer it to see what he wanted.

"Hello." I could hear him clear as hell. He talked about his head hasn't been in a good place, and he apologized for not seeing Liam more. Alyssa was so sweet she told him it was good and then he started asking bullshit questions about her and they baby. How they've been, does he keep her up at night? The sick ass fuck even had the nerve to compare Liam to how Maine was when he was born. I was glad she didn't mention me over here, but I got annoyed when he asked to see Liam.

"Um ok just let me know when and where. I go back to work next week, but after work I'm open. Ok cool, bye." She hung up and looked at me.

"That was odd and out the blue. I wish Shauney would come around like Malcolm is trying to."

"Yea that would be cool. Aye I'm not trying to tell you what to do. But I think you might wanna wait a little before leaving Liam alone with Malcolm. You know at least until Malcolm learns him." I had to say that shit in the calmest way because I didn't want her to think I was trying to tell her what to do with Liam.

"I wouldn't let him keep my baby. I mean Malcolm has never done anything to me, but I don't know him or Shauney that well. Jermaine and I were mostly at my house. Whenever we were at his house, I stayed in his room, and that was it. I only trust my family, Hazel and your mama with Liam. Speaking if your mama will she be at your grandma's?"

"Nope she'll be at work, but by the time we're done, she will be off. We can swing by her crib then." Alyssa smiled and kissed me as my light went off on my iPhone.

"Who is Ranita?" Alyssa snatched my phone off her nightstand before I could answer.

"Oh this the Facebook bitch." She gave me my phone.

"Answer it." I laughed but she wasn't playing so I did just to get some humor.

"Sup ma."

"You really ain't shit nigga. How you gone leave me at Amelia party and then just drop off the face of the earth?"

"I ain't drop off shit I just dropped into some pussy. I got a girl now ma, so we done here." I hung up and put that bitch on the block list.

"Sada don't make me have to fuck you up. Keep ya bitches in check." I cupped that pussy from the back and pulled her to my chest.

"Shut the hell up talking like that. I got one bitch who about to get all of me and then some so chill. I do however see Mario still under your pictures on Instagram. Tell that nigga he'd best to move the fuck on. You ain't available Alyssa so let these niggas know." She unlocked her phone and took some selfies of me and her.

"We look really good together. Especially this one, I might not post this one." She giggled.

"Why not? That shit looks hood."

"Sada you holding my pussy outside of my leggings."

"Because it's mine. Post it, tag me in all of them." She did it, and as she packed Liam diaper bag, I commented under all three of them. Sad social media was a way to make a statement, but hey, it's the times we living in.

"You gotta chill fat, my grandma is cool peoples." We pulled up to my her place, and I was taking Liam car seat out. Alyssa swore he was heavy but to me if felt like he wasn't even in the seat. Hot as shit outside she dressed him in a Polo onesie with some cute ass things that covered his hands. Lil homie had so much hair under his POLO hat, swagged out as hell.

"I know bae, and I'm trying to calm down, but I can't help it." I just chuckled and shook my head. Signing us in we caught the elevator to my grandma's floor.

"Aw shit." I meant to say to myself, but it came out. Alyssa probably didn't hear me because she didn't say anything. Both the nurse hoes I fucked were behind the desk. I hate when bitches do this shit, they gave me the stink eye and looked Alyssa over hard as hell.

"Good afternoon ladies." Alyssa smiled at them.

"Hi, I'm sorry are you on Mrs. Willis's visiting list?" I looked at the redbone hoe and almost smacked her.

"Tha fuck you talkin' about this ain't no damn prison." She gon' look at some shit on her computer screen.

"I'm sorry, but we have residents to protect. If she is not an authorized visitor, then she has to leave." Alyssa looked at both the nurses and then at me.

"Oh, I get it. Y'all fucked him, and now it's salt in ya diet because he's here with me." She giggled.

"You hoes are sad. If it wasn't me it would have never been either of you." Alyssa kept her eyes on them.

"Bae which apartment is your grandma's?" I pointed to the one on the right. We walked past the nurse's station and to her door.

"You know that shit was sexy as hell. I can't wait until next week." I squeezed her booty hard and almost bit my lip off.

"Hey, gorgeous." I smiled big anytime I seen my grandma or mama.

"Oh my goodness what a surprise!" She stood up and hugged me. Kissing on my cheeks like always and I kissed her on her cheek. Grandma moved like she wasn't in her sixties.

"Well, who is this beauty?" She looked at Alyssa.

"Grandma this is Alyssa, my girlfriend." I sat Liam on her couch and took him out while her and Alyssa hugged.

"And this is Liam, her son."

"Oh my Lord look at him." She went to her kitchen and washed her hands. My grandma sat down in her recliner, and I put him in her arms. She was smiling so hard at Liam, it made me and Alyssa smile hard.

"Have you ever seen anything more precious. Let's you know GOD is real." She looked at Alyssa.

"You are very blessed young lady."

"Thank you so much." Me and Alyssa sat down on the couch.

"So we know who I am, now tell me about you, Ms. Alyssa." She got to telling my grandma about her family, what she does for a living and what she likes to do for fun. She even told her about Hazel. I enjoyed them talking and seeing my grandma hold Liam. Alyssa seem to loosen up more until.

"Ok well, what about the child's father? Is he ok with Sada being around him?" Alyssa looked at me scared and nervous as hell. Since this was my mama's mama, she had only met Maine a few times.

"Um, well. It's a little complicated."

"Grandma the thing is---" She held her hand up.

"Now Sada you know me, stop beating around the bush and just keep it real. I want to hear it from her." I looked at Alyssa and chuckled because she was shocked to hear my grandma talk that way. I told her she was a different breed.

"Well, the father of my child was killed when I was two months pregnant. His um, his name was Jermaine." Alyssa dropped her head, and I grabbed her hand kissing it.

"That's that boy on your father side of the family right?"

"Yup that's him, but it's not what'chu think grandma. We wasn't messing around or anything. I fell for her a few weeks ago. We started being around each other, and I noticed she had a personality. There was so much that I didn't know she had because she was with Maine and I didn't look at her as anything but his woman." She continued to rock Liam in the chair. I could feel Alyssa eyes looking at me.

"Mrs. Willis I do care for your grandson. I can see myself loving him, and we both know what it will look like to others. But as long as we know what it is then that's all that matters.

"Let me tell you something. I met my daughter, him and Mac's father. We used to hang out at this underground club downtown called the Joint. I would go with my girlfriends, and a way we made some money was by keeping men company." Alyssa's mouth dropped, and my fuckin' face turned up,

"Grandma I don't wanna hear this shit." She laughed and kept talking like I wasn't her grandson.

"Oh please boy you'd be surprised. You young people, think the shit y'all doing is new. Y'all just gave it a different name. Anyway, I was sitting at the bar with my girlfriend waiting for my next job. His grandfather walked in with his best friend. Long story short, I went with his best friend, and my girlfriend went with his grandpa. I ran into him outside of the club one day at the store. We started talking, and before I knew it, we fell in love. My point being, you can't help who or how you fall in love with someone. As long as you're not hurting yourself or others then, fuck'em." Me and Alyssa fell out when she said that.

"Plus it's good to see this nigga stick his dick in one female. He done fucked half the damn staff here. Now, I know I'ma have to snap on one of these nurses now that they see he's taken."

"All you gotta do is call me if one of them mess with you, Mrs. Willis. Me and my girl will be up here fucking shit up." My grandma laughed.

"I knew I liked you." Like I knew, Alyssa and my grandma hit it off. We chilled and kicked it with her for a while. Liam woke up only for a few minutes, and my grandma hogged his ass from us. Alyssa had a great time, and she opened up to my grandma about a lot. I enjoyed watching them get along, and of course, my grandma had to talk some shit. Today made me realize that me and Alyssa could be the real deal. I just hope I didn't fuck it up.

"I really enjoyed myself today." Alyssa turned her bedroom light off and crawled in her bed. I watched her turn the baby monitor on so we could see Liam. Alyssa wasn't nervous the first time I spent the night. It made me feel like she been feeling me for a while just like I had been feeling her. The touch of her hands and her skin was everything.

"I'm glad you did. I told you my grandma was cool peoples."

"I absolutely adore her, and she blunt as hell. I can't believe she use to sell----"

"Come on man, don't." She started laughing, but I was grossed the hell out.

"Change the damn subject. You see our pictures got nine-hundred likes? The comments funny as hell." People were shocked, asking how long we been together. Muthafuckas were just nosey as hell, but we didn't give a fuck.

"Yea I saw it. It's funny as hell because I could tell people thinking the most. You see Laurie ugly ass gon' say wow. I swear I hate her." Laurie was this bitch Maine fucked when him and Alyssa were broken up. The bitch always had some shit to say. I looked at Alyssa and kissed her lips.

"Fuck them," I said in between kisses. It got deep as she climbed on top of me and started kissing on my neck. Them soft lips felt so good, she started nibbling on my ear which was my spot. When she worked her way down and pulled my dick out my boxers, I was shocked.

"Lyssa you know I can wait until next week to do anything?"

"I know, but I want to do this." I bit my lip watching her take her top off. She didn't wear a bra and when her titties touched my thighs. That shit felt so good because they were soft, voluptuous and she had some chocolate ass nipples.

"Shit." I groaned, and my head went back on the headboard. Alyssa had a tight grip with her hand around my dick and her warm mouth taking it in and out. Them little-manicured hands had too much dick in them. Them noises I loved to hear were taking over the room and then she moaned with it. This bitch was rockin' my fuckin' world with this head. When she put my balls in her mouth that took me out the game.

"Fuck," I grumbled as my hand squeezed her hair, she was a pro. Her pace speeded up, and that mouth got wetter. I felt my nut building up, and her hand massaged my balls while that mouth worked its magic.

"Oh shit!" Swear to God my toes cracked like firecrackers. This had to be the best nut from head I ever fucking had.

"If you eva in ya life suck my dick that good again." I was breathing hard as she kissed up my chest.

"You didn't like it."

"Hell yea I liked it, that shit just fucked my head up. And you swallowed every drop, fucking GOAT fat fat." She giggled and pecked my lips. I watched her sexy ass get up and brush her teeth. She came back with a rag and cleaned me up as well .

"Casada."

"Sup."

"I'm feeling you tuff as hell."

"That's a good thing right?" She shrugged.

"I feel like I can't keep you. Like---" She dropped her head and looked heartbroken.

"Aye." I made her look at me.

"I can't predict the future, but I can promise you that I'm good. I get why you feel this way, and a nigga is still in the streets heavy. But we here now and I don't want you focused on a bad outcome. A'ight." She was about to say something, but I shut her up by kissing her. We made out for a while until we fell asleep. I wasn't letting this go right here. I was going to do everything I can to make sure I didn't leave Alyssa. At least not by choice.

Hazel

"Kahlil stop calling my damn phone."

"Well stop hanging up on me and blocking me." I let out a loud grunt. This idiot called me so much and texted me even more. I hated talking to him like he was some lame because in reality he wasn't. He's a cheating asshole, and for that reason, I wanted nothing to do with him. He just wouldn't get the hint.

"I do that for a reason. We are done, and I thought I made myself clear before I left." I put my work shoes on and made sure I had everything I needed. I was loving my job and although things got a little hectic at times. I was cooking which I adored.

"All I want to do is talk to you. I miss you, and we need to talk."

"Ok Kahlil, I have a few minutes before work. Talk." It didn't make a difference what he said, we were done.

"Sani talking about she's pregnant. I swear to God Hazel it's not by me. I always wore a condom."

"Wait a damn minute, you're calling me to tell me that the bitch you cheated on me with is pregnant? Are you fucking crazy!?" Yea I yelled because no one could possibly be this stupid.

"Didn't you hear what I said, it's not my baby."

"I don't give a damn Kahlil! Look, it's my fault for even hearing you out. Don't call me anymore. I'm done, I'm happy, and I've moved on. Fuck off!" I hung up on his nasty stank dick ass. I blocked both his phones this time then blocked him from social media.

"Kahlil is trash," Alyssa said when I got downstairs to the kitchen. I told her what happened as I made me a bowl of *Cookie Crisp* cereal.

"Girl trash is a compliment. That bitch gone hurry up and put his ass on child-support. Stupid ass nigga."

"I know right, he to fine to be so dumb." I agreed as I put some cereal in my mouth.

"Who the fuck is to fine?" Sada came in holding Liam on his chest. I chuckled because he was bothered as hell by Alyssa's comment.

"So damn nosey," Alyssa smirked, and he kissed her on her lips.

"Yea a'ight, watch I fuck you up if you play with me."

"Aww y'all are so cute." I smiled big, and Alyssa waved me off blushing.

"What's up sister-in-law. I see you still giving my brother a hard time."

"Sada for the last time I am not with your brother. He wants to have it all, me and these hoes. Nope, I don't share, and he seems to be fine with that because he hasn't called or texted so." I shrugged and put some more cereal in my mouth. Sada laughed, and Alyssa sat his plate of breakfast on the table as she put Liam in his swing.

"Thank you fat." He said to Alyssa, and I couldn't help but smile.

"You need to learn something about my brother. When he's quiet, that ain't never uh good."

"And I suppose you about to feed me some bullshit about how you can tell he like me and blah blah blah."

"I ain't gone tell you shit. Just watch what the fuck happens. That nigga crazy as hell, we both are." Alyssa sat down with us and was giggling.

"I'm taking my ass to work. Y'all can sit here and talk shit alone." I hugged Sada, hugged my best friend and kissed my God son.

***

"That looks beautiful Hazel, the presentation always goes noticed." I cheesed hard when one of the head chefs's complimented the dish I just made. Seasoned chicken breast in top of some collard greens and some pureed sweet potatoes. I had a special honey glaze I decided to drizzle on top of it. The one thing I liked about working here is that certain dishes on the menu can change spontaneously.

"Thank you so much. We had a serious lunch rush, and I thought we were going to crack." I joked but was low key for real. A kitchen runs smooth when everyone is on one accord. Sometimes the waiters and waitress don't communicate with us cooks right. The kitchen falls apart, and orders pile up. Today was similar I thought the other head chef was going to fight this one guy waiter we have. He was lazy and took to many bathroom breaks. But we got through it and the overall day was good.

"Hazel you are a delight to work with honey." This waitress Jackee said to me while we were in the women's locker room. My shift was over, and I was taking my hat and hair net off.

"I love working with you too. It's always a shit load of laughs." We were talking when my phone rung.

"Ok girl I'll see you Sunday." She said and walked out. I answered my Bluetooth while I took my pants off. I hated walking around in my uniform after work because I smelled like food. Plus if you leave your uniform here, it gets washed and dried. I brought some floral shorts, a crop top, and some sandals. I had just took a shower a let my hair air dry. Meaning big, curly and freezy, but whatever.

"What Mackenzie?" I answered my phone, and I swear I had to hide my smile. I hated that I was so into his difficult ass.

"Tha fuck you mean what, you betta check that shit." I rolled my eyes and put my DKNY bookbag on. I walked out smiling and waving to everyone.

"I don't have to check nothing."

"I like how you smiling while talking to me." I smacked my lips.

"Ain't nobody smiling so please don't think so much before you hurt yourself."

"I never thought you were a liar. I can see you smiling." I stopped walking and froze.

"Why the fuck you so scared of me. I told you I would never hurt you. Unless I'm hurtin' that pretty pussy." I looked around and didn't see him.

"Where are you? Why are you lying?"

"I would never lie to you angel face." Ugh, his voice was so deep, and it fucked my ears so good.

"You look good as fuck but them shorts to damn short. I can see the start of your fat ass cheeks." I still looked around and started walking a little.

"Mac stop playing." I started whining and stomping a little. He did that sexy low chuckle, and I tried not to bite my lip.

"You so fucking sexy." I turned around when I heard that voice close. There he was, looking like a gift from Jesus himself. That jet-black full beard, them thick waves in his head. Those full lips, hard body, and all those tattoos. He had on some basketball shorts, slides, and a beater. His watch was nice as hell, and his diamond studs in his ear completed him.

"I'm used to you calling me Mackenzie." He smiled, and I rolled my eyes to keep from smiling. I turned and walked out the door where the employees parked. Of course, he grabbed my arm and turned me around.

"You just gone walk away and not acknowledge me?" He looked big mad.

"Hi, Mackenzie. Now, how may I help you?"

"I can't come see you?" I laughed and put my book bag in my back seat.

"No, you can't. I haven't heard from you in days, so again I ask. How may I help you?"

"I miss seeing you and talking to you." I gave him a dumb look.

"Anddd you miss fucking me, gon' and say it."

"You right I do miss fucking you. I miss making you cum, hearing you call my name and the taste of your pussy."

"Wow how sweet, I feel so important," I said sarcastically.

"Look, it's a lot of bitches willing to offer you some pussy. Go fuck them." I folded my arms with an attitude.

"That's what I been doing, but my dick is craving you. Nigga got a mind of its own." I shook my head at him.

"You're disgusting Mackenzie. I'm not fucking you ever again. I want more, and you wanna be a hoe."

"I don't Hazel." When he said my name, I always felt like he was checking me. He stood in front of me with his hands in his pocket. His face was just perfect, and the lip biting thing was so much.

"What do you mean you don't?"

"I miss talking to you. I thought I still just wanted to do me and not complicate shit with us but naw. I want you to be my woman, and I also wanna fuck." I couldn't help but bust out laughing when he said that.

"You just flood me with romance." I joked. His aggressive butt put his hand around my neck and pulled me in for a kiss. I wanted to fuck right then and there. That was some of the sexiest shit I ever had done to me. His hand stayed around my neck when he broke out kiss.

"You my woman now and I'm ya man. Don't make me fuck you up Hazel." He bit his bottom lip, and I nodded.

"Same here homie, don't play with my feelings."

"Never." He pecked my lips again.

"I wanna take you somewhere." His voice was deep and low.

"Ok, where to?"

"It's a surprise so follow me. We gone drop your car off and then you're riding with me. When were done with the surprise it's back to my crib. I need to dig in them guts." I laughed and hit his arm. We kissed some more then I was in my car following him to my house.

"Umm, why are we here?" We walked in this retirement center, and I was so confused. All I know was he had me change when we got to my house. I kept my hair, earrings, and sandals on. I just put on a long fitted maxi dress.

"You'll see, come on." We walked to some elevators and took them to the third floor. Getting to a door, Mackenzie knocked and then used his key. When he opened the door, it smelled so damn good my stomach started growling. He held my hand, and when he called out grandma, I looked at him shocked.

"Is that my big Mac coming to see me." This beautiful woman with black and white long hair came from the back. She hugged Mackenzie and kissed his cheek. Her smile looked like his and his brother. Then another woman walked out the bathroom drying her hands.

"Hey, mama." *Mama!* I thought to myself. Shit now I felt like I was about to faint.

"I didn't know you were here." They embraced, and I smiled because they all had the same complexion and smile. His mother just had the same eyes like Sada. Them ones that were the devil and probably made people weak at the knees. My baby had his grandma's eyes. Dark, deep and they grabbed a hold of you.

"Yea I got off work early." They both looked at me and then at him.

"Well cool I can knock this out in one visit. Mama, grandma this my woman Hazel. Hazel this my mama and grandma."

"I know you not about to shake our hands like this is a job interview." His mama joked. I was so nervous, but their hugs calmed me down because it wasn't forced or fake.

"Nice to meet both of you. I apologize I'm just nervous. He kind of sprung this on me." I looked at him, and he smiled.

"I figured he did because you looked like a deer caught in the headlights, but it's all right. We good people." His grandma said as we all went and sat down in the living room.

"Well shit, I need to play the mega-million. First Sada and now you."

"Yea I was a little skeptical when I saw it was Alyssa but talking to her and hearing their story. I get it. I told her about me, y'all dad and Shauney. Shit happens, but they didn't hurt anybody so." His mama said and shrugged her shoulders. Already I liked both of them. We got the small talk out the way. I told them about my family and how I grew up. We talked about school and how me and Mackenzie met.

"That nigga rude as hell just like his dad was." His mama joked, and he waved her off laughing.

"I was ready to punch him, but for some reason, he stayed on my mind," I admitted which I knew he was about to rub it in my face later.

"Yup, that's how his dad got me. That rude shit is a turn on for some odd reason." I had fun, and his grandma cut into her apple pie she baked with some vanilla ice cream. I had to get the recipe to her crust because it was delicious. Now we were in his car going back to his house. His hand stayed on my thigh lightly squeezing it.

"Thank you for that, I had fun." I was still smiling at how cool his grandma and mama were.

"You're welcome angel face. I just wanted you to see that I'm for real." His phone rung and like all women do I side-eyed it trying to see but I couldn't. He turned the radio down, grabbed my hand and kissed it.

"I got something to tell you." He said and still kept our fingers interlocked.

"Ok."

"It's this girl name Quinn I used to fuck a while back. She's eight months pregnant and from what she says. It's mine." I tried to snatch my hand away, but he held it tighter.

"Can you hear me out, it ain't what you think."

"Bullshit, this girl might have your baby, and you kept it from me. So what, she crazy and I gotta deal with that. Nope, if that's the case, I could have stayed with Kahlil." This crazy nigga pulled over fast as fuck on the damn freeway. My heart raced because he was oblivious to the other cars as he turned his hazard lights on.

"Mackenzie you can't----"

"Don't disrespect me like that and compare me to one of your pussy ass niggas. I'm a different breed than them."

"So why are you just telling me then?"

"Because I don't know if this baby is mine, so I thought I wasn't going to say shit until I find out. That's my fault because you have the right to know. But that's my only wrong in this. I ain't touched that damn girl in months and don't want to. She pregnant and that's it. If it's mine, then I'mma do what I need to do. If not then I'm sending her ass the fuck on her way. Don't let nothing like this keep you from me, Hazel." I heard him loud and clear. His honesty was appreciated, but it's just something I can't deal with.

"It just sounds like too much. That girl just called you three times back to back. Naw I'm good Mackenzie, but we can be friends though." He looked at me for a second and didn't say anything. He turned his hazard lights off and pulled off back into traffic. His mood seemed calm, not mad or even bothered. He turned the radio back on, and his hand went back on my thigh. I don't know what that meant, but as long as he understood that we can't be together, then I was cool.

***

"Ahhh…ahhhh fuck baby." This nigga had been fucking me so good for the past fifteen minutes. We came in his house, and I thought we were about to talk. It started with him eating my pussy so damn good with my back pinned against his dresser. Then before I knew it, we were naked, and I'm face down ass up. He had both my hands behind my back fucking me like every woman should be fucked.

"Talk that shit now Hazel." He pounded harder, and I was cummin' to the point where my clit was tingling. All I could do was moan and bite my lip.

"You ain't leaving shit and we ain't no friends. You mine, say that shit." He slapped my ass so hard that I know my light skin was read.

"I'm yours, oh God I'm yours." Yea I meant that shit, I was Mackenzie's and between him and his dick. I was about to be crazy over him.

"Yea, I like hearing that." He let go of my hands and wrapped his hand around the front of my neck forcing me to kiss him.

"Let me taste that pussy again." I nodded out of breath and crawled on his bed on my back. I don't think it dawned on either of us that he wasn't wearing a condom.

"Ooooo Mackenzie daddy. Ssss right there." He had my legs so far apart, and his head was all in my pussy. I arched my back and ran my fingers through his waves. They were so soft and thick which made me cum harder. Everything about him turned me on and made me wet. The way he was kissing and sucking on my thighs had me throwing my head back and closing my eyes.

"Swear yo' pussy is the best I have ever tasted." His soaked beard was so sexy as he pushed both my legs back and put that thick dick back in me.

"Ughh." We both moaned, and he bit the heel of my foot. He was so deep in me, and his pace was perfect.

"Shit," Hearing him grumble made me tighten my walls around his dick. I knew he loved that and I did to.

"I wanna ride daddy, let me ride your dick." I moaned out, and he nodded his head. I hadn't had a chance to ride him yet, but something in me was up for the challenge. I got on top of him and kissed his lips nasty as fuck. Our bodies were soaked, and I wanted to sleep like this all night. I grabbed his hard dick and slid down on it slowly. Biting his neck, he squeezed my ass cheeks for dear life. I did a few slow grinds until he was in me nice and snug.

"Ahh shit, mmhmm." I threw my head back, got in a squat position and rode his dick like my life depended on it. My hands were flat on his bed, and this was the best. I don't even smoke, but I would imagine this is how weed felt. I was on a high, and his hands were moving all up my stomach and squeezing my titties.

"Ssss. Fuck. Mackenzie."

"Ride that dick baby, just like that. Look at'cho cum all on my dick." Oh my goodness his deep low voice was making my nipples so damn hard. I licked my lips and finally was able to sit my head up and look at him. His fuck face was just too much, like always that hand went around my throat and he pulled me down to kiss me.

"Mm!" I bounced on his dick and the slapping sounds mixed with our wet bodies were so erotic. Damn, we'd make a good ass porno tape. I had a surprise for him that I knew he was about to love. I hurried and climbed off his dick and took it in my mouth. I sucked it with no hands and tightened my jaws. In no time he came in my mouth, and it went down like soft served ice cream.

"Fuck!" How is it that he can fuck this long, cum that much and dick still not go all the way down. I rolled over on my back by his legs. I just knew in the morning my legs and pussy muscles would be sore. I got up and went to his bathroom. Luckily I left my toothbrush over his house. Mackenzie came in behind me and put his hands around my waist. He kissed my neck then cleaned himself up, and I let him clean me up too.

"Does it feel good having a girlfriend?" I asked him with my chin on his chest.

"Yea, I can dig it. Like I told you, I had some before it just always turns to a mess."

"You think we'll turn into a mess?" I asked him because I wanted to see if he had any faith in us.

"Naw, I think I'mma be stingy as fuck with you. We got a good vibe, I can be around you and not fuck. Although I haven't but I know I can." I chuckled as he continued.

"I know if I don't keep you another nigga gon' come along and snatch you up. Shit won't end well if that happens so I gotta make sure I do right."

"It's just funny how you can sound psychotic and sweet at the same time." I rubbed his waves and then the side of his face.

"I just speak the truth how you take it is how you take it." That sexy bottom lip went in his mouth again.

"I'm hungry as hell." I smiled when he said that.

"Come on." We both got up, I put his beater on, and he put on some boxers. I was excited because I had never cooked for him before.

"Yea, your mama, definitely shops for y'all." When I opened the refrigerator and saw all the ingredients I needed, I was shocked. Especially since two men lived here. I grabbed some flour, eggs, milk, cream cheese, and some strawberry syrup. I got to work on our food.

"Who taught you how to cook?"

"My mama and my dad but mostly my mama. She loves cooking and beyond the soul food. She was a feature on *Rachel Ray 30-Minute-Meals* show and on *Barefoot Contessa.* She never did open up her own restaurant though. I think she never wanted to but not me. I want a very intimate restaurant here, in New York, California, Paris, London, and Italy." He stood there leaning against the wall just listening to me.

"Those some dope ass dreams to have baby. I'mma make sure all that happens." I crumbled up the cream cheese and smiled big at what he said.

"So, what about you? What dreams do you have?"

"I want to open up a center for children who have parents incarcerated. I feel like society forgets there are children out there whose parents are in jail. They tend to not sympathize with a person if one of the parents is locked up instead of dead. Prisoners don't get sympathy, but nobody understands the child ain't got shit to do with all of that. Some kids don't even see their parent locked up for a bunch of reasons, they miss out on a role model, and some feel lost. I wanna come in and fix all of that as much as I can."

"Wow. I have never even heard of anyone who wants to do that. I think that's amazing and a lot of kids can benefit from that. You can always start off small like coach a team. Pick football or basketball, and I'd coach the cheerleading team of girls. We can have games against other little league teams. Do field trips, and if their parent is locked up in Michigan, we can look into taking them to visit them." I started plating our food and drizzling strawberry syrup on it. I looked at him because he was so quiet.

"What?" He was still leaning against the wall looking at me, but his eyes were low, and he was biting that sexy bottom lip again.

"Nothing I just think that's a good idea you came up with." Smirking I took our plates to the kitchen table, we said grace and dug in. I made us some cream cheese stuffed pancakes.

"This shit slaps angel face." A mouth full he complimented the food, and I blushed.

"I'm glad you like it, I'll cook for you more often."

"Hell yea, come here." I leaned over my plate and kissed his lips. We were interrupted with some aggressive knocks at his door.

"What the fuck." His whole mood changed so fast, and the expression on his face was like none I've ever seen. This nigga grabbed a big ass shotgun from behind the couch. My eyes bucked and he looked at me.

"Go in the kitchen and stay there it's a .9 in the jar that says 'cookies'. If need be just point and shoot." I flew to the kitchen and stood there looking at that cookie jar. I've never shot a gun before in my life, but I'd learn today if me or his life was in danger. He walked to the front without a fear in the world. I heard him open the door and a female started going in.

"I gotta pop up on you at nine at night Mac! Like what the fuck, am or am I not your baby mama!?" Then I heard a second female voice.

"He probably got some bitch up in here." Nope, I wish I would stay in this kitchen like some scary hoe. I emerged quick as hell with my arms folded in the flesh.

"I fucking knew it! Who the fuck is this Mac?!" The one with the round belly I took it was Quinn although both the bitches looked pregnant.

"You come barging in my shit with Baby D fat ass behind you. Both of y'all betta get the fuck out my shit."

"So you'll put me out, the one carrying your child but this hoe can stay?"

"No hoes in this direction sweetheart but I am his woman. You think because you carrying his baby you got some rights to him? I think the fuck not." I stood there and didn't for one second look or feel intimidated even when she started talking shit back.

"Bitch I do have rights to him that's my baby daddy!"

"Might be your baby daddy!" I shouted back, and the fat bitch with her gone try to step to Mac.

"So you telling these hoes my sister business?!" Mac lost it.

"You betta get'cho built like a M ass outta my fuckin' face." He had the shotgun still in his hand but pointed down. His expression made Baby D ass think twice. Next thing I know, Quinn tried to come for me. She yelled almost hitting me but she missed, and I pushed her. I really didn't want to because she was pregnant so I just pushed her on the couch. Her fat ass linebacker tried to run my way, but Mac pushed her against the wall with his arm on her neck.

"Quinn, take yo' sister and get the fuck outta my crib. Holla at me when the baby born so we can get this DNA test out the way. You need to respect Hazel because if this child is mine." He pointed at me.

"That's gon' be his stepmama. Now apologize to her and leave my crib." Quinn got off the couch and turned her nose up at me.

"You must be out of your mind if you think I'm apologizing to this bi---" Before she could finish her sentence Mackenzie cocked the shotgun and put it to her sister's neck. He didn't even speak he just gave her this menacing expression. I stood there thinking there is no way he would shoot this girl. I thought Quinn would call his bluff, but she turned towards me and said.

"I apologize for coming at you the way I did." I nodded my head, and she looked at Mac like she wanted to smack him but I wish the fuck she would. Stomping out the door, he looked at her sister.

"You too. Apologize for charging at my woman. Tell her next time you'll act like a gentleman in her presence." Was I wrong for chuckling a little?

"I apologize for charging at you."

"And?" Mackenzie said, and I couldn't believe he wanted her to say this.

"And the next time I see you I'll act like a gentleman in your presence." He moved his arm from her neck and lowered the shotgun.

"Now get the fuck out and tell your sister I'll see her in a month." She left, and he slammed his door and locked it. Putting the shotgun back behind the couch he walked up to me and put his hand on the side of my face.

"You good?"

"I'm fine. I'm sorry for pushing her, but I didn't want to hit her."

"You ain't got to apologize for shit angel face. She came at'chu like she wasn't pregnant. Come on let's finish eating." He kissed my lips, and we went back to our food.

"You weren't really going to shoot her, were you?" I fed him some pancakes after I warmed them back up. He chewed his food and licked them sexy ass lips.

"I would've blew her fat ass stomach off." Those eyes didn't have one ounce of deception in them.

"And this is only the 'liking you stage'." That eyebrow arched and instead of running for the door. I just pecked his lips a few times.

"Mm."

Kiss.

"Mm."

Kiss.

"Mmm. Yea let's finish this food up. My dick hard again." I giggled and the rest of our night consisted of fucking and eating.

Quinn

I have been crying for three days now. Mac didn't give a fuck about me or the fact that I was carrying his child. Then he had the nerve to have some new bitch that he claims is his woman. As if I haven't been wobbling around for eight and a half months with his son. I have never even seen this hoe Hazel before in my life. I know every bitch in Detroit that Mac has fucked, but this trick is a new face. Nobody moves to the hood they usually move out, so I had to do my digging. And behold, she's best friends with that black ass bitch Alyssa. I have never liked her ass because she's never liked me.

I lowkey laughed when Maine died and left her ass. Then the nasty slut gone hook up with his cousin. And you hoes wanna judge me! I bet that baby was never Maine's. Sada nasty dick ass is a new low. Anyway, little Ms. Hazel bitch is from Grand Rapids and according to her pictures. She likes to cook, and I guess pretend she's a model because the selfies she takes looks like it. I ain't gone lie, she cute and all but out of all the niggas in Detroit why the fuck she had to put her dick suckers on my baby daddy.

To make matters worse, Mac pulled a gun out on me and my sister. I looked that lunatic in the eyes, he would have shot Starrenna without a doubt. I knew Mac wasn't playing with a full deck, but damn he proved it that day. I've probably watched his Insta-Story about ten times. She was on it, and they looked like a real-life happy couple. He was kissing on her, touching and hugging her. Then him licking her ass cheeks while she had some boy-shorts on.

Like ugh, that shit isn't for the cameras. I hated that bitch and didn't even know her. The only communication I got from that nigga was asking if I was good or if I needed anything. He stopped by my mama house and gave her rent money, but he didn't even ask to see me. As of today, I feel like fuck Mac and his bitch.

"Damn, I haven't seen you in a while." Malcolm opened his door with an open robe and some boxers on. No matter how I felt about him, he was always so damn fine. No denying that I just never took him serious. One because I wanted Mac and two because he was a bigger hoe then his nephews.

"Can I come in?" I asked him as I batted my long eyelashes. He stepped aside and let me come in.

"So you were right, about Mac." I put my purse on his couch and leaned against the wall.

"He never has or will love me. In fact, he has a new bitch. I'm completely done with him." I looked up at Malcom, and he had a stern expression.

"And I take it now that your flat on your ass you think I want you." My nostrils flared, and I got an attitude.

"I don't care rather you want me or not Malcolm. I only came to tell you that you were right." He started laughing.

"You lying and you know it. You came to tell me that and to give yourself to me. The thing is, I don't know if I want it anymore. You have his baby in you, what makes you think I wanna look at that every day?"

"Malcolm please, I'm realizing you were always right and always trying to be there for me. I messed up." I walked closer to him and touched his face. When he didn't deny my touch, I knew I had him.

"I want to be with you and only you. No back and forth and no games."

"You mean that shit?" I smiled and kissed him
hungrily. He picked me up and carried me to his bedroom.
We both got naked and went back to kissing. Malcolm
wasn't the best kisser, he sucked on my lips to damn hard
and sometimes his breath would be stinking. But today it was
good he just pulled on my lip like he was trying to break it
off. He opened my legs and started fingering me. I never
liked that shit, but something about the way Malcolm did it
made me cum so damn good at least twice. I grabbed his bald
head and let his fingers work their magic.

"Cream on these fingers and tell me this my pussy."
He was hitting my spot, and I felt myself cumming.

"It's your pussy Malcommmm. Arghh!" I came so
good, and he started eating me out. That bald head was going
crazy, and so was I. I got ruff with it and pressed his face so
hard in my pussy. I was biting my lips and growling because
he didn't ease up. I came again, and I felt it coming right
back. I rose up a little off the bed and my legs wrapped
around his neck so damn tight.

"Ahh shit!" My goodness, I fell on his bed, and my
chest was going in and out at a rapid pace.

"I'm about to fuck you so good Quinn." He stood up
and stroked his dick.

"Where can I put this nut?" I opened my wet pussy
lips wide.

"Inside of me." Malcolm smiled big, leaned forward and started kissing me while sliding his dick in. Malcolm fucked me so good that I tapped out after I came for the third time when he was hittin' it from the back.

***

I woke up because I was hungry as hell. The baby had me peeing so much so before I head to the kitchen I went to pee. Me and Malcolm had some good sex. Nowhere near how Mac used to fuck me, but I needed to get over him. I wasn't about to become second or third because my baby would come before me. I didn't mind that but what I did mind was coming after some bitch. With Malcolm, I'd always come first, and I had my baby, so it was all good. That nigga loved my bloody tampon, so I knew he'd except me and him.

I was ready to move out my mama's house and since Mac was out. Malcolm was a great second best, he had money, a big ass house and I was everything to him. Why the fuck not. I flushed the toilet and washed my hands. Grabbing his shirt and a pair of his boxers I put them on so I could head downstairs but I heard voices. Stopping at the top of the steps a wall hid me as I started ear hustling.

"What do you want us to do? The east side is where we getting our most money." I didn't know who the fuck that was talking but then I heard Malcolm's voice.

"What the hell you mean 'what I want y'all to do'? Keep selling my shit, I was just informing you to pay attention on the streets. Them east side niggas know y'all out there, and they sent my nephews to make us stop." Then another voice spoke.

"I'on know Malcolm, I think we should say fuck the east and stay with the areas we have."

"Tha fuck did I just say!! I ain't scared of no damn body! I been waiting to take over Detroit for a while and not nobody about to fuck with my plan. Not my punk ass nephews, hell I had y'all kill my own son because he wouldn't get down with me. I keep y'all safe from Mac and Sada, trust me when I say them east side niggas ain't gone do shit. I need this product to be pushed out, and then we make our move. I got some eyes on the over there and when we meet back up, we making our move on the east. Robbing and killing all of them and that's how we will take over east and west. More money will come pouring in, just hang tight." I heard him give them some fives and dismiss them.

The front door closed, and I hurried back in the room to lay down and watch TV. I couldn't believe what I had just heard. Maine was Malcolm's flesh and blood. How the hell could he have him killed like that? And why are Mac and Sada still alive? This shit was crazy, and I wanted no parts. If he could kill his own son, then he could kill me and maybe even my child. No fucking way, I needed to think of a plan. One that will get me far away from Malcolm. A plan that will put some zeros in my bank. Right now a bitch was looking at 45K in my bank account, and the K is silent, so I need to think of something. Malcolm came back in the room and took his clothes off. He climbed back in bed with me and went under the covers. I closed my eyes and enjoyed the head especially when a plan came to my mind just that fast. I knew what I had to do.

Alyssa

"Why you acting all scared fat-fat, huh?"

"I'm not scared Casada; it's just." He started kissing on my neck and then my lips mid-sentence.

"It's just what bae?"

"I-It's just been a while and you------ Ughh." Today was the first day me and Casada have had sex together. I'd been back to work for a few weeks now, between my schedule and his we hadn't been able to meet in the middle. By the time we'd get in bed it was to sleep. Being Casada's `He loved my son and always picked him up from my mama's and brought him home. My mama is still a little side-eye about us being together, but she knows what comes with me is him. Now we were at his house in his bed, and he was putting his big dick in me.

"Let me in bae, you done sucked this dick more than enough. Now you acting all scared and shit." He slid in me a little more. I was tight, and he was so big.

"Sucking is different from fucking bae." I rolled my eyes in the back of my head because now he was all the way in and oh my goodness it was hurting so damn good. Then he started moving slow and them lips kissing on me was just, mm!

"There we go fat-fat, open that pussy for daddy. Shit." I spread my legs wider and he grinded in me deeper. How the fuck is it he felt this good, like oh my God my body just went in sync with his. These kisses he was showering me in was making me get wetter and wetter. He was grumbling all in my ear, and his dreads were all over his face.

"Ugh, you feel so good. Ugh. Fuck me. Mmm just fuck me." I moaned, and he did just that. He started biting on my neck and sucking on it. Then he took me out the game when he started talking nasty in my ear mixed with his bomb strokes.

"This pussy mine, ya hear me, Alyssa. This wet tight ass pussy is mine forever." He licked my ear and continued.

"Cum on this dick, I want this chocolate pNJussy to cum on this dick."

"Casada….ahhhh….ahhhh." I came so good, he pulled out and flipped me over.

Slap!

Slap!

"Toot dat ass up bitch." He slapped both my ass cheeks and my freak ass started shaking them.

"You like that ruff shit huh?" He rubbed his hard dick up and down my ass crack then he started rubbing it between my pussy lips. I had a deep arch in my back, and my face was in his mattress. He slid in and not a little at a time. The whole ten-inch was tickling my guts, and he just held it there for a second.

"Shit," that got me when he said that with his raspy voice. Then he started gripping my hips and pumping my pussy up with good dick. I bit his sheet hard to keep from screaming. The ass slapping, when he'd grip my waist tight, and just the feel of his dick had me going cross-eyed.

"Slam that fat ass booty on this dick. Bae." I moaned so loud in his sheet as I threw my ass back over and over. He grabbed my neck and pulled me to his face.

"Look at me." I looked on the side of my face where he was, and he was looking so good then he kissed my lips nasty. Still fucking me so good he said.

"You love me?" He kissed me and bit my bottom lip a little, I couldn't even talk because I was cumming so good. He had a hold of my neck, and he was making me look at him still.

"I said do you fuckin' love me? Dick got'cha tongue." He literally put his tongue down my throat when he kissed me again.

"Ugh yes, I love you, Casada." Finally finding my voice, I answered and he smiled big. A few more pumps and we both came together. The orgasm was so good I was shaking. Casada kissed and licked all down my wet back. He squeezed my ass cheeks and then kissed my ear.

"You meant that? Do you really love me?" Out of breath I looked at him and licked his bottom lip.

"Yes Casada I meant it, I really do love you. I was just scared to tell you first." I confessed.

"Don't ever be scared to tell me shit. A'ight." I nodded as he got up and pulled the condom off. He cleaned himself and then came back and cleaned me up. We laid in bed naked, and I was on my way to sleep.

"Fat-Fat."

"Yea?"

"I love you too." I smiled big and kissed his chest. Sleep came in no time.

***

I got out the shower and took my hair out my shower cap. I was still wearing my real hair in the wave pattern. August is the hottest month of the summer for Michigan but the way this weather was set up who the hell could tell. Every day was hot as hell, so I decided not to wear any make-up. I wore a long fitted maxi skirt and a bandeau top with some wedges. Casada was knocked out, but he told me to take his Magnum to work since he drove me over here. I didn't have to be to work for another three hours, but I wanted to leave early so I could see Liam at my mama's house.

He spent the night with her, and I was missing my chubbs. I had to work eight hours today and no way could I be away from him all night and all day. Liam had a stalker for life, and it was me. I walked downstairs and opened the door leading to Mac's part of the house. Hazel spent the night, and I knew by now her ass was up. When I saw Mac sleep on the couch. Aw shit. They must have gotten into it. I walked to the back in his room and knocked on the close door. Hazel said come in and I did.

"Good morning." She was laying on the bed watching TV. Her hair was wet, so I took it she had just got out the shower.

"Hey boo, you ok? I saw Mac sleeping on the couch. Do I need to kick his ass?" I sat on the chair in his room. Hazel rolled her eyes and waved me off.

"Girl he so dramatic. I farted in bed, and he swore up and down I killed him." I laughed my ass off, and so did she.

"I know his ass be dropping some deadly ones because his brother fucking does."

"Ok! Like nigga my bad, I underestimated the fart." I was still laughing listening to Hazel stupid ass.

"I'm for real bitch, I thought the fart would whisper in my panties, but I guess I was wrong." I literally rolled out the chair on the floor laughing so damn hard. That was the funniest shit I've heard in so damn long.

"Bitch I hate you." I wiped the tears from my eyes holding my stomach.

"So we haven't had a chance to catch up. Guess what?" I got serious when Hazel said that because she rolled her eyes.

"Oh Lord what happened?"

"Mackenzie told me this girl is pregnant and it might be his baby?" My eyes almost popped out my head.

"Ima leave, come back in and pretend you didn't just say that."

"Don't bother the tea will still be the same. It was before me, she about eight and a half months."

"Bitch stop! Who is the girl?" Hazel shrugged her shoulders.

"Some bitch named Quinn." When she said that I almost melted in the chair.

"Get the fuck out Hazel! I knew they were fuck buddies, but I never knew he would slip up like that. I know that bitch think she on top of the world. He ain't been with her in so damn long."

"You know her?"

"Nope, I just seen her a few times over here when I used to be with Jermaine. I never cared for her because she fucked anyone with money. As long as she never comes for you then we all good." Hazel tilted her head and smacked her lips.

"Bitch too late for that. Her and this Tee Grizzly looking bitch came over and tried to step. Mackenzie handled it, but I pushed Quinn on the couch when she tried to swing at me." This was too much for one morning.

"Well, then we know what we gotta do when she drops that baby. Stupid ass hoe wanna take swings, naw bruh. We whooping her ass for that and the big bitch that was with her. That's her sister Starrenna . She fucks with this wannabe gangsta nigga named Freddy. He always at the strip club and casino blowing money and claim he about that life. Lame as fuck. I can beat them hoes up in my sleep."

"All I know is if this baby is his she ain't got no choice but to chill the fuck out. I'll be in her child's life because I'm with Mackenzie but if she oversteps again I'm knocking her ass out." I looked at her shocked as hell.

"Wow bitch, Mac must got that pipe. I'm so surprised you didn't dip on his ass." She giggled and said.

"Nope, I'm a mother first." We both laughed when she said that.

"He put that dick on you and fucked you into staying put." She blushed and nodded her head. The door opened, and Mac walked in.

"What up doe sister-in-law." He looked at Hazel.

"Good morning shitty ass." Hazel pouted, and he got up in the bed with her. She tried to touch him, but he blocked her.

"Don't be doing my best friend that way nigga." I talked shit from the chair I was sitting in.

"You ain't smell that foul shit that came out her ass. She smelled like a grown ass diabetic man." I tried not to laugh because Hazel feelings were hurt, but that was some funny shit. Mac looked at her and saw her face. His ass changed it up real quick. I really tried not to laugh when she was crying because she was playing him. He made her straddle his lap.

"Angel face stop crying. I was just fucking with you."
She sniffed and wiped her face.

"No you weren't, you slept on the couch and
everything."

"A'ight I won't do that again, next time I'll just fart
with you." When she started giggling and kissing him, I
knew that was my queue.

"Ooook by brother-in-law, bye best friend." I saw
both of them chug me the deuces and I just closed the door.
Nasty asses.

"Hi, my chubbs." I picked Liam up out his crib my
mama had over her house. I came straight in, washed my
hands and went for my baby. His hair was so curly and big
now, and he was chubby as hell. Jaws were chewable, and he
was only three months. He stayed up longer now with those
eyes like his daddy. I was in love like never before when I
was around my baby.

"You know mommy loves you so much? Well she
does, she loves you so damn much." I kissed all over him.
Then I changed his diaper and put him on a new sleeper. I set
on my mama's bed and breastfed him. This was my favorite
thing to do with him because it was a bonding moment. His
little hand would hold my finger, and we'd just stare at each
other.

"So is that boy coming to pick up Liam?" I rolled my eyes when my mama walked in the room trying to be funny with her question.

"I don't know what boy you're talking about, but Casada is coming to pick him up then he's picking me up from work." My back was facing her as I was burping Liam.

"Well you know what I mean, how long do you think he will do this before he gets bored?"

"What is your problem today? Are you trying to make me have a bad day?" I finally turned to her.

"No I'm not, but I am being honest with you. Y'all are twenty-one-years-old. You are responsible because Liam is your flesh and blood. He's your son so as soon as you peed on that stick." She snapped her fingers.

"Instantly your mindset was different. He will not think like you because he doesn't have to. He's not Liam's father, so he can walk away anytime. Do you understand that?" I laid my son down in his crib and looked at my mama.

"What I understand is if Jermaine was alive, he could have walked away, and he was my boyfriend and Liam's father. If I was engaged or married, the guy still could walk away. It happens all the time mama. Men leave women, and women leave men. I completely understand that. Anybody I decide to be with can walk away at any time, but guess what mama? If they ever do, then I'll be ok. This little boy will be ok because you didn't raise me to have my child around every man I meet. I'm twenty-one years old and have only met one of your friends, and you were with him for a year. The possibility of heartbreak just comes along with dating. At the end of the day I'll be fine because even though Casada makes me happy, he is not my happiness." I kissed Liam on his jaw one more time and said goodbye to my mama.

She annoyed the hell out of me and trust me just because I said what I said. She is still going to talk shit. As long as she wasn't rude to Casada, then I was cool. I was hungry as hell since I didn't eat at my mama house. I was leaving her house headed to Greenfield-street, so I could drive it down all the way to work. ,I decided to stop at the gas station and grab me a honeybun and a Red Bull energy drink. I hated this gas station on Fenkell and Whitcomb and so did my mama because the outside of it was a slum. It was deserted, and the owner didn't care, but he let niggas sell drugs out of it because they gave him a profit. It's a little hidden and just needs to be shut down. But I just needed a little something on my stomach.

I grabbed four dollars, my phone and headed in the store. I walked in, and the clerk spoke to me, and I spoke back. I looked around and was pleading that they had my drink. Smiling big when I saw it I grabbed me a honeybun and a bag of hot Cheeto Puffs. My total came up to three-dollars and some change, so I gave him the four and told him to keep the change. I opened the driver's side and put my items on the passenger seat.

"Alyssa." I turned around just before getting in the car when I heard my name being called.

"Oh, hey Mario." Oh goodness, I had been ignoring him for a while because he wouldn't catch the hint that I didn't want to talk to him anymore. I even said the words out my mouth that we needed to shill on talking, but he still tried to reach out to me.

"Hey yourself, I see you looking good as hell this morning." I gave him a fake smile, and he stepped closer.

"Thank you. Well, I need to get to work so---"

"Hold up, hold up I just want to talk to you damn." When he slammed my door, I jumped a little.

"I just want to know why you played me? I didn't do shit wrong, never disrespected you and I didn't even want to only fuck. I actually wanted to make you my lady." He was so close to my face I could smell the liquor on his breath, and it was only ten in the morning.

"Mario please step back a little." I was starting to get scared.

"Why can't I be on you, huh? Oh yea that's right, you're with that bitch ass nigga Sada." His hand traced around my face and then my chest.

"It wasn't planned being with him. We weren't even friends for a while, it just sort of happened." He shook his head while I was explaining. Which I would never but at this point Mario was scaring the shit out of me.

"But you're still with him now when you made me think me, and you were building something. I ain't never been like this about a bitch. But you Alyssa." I closed my eyes and tears started to form when he slowly started pulling my skirt up. "You I think about, dream about and even jack off to. And you fucking played me." That last part he gritted his teeth and said.

"Mario please don't do this to me. I didn't play you if you felt I did then I apologize. But I know you, you're not a rapist so please just stop."

"You don't know shit about me because you didn't give us a chance. But you let Sada bitch ass get all up in. Up in what the fuck was supposed to be mine." His hand was now under my skirt, and he touched my pussy outside my panties.

"You won't even get fuckin' wet for a nigga." He let my face go and then I felt a hard steel on my hip.

"Get wet for me Alyssa. I want you to call my name and get wet for me, or I swear I will kill yo' ass right here. I don't care about going to jail." You could hear the tear in my panties, and his fingers started going inside of me. I was dry as hell because this touch was not one I ever wanted. We were just friends kicking it, he never asked me to be his girl or even hinted that he wanted me. Me and Mario have never kissed, went out or anything. We laughed and chilled at Butzles, exchanged numbers, sent a few texts, and that was it. The next time I saw him was at Amelia's party. The hard steel pressing harder in me made me snap out of it.

"I said get fuckin' wet. I know you don't make that hoe ass nigga Sada ask twice." When he said my bae's name, I closed my eyes and thought about him. Our first-time last night having sex with each other. I thought about his touch, voice, kisses and how he felt inside of me. How he just knew my body and I didn't have to say a damn thing. I thought about how sexy his moans were and how them dreads would be all over his face. This was about to help me not get killed by this crazy nigga.

"See I knew you had it in you." I tuned this stupid nigga out. His dumb ass thought he was doing this to me. Little did he know thoughts of my man were getting me through this. Then I couldn't keep the image in my head because Mario started breathing hard as hell. I thought he was about to pass out. I finally opened my eyes, and he had his closed with his mouth open. His fingers were so ruff, and I felt myself drying up.

"I need to feel how good this pussy is. I know it's good, I just need a minute inside of you." I broke down then.

"Mario please---" his eyes shot open.

"Shut the fuck up. I'm getting this pussy, and you betta call my fucking name." He pulled his fingers out of me and roughly grabbed my face.

"Stop that fucking crying before I end your life." He then licked my tears and I almost threw-up. Removing the gun from my hip, he set it on top of Sada's car, and I heard him unbuckle his jeans.

"Oh my God, I can feel you already. I'm cumming in you too and if you get pregnant, you betta have my baby." Hell no, I'm not about to be this person. I've never been touched on or forced to do anything sexually that I didn't want to do. I thought quick on my feet when I saw him pull his dick out. My skirt was still up, and my legs were free, I looked on the side of me and saw his gun. When he started stroking his dick with his eyes closed, I eased my hand up and grabbed his gun so fast. He moved his hand from his dick, and I kneed him so hard in his balls, and then I hit him in his face with his gun even harder. That nigga fell back into the garbage can that was by the gas pumps.

"Ugh! You fucking bitch Ima kill you." I didn't even give him a chance. Moving fast as hell I jumped in the car, started it and pulled off. I was shaking so hard as I threw his gun on the floor. What the fuck just happened. I started off having a good morning, I saw my baby and all I wanted to do was head to work. Speaking of work, I don't even know where I was driving to. I pulled off with only the thought of getting far away from Mario's ass possible. My tears were falling non-stop at what he did and what he could have done. I turned down the next big street and knew exactly where I was going.

Sada

I woke up and rolled over to Alyssa gone. I forgot she said she had to work and was leaving early because she wanted to see Liam. One of the things that turned me on was how much she loved her son. Making her, my woman was a good ass decision. I know we young as fuck, and a nigga like me still has some immaturity in me. But I do love Alyssa, and I don't want her with nobody else. I like kicking it with her without knowing she was being phony. So many bitches I talk to act fake as fuck. Some come real and let me know they just wanna fuck just to say they smashed me. Some come as gold diggers in disguise, but once I smell that shit, I get they ass away from me.

Then some try to act like they the homie knowing they want more but think being my friend first will make me wife them. Big fucking mistake, if you act as the homie, Ima treat you as such and ain't no coming back. Alyssa was my woman and my homie. We vibe on a whole other level that I fucked with heavy. I got up and headed to my bathroom to take care of my business. After I was done pissing, I washed my face and brushed my teeth. I grabbed my other rag and put some soap on it so I can clean my dick and balls. Before I did, I rubbed under my balls and like I knew, they smelled just like Alyssa's pussy. Clean but sweet at the same time. I grabbed my black sweatpants and turned on my A.C. as I headed to the kitchen.

"Damn."

I spoke out loud because me and Alyssa did all that damn grocery shopping for her crib and mine and I still forgot milk. I hate that shit; you'll spend over a hundred dollars and still forget shit. I knew for a fact that Mac had some since Hazel was always cooking. Putting my slides on and grabbing my box of *Coca Puffs* and headed downstairs. I got to the kitchen, and just like I thought, they had a gallon of milk. I sat down and decided to eat my cereal down here instead of taking the milk upstairs.

"Got damn you get so fucking wet for me baby. Shit." If you could see my fucking face right now.

"Cum with me daddy…P-Please cum with me."

"Tell daddy where you want this nut."

"My mouth. Oooo shit cum in my mou---"

"AYE!! SHUT THAT SHIT UP! THIS IS A CHRIST FILLED HOME!!" I finally had enough even after I turned music on from my phone.

"Nasty muthafuckas!" I yelled again and went back to eating. About fifteen-minutes and three bowls of cereal later Mac came from the back. I shook my head, and he gave me the middle finger.

"Where the hell is the other sinner at?" I joked while drinking my milk.

"Her scary ass in the back. You know I'on got no shame in my dick, but her ass is embarrassed." I laughed, and so did Mac.

"Hazel get'cho ass out here and take the walk of shame!" I cracked up when she emerged, and her face was red.

"Unholy ass sinners." I shook my head in shame at her, and she covered her mouth laughing. Mac came and put his arms around her.

"Fuck you nigga. Don't forget yo' bedroom is over my bathroom." I shrugged my shoulders.

"I was trying to take a nap, but your brother kept messing with me." Hazel finally spoke and wasn't red in the face.

"She was loving it."

"All I gotta say is, I hope you brushed yo' teeth." I laughed because she turned back red and screamed laughing in her hand.

"Leave me alone brother-in-law. I'm about to make a Dutch baby for us do you want one." I gave her a puzzling expression.

"What the hell is a Dutch baby?"

"Shit don't ask me, I stop asking her about the stuff she cooks. As long as it's good, I just say ok." Mac said, and Hazel smacked her lips.

"Y'all annoying. A Dutch baby is a puffed baked pancake that in the center of it can be filled with anything. I'm filling mine with sliced strawberries, whip crème, and raspberries. Eggs and bacon will be served on the side.

"You had me at strawberries. Hook that shit up sis." Hazel kept us full all the damn time. On some real shit, she needed her restaurant and Alyssa needed her own boutique. They just had gifts that many people didn't discover until later in life.

"I got an idea on how to handle Malcolm. Well, part of it but it's still something I wanna run by you and Clip." Mac whispered to me while Hazel was cooking.

"Cool. I been thinking how we can handle him and his crew to but I ain't came up with shit. Plus you know them east side niggas impatient."

"Naw I kept shit G with them, and they know I don't move fast or sloppy. They want bodies, so it takes time. I got this shit in the bag." I nodded just as someone knocked on our front door.

"I swear if that's your baby mama trippin' again I'm throwing her ass in this oven." Hazel stood in the kitchen looking heated with a big ass skillet in her hand.

"Keep yo' woman in the kitchen. Damn girl crazy just like yo' ass." I laughed shaking my head. I looked out the window and saw my Magnum in the driveway. I know I gave it to Alyssa to drive to work so what the hell was she doing here? I opened the door, and she crashed into me.

"Bae, what's wrong?" I slammed the front door with her hugging my waist crying. Mac and Hazel rushed to the living room.

"Best friend what bitches do we need to fuck up?" Hazel said already putting on some gym shoes.

"No it's----- It's not that." She was balling, and Hazel ran to the back and came back with some Kleenex cleaning her face.

"I-I-I was on my way to work, and I stopped at the gas station on Fenkell and Whitcomb." Alyssa was crying so hard her eyes were puffy, and she was stuttering.

"Calm down bae so you can talk. I'm right here so you good, just tell me so I can handle it." She nodded her head fast and took a deep breath.

"I was coming out the gas station, and Mario approached me." She said his name and my body became numb and my heart was racing.

"He started walking up on me telling me I played him for you. How he thought we were working on building something." She looked at me with sad eyes.

"Bae, I swear I never led him on or anything. We didn't fuck, kiss or even go out, so I don't know why he thought that." She sniffed and continued.

"He put a gun to my hip and lifted my skirt." She broke down, and I hugged her tight.

"Oh my God," Hazel said low with her hand over her mouth and tears coming from her eyes. Mac looked at me and went to the back. I was so fucking heated that I couldn't even say anything. I consoled my girl and calmed her down.

"Look at me fat-fat." She did, and I wiped her face.

"I'm not about to make you relive that horrible shit. But I gotta know---" She picked up her purse and pulled a gun out.

"I kneed him in the balls and hit him with his own gun. Here." She gave it to me, and I was relieved because I didn't know how far he had got.

"He had his fingers in me Casada, and he made me say his name."

Hazel came and hugged her then, and I had to go to the kitchen and take a shot of Patron. This muthafucka came for my woman. Touched her, scared her and almost raped her. Hell in my eyes he may have not penetrated her, but he still did things that she didn't want done. My hands were so hot that I had to close my eyes for a second. I was killing Mario, no question about it. It was just a matter of how.

"Let's roll bro." Mac walked in the kitchen in some red sweatpants, gym-shoes, and a black t-shirt. He tossed me a black t-shirt and socks. I put that shit on and hurried out the kitchen.

"Bae I'll be back." I kneeled down to her cute ass face. I hated this shit happened to her. Pussy came easily to any nigga with a dick. You just had to know what to say, hell if you had no game. Then go by some damn pussy. But to make a woman do anything that she doesn't want to do just so you can get your rocks off. That shit is disgusting as fuck and my girl sitting here because she was violated. It was time to get my hands dirty.

"Ok, Hazel is taking me to get Liam so I can go home. I don't want to tell my mama which is why I didn't want to go to the police." I kissed her a few times. I really wanted her to come back here. But her comfortability was more important right now.

"I'm glad you didn't go to the police. Let me handle this, and I promise that nigga will pay." Kissing her again it was then that I realized I really loved Alyssa and Liam. As soon as I was done, I was getting right up under them. Mac hugged and kissed Hazel, and both of them told us to be careful.

"Mario lives on Mendota and Puritan. Ain't shit on Purtian but some bum ass niggas I'on even know why Alyssa fucked with him in the first place." I balled my fist up tight as hell.

"Don't even trip, that muthafucka finna pay. I got an idea." We took my truck, but I let Mac drive because I was to pissed right now.

"Aye, come here sweetheart." He pulled over at this abandon liquor store on Fenkell where some crackheads and prostitutes were at.

"You wanna make three-hundred dollars?" She smiled big as hell with her fucked up ass teeth.

"Hell yea, what I gotta do?" Mac unlocked the back door, and she got in.

"Shit man this bitch stink," I said not caring that she heard me.

"I know and well get'cha shit cleaned later." He looked in the rearview mirror.

"All you gotta do is take a ride with us. We'll drop you off where ever you want after." Mac reached around and gave her a hundred dollars. Swear the shit people were willing to do for money was funny as hell. This lady didn't know us or know what the hell we were getting her into.

"This stupid ass nigga at home to," I said when we got to Mario block. His brother was killed last summer, and he threw a big ass party after his funeral. That's how I knew where he stayed. His car was parked in the driveway with another one parked in front of it.

"That's a bitch car." I looked at Mac and pointed out.

"I can see the pink steering wheel cover and beads hanging from the rear-view mirror." As I spoke Mario door opened, and the bitch came out. They kissed, and she walked off the porch. I was glad because we would have killed her ass to and all she would have been guilty of was being at the wrong place at the wrong time.

"He just got some pussy so let's wait about fifteen minutes. He gone shower, smoke and then eat. Perfect time to make our move." This is why we killed niggas for money and did shit clean. Mac ass was always planning and smart with his moves. I had to crack my window just a little because this damn bum was foul as fuck.

"Let's move." We got out, and Mac turned to the bum.

"Stay behind us. You'll get the other two-hundred when it's all done." Her high ass agreed, and we started walking towards the front porch.

We both pulled our gun with the silencer out once we were close enough to the screen door. The fool had his shit unlocked, but the big door wasn't. We squatted down once I got the door unlocked. Mac taught me when breaking in someone shit you never knew if they had heat on them or not. Squat down because nine out of ten times if they did shoot at you it would be in an upward position. We got in, and the living room was clear. There was no upstairs, so we had one floor to focus on. The high smell of weed was getting stronger. Mac was right, that nigga had smoked. Once we got passed the living room, we stood up straight and went to where the TV and weed was coming from. Sure enough, he was sitting on his bed eating a sandwich.

"What's up my nigga." I walked in smiling, and he looked like he was about to choke on his food.

"What the fu---"

"Don't even think about it bitch." Mac hurried and grabbed Mario's gun on his nightstand.

"Now you wouldn't have any idea as to why I'm here do you?" I asked him like I didn't know.

"Oh, I remember." I balled my fist up and hit him in his nose hard as fuck.

"Fuck!" He yelled as blood gushed from his nose.

"You not only touched what was mines but you tried to rape her as well. All because she chose a real nigga to be happy with over you."

"Fuck you nigga, you and Mac think y'all can do what the fuck you want. I didn't do shit to Alyssa that she didn't want." I hit him again, and I was about to shoot him, but Mac stopped me.

"Shooting him is to easy. Come here, sweetheart." He looked at the bum ass prostitute we picked up. He had her get on the bed and pull her dress up. I almost threw up because her pussy was so hairy it was poking out her panties. I caught on then and with my gun still on Mario I said.

"Now, eat that pussy good, and you better make her cum. If not, it's lights out for you my nigga."

"Ain't no fucking way I'm putting my mouth on this nasty bitch. I don't know what the fuck---"

"I don't give a fuck what'chu don't wanna do. Did you give a fuck what Alyssa didn't want!? Naw, go, and this is the last time I'm gon' tell you." He looked at the skinny crackhead laying on his bed. She was dirty, smelly and pussy probably smelled even worse. Mario turned around with his face balled up. She opened her legs, and he started eating that nasty ass cat. Mac and I were cracking up. Then the crackhead moaning was even funnier because her voice was baritone and horse as hell.

"Come on man can I stop now?" Mario was actually crying, and then this fool threw up.

"You cum yet sweetheart?" Mac asked her.

"He needs to suck a little harder."

"You heard her nigga, suck on that clit." Mario coughed and went back to eating it. This shit was funny as hell, and when she came, Mario leaned over and threw up so damn much all on his bed and floor.

"Good job homie. Gon' and get dressed sweetheart." She got up and put her dirty panties back on.

"Go wait in our truck and we'll pay you when we come out." She left, and Mac looked at me and nodded towards Mario.

"Handle yo' business." He told me. I went over to Mario who was still coughing and spitting all over. I hit that nigga a few times and took out my anger on his face. He rolled over and fell all in his throw-up. After I beat his ass, I stomped on his dick a few times.

"I'm sorry man! I'm sorry!" Blood was all over his face and between his legs because I had stomped his shit in so hard.

"How many times did she plead with you and you didn't listen?" I stepped on his dick again.

"Ughh!"

"You touched what was mine when she didn't want you to." I stepped down harder, and he pleaded again. I pulled my gun back out and put it to his head and pulled the trigger.

"Shit felt good as hell." I put my gun up, and Mac gave me some dab.

"It should, punk ass nigga tryna rape somebody." Mac opened Mario nightstand and saw a knot of money. We got back to that car, and he gave the bum the knot he took. She wanted us to drop her back off on Fenkell, so we did and headed home. Mac had to go to work, and I needed to shower so I could head out to Alyssa and Liam.

***

"You da real MVP lil homie. Ain't no damn way I'd eat this shit." I threw the two jars of baby food away.

Alyssa gave me two jars of this squash and pears baby food to feed him. He was strapped in his bouncer with a bib around his neck. He ate all the food as if he hadn't eaten since birth. Lil homie was chunky as hell and cute too. My mama had been calling me about seeing him again, so I had to ask Alyssa when she wanted to make that happen. After I fed him and gave him a water bottle. I changed his diaper, and he passed out in my arms. I don't know, but for some reason, I felt connected to Liam.

I think because I seen him born, so I felt like we had a natural bond. I always wanted to make sure he was good, and I stayed buying him shit. As little as he was, he had a way of making my day good as hell even if he's sleep. I had turned my smoke room into his area at my house and didn't even mind. I laid him in his crib and went into Alyssa's bedroom. She was laying down watching *Bob's Burgers* laughing. I pulled her covers back, and she had on one of her short gowns, and I could tell no panties. I put my arms around her waist and kissed her neck.

"Liam knocked out in his crib. You was right, he ate and drunk everything. Lil chunky ass." We both chuckled, and she turned towards me. All that chocolate smooth skin was glowing.

"Thank you, Casada, for everything." I knew she meant more than just feeding Liam.

"Nobody will ever hurt you and live to see another day. I'm sorry that shit happened to you and I'm glad your boss didn't trip about you missing work." Her soft hands were all through my dreads.

"It wasn't your fault. Mario was on some crazy shit."

"Naw it was my fault. Had I not been trippin' when we first kissed and pushed myself away. You never would have got mixed up with him." She climbed on top of me, and that warm pussy was bare on my dick.

"I love you, Casada. None of that shit was your fault and at the end of the day. We got the it right now."

"I love you to fat-fat. Now that you woke my dick up I need you to put him back to sleep." I pulled her shirt over her head and my mouth watered looking at her chocolate titties.

"Put that pussy on my face." I laid back on her bed and watched her sexy ass scoot up. That bald pretty ass pussy came down, and I got to work. Alyssa had no scent and a water taste. Something that I knew I wanted to eat every damn day. I kept my arms locked around her waist so she couldn't move. My head game fucked Alyssa up, and she always tried to tap out. Not right now though. I wanted to make her cum over and over.

"Oh, bae…ssssss. Shit Casada." I unwrapped my arms and gripped her juicy ass booty cheeks with my nails. My tongue was making waves on her clit. When she fell forward, I slapped that ass making it jiggle in my hands. Alyssa came all in my mouth, and I loved it. Gripping her thighs, I slammed her on her back and climbed on top of her. She was moaning and breathing hard from cumming.

"Arghh!" She called out when my dick was inside of her. I grabbed her jaws and turned her to me.

"You belong to me forever Alyssa." I filled her up with dick while kissing her nasty and speaking facts.

"I'm yours ugh shit I'm yours." She came hard, I pulled out and started stroking my dick with her juices all on it.

"Fuck you got the best pussy. Ssssssss." I went back in her deep as hell. I bet if I stuck my tongue down her throat I'd tickle the tip of my dick. That's how deep I was in her. She pulled me down to her so we can kiss and them muscles gripped my ten-inches like it was mad at me.

"I pulled out again and got up. Standing at the foot of the bed I pulled her to the edge and flipped her over. She gave me that signature arch she had, and I ate her out from the back for a second. After I had enough, I stood back up and went in her pussy from the back.

"Throw that chocolate ass back fat, throw it back." She did what I said and them juicy ass cheeks plus the slapping our bodies were making was music to my ears. I gripped her waist and fucked her hard and good.

"Ahhh! Shit, shit I'm cummin'!!" I pushed her ass back while she squirted everywhere, and I nutted all on her ass cheeks and back.

"Fuckkk!!" I don't even know how I was still standing as hard as I bust. After we cleaned up, we got back in bed and watched a movie. I could get used to life like this with Alyssa and Liam.

Mac

"What up doe ma, you good?" I decided to answer the phone for Quinn since she was finally acting like she had some damn sense. I knew she was almost due, so I made sure to communicate at least once a day. Even though when I did the bitch gave me nothing but attitude.

"I'm fine. Is it ok if I meet with you tomorrow? I really need to talk to you about something, actually, can Sada be there too."

"What the fuck do you have to talk about that involves my brother?" She groaned out loud.

"Mac the way you disrespected me the least you can do is what I asked. You got a new bitch on me when I been fucking you for a while."

"You stay in yo fucking feelings, you was never gone be my woman rather the kid mine or not. Be at my crib at three tomorrow and don't be late." I hung up on her stupid ass and turned down Hazel's block.

Me and her been rocking tuff and I was about that shit. I thought I would have fucked up because a nigga like me loves bitches. Pussy was thrown at me all the damn time, and I usually catch that shit with my dick. But I found myself turning hoes down and feeling good about it. I liked what me and Hazel were doing, and I didn't want to lose it. Plus, my mind stayed on her leaving me if I fuck up or her retaliating if I cheat. That shit bugged me because I always took myself as a move on type of man. A bitch cheat on you, let her know you know what's up. Fuck the nigga up if you see him and move the fuck on.

If I cheat and get caught, let the girl cuss my ass out and then move the fuck on. But with Hazel Monroe, my angel face, she changed the game for me. Some shit go down like that with me and her. Without a doubt I'm killing the nigga, fuck her up, and she still gon' be my bitch. If I cheat on her, she can do what she wants to the bitch. Hell if she wants me to kill the hoe, I will. But Hazel still would be mine, she betta go on a pussy strike or something but leaving me was out the question. She had me out the bag, missing her when we were apart, thinking about her and my dick stayed hard whenever she was around.

"Hey, Mac." Alyssa smiled at me when she opened the door.

"What's up Lyssa." I smiled at Liam in her arms.

"What up nephew, yo' mama still stuffing food in them cheeks?" I joked because lil nigga had the fattest jaws.

"Shut up don't be talking about my baby. Yo' brother just left for work."

"I ain't looking for that fool. Where *my* baby at?" She pointed upstairs, and I headed up.

"Ok, so I'll meet you at *Red Lobster* in thirty minutes. Love you bye." My eyebrows furrowed when I heard her on the phone. So many questions ran through my mind. It'd only make sense to ask her what was up when I came in, but naw, I wanna have some fun today.

"Angel face," I called her name as soon as I hit the last step. She came around the corner and looked shocked as hell.

"Hey baby, I thought you had to work." She had on a robe, her hair tied up and some house-shoes on.

"I got some street work to do today, Chrysler tonight." Usually, she would rush me but she didn't this time, she just looked nervous. Yup, today was about to be fun as hell.

"O-Oh ok well that's cool." She turned and walked to her bedroom. I followed hot on her ass. She had an outfit laid out on her bed.

"Where are you going?" I moved her clothes over and sat on the bed.

"I uh, I have a meeting at work to go to." Boldface ass lie.

"That's what's up, well I was catchin' lights so I can come and see you." She turned to me smiling. Her beautiful ass face made me forget that she was lying to me.

"Aww, you missed me, baby?"

"I mean yea I did but seeing as uh nigga ain't got no love shown yet." She rushed to me and straddled my lap. Even mad at her my dick and body responded to her touch and lips.

"I miss you too Mackenzie." I kissed her hungrily and squeezed her round ass booty. She climbed off and went to the bathroom to fix her hair.

I was able to get a look at her outfit she had out. It wasn't nothing special, some skinny jeans, this graphic tee with some skulls on it and I knew it was going to be off her shoulder because of the way it was slanted. I checked to see what kind of panties if any she was wearing. They were some basic black boy shorts with a matching strapless bra. An idea came to my head, and I made my move before she came out the bathroom. Last week me and her took a trip to *Adam & Eve* sex store. I don't play that dildo shit, but I loved lingerie, so I let her pick out some.

We also picked out these sexy ass panties that had a vibrating pussy patch on them. Them bitches ran me fifty dollars, but the sales ladies told us they were discreet, lace, and came with a controller that controlled the sensation. Plus they had this clit pressure that intensified the pleasure. The panties looked a lot like the ones Hazel had on her bed, so I went to her dresser and opened the top drawer. Like I knew they were right there with her other panties. I opened the box and took the panties out, switched them with the ones on her bed and put the controller in my pocket.

"A'ight angel face Ima get outta here and let you finish getting ready for your meeting at work." She came out the bathroom with her pretty ass hair down and some behind her ear.

"Ok, can you come back here when you're done?" She grabbed a key from her nightstand and gave it to me. "Alyssa knows, one for the downstairs door and the other for the door up here."

"I can make that happen." I pulled her to me and kissed them soft lips. Her ass was like butter in my arms like she should be.

"I'll text you, baby." I slapped her ass and headed out.

I definitely would be at her crib later because like I said earlier. She cheat, I'm killing the nigga and fucking her up, but she still would be mine. The key word here is, mine. Hazel Monroe was Mackenzie Willis woman, and that's how it was going to stay. I got outside and sat in my Magnum waiting for her to come out and head to her destination. I was disappointed in Hazel right now. I made it clear to her that I was a crazy ass nigga and not to fuck with me. I told her I wouldn't play with her feelings, so I don't know why she took that as an invite to play with mine.

But here we are, and there she is coming out her house getting into her car. I started mine and took off a few feet behind her. She said she was going to Red Lobster and I bet it's the one on Michigan Ave. Whichever one it didn't matter, she drove, and I followed. She turned, and so did I, she stopped and so did I. Wasn't no way I was losing her, and I didn't mean just in this traffic. Hazel ended up at the Red Lobster in Westland on Ford Rd. She got out and went in, and I was behind her leaving a nice distance. When I entered, I looked around and saw she was sitting in a booth alone looking over the menu.

"Hi welcome to Red Lobster, will you be dining in alone today?" The greeter asked me.

"Yea it's just me. I already know the booth I want, come on." She looked skeptical, but I didn't give a fuck. I knew the perfect place to sit, I could still see her, and if I'm lucky, I could hear her.

"Ok, well your waiter will be right with you. Enjoy." She set the menu down in front of me and left. I watched Hazel go through her phone and twirl her hair. My girl was so fucking sexy, but her stupid ass was about to learn a life's lesson today. My phone vibrated, and it was her ass texting me.

Angel Face: I miss you, baby,

Even on some foul shit she still kept me on the brain. I texted back.

Me: I miss you more gorgeous.

I looked up at her, and she was smiling big as hell. I wanted to see what she would say so I hurried up with a follow-up text.

Me: How ya meeting going?

Angel Face: Boring.

Just as I was about to text back, some white muthafucka approached her table. This man was older, and when Hazel saw him, she gave him a smile. Standing up they hugged, and I couldn't really hear what they were saying. All I knew was he had his hands on her. It took everything in me not to flip this damn table over. Her smile was so damn big that I grew just as jealous. She only smiles that big for me, not no old white guy. They sat down laughing and started ordering food. My fist were balled up so damn tight, and I didn't stop looking at them until my waiter came. The dude she was talking to back was facing me.

"Hi, my name is Jude, and I'll be your waiter for the day. Can I start you off with something to drink?"

"Yea, let me get a Pepsi, and I already know what I want to order." She smiled at me and took her pad out." I ordered my food to go and kept my eyes on Hazel. Once the waiter left, it was time to play. Taking the controller to the panties out my pocket. The dialer on it went from 0 to 5.0. I take it from the pictures it was an intensity level, and the numbers were for speed. I turned it on and put the intensity to low vibrate and the speed at 1. She didn't really notice it except an expression she made. I turned everything up one more notch. That didn't go unnoticed to her ass. She moved around in her seat and cleared her throat. I cracked up because her cheeks turned a light red.

"You ok Hazel?" I finally was able to hear her old nigga's voice. She smiled and played it off.

"Yea I'm fine." Smiling and shit in some scrub ass muthafucka's face, knowing damn well that smile is reserved for me. I went up another notch on both levels. This silly ass girl dropped her fork and started twitching a little more.

"You gone learn who the fuck you belong to," I mumbled out loud to myself but still laughing because angel face was fucked up. I turned everything off when my waiter came with my food and my pop. Once she left, I had to get my shit together because I was cracking up. Looking at Hazel, she was coming around and trying to get back to her meal. They went back to talking, and that smile came out again. I turned the controller back on and went to medium intensity and 3.0 in speed. She was drinking her tea and almost choked on it. I laughed hard as hell at her expression. I could see her chest going in and out and her breathing change.

"Hazel honey are you sure---" He called her name and then called her honey. I got pissed off and turned everything up to the capacity.

"Holy sh-shitt. I uh, whew. I need to go to. Oh my God." She hurried and got out her seat.

"I-I-I'll be right back." She kneeled over and flew to the bathroom. I laughed my ass off because she jerked all the way to the restroom. I left my food and went to follow her. Turning the controller off I could careless if someone else was in there with her or not. It was a Tuesday afternoon, so the restaurant didn't have even a small crowd.

"You look like you havin' some problems." Hazel was slumped over the sink breathing hard and looking flushed.

"What are you doing here?" She asked me, and I turned the controller on making her jump because I left everything turned up.

"Oh my fucking God!" She yelled, and I turned it off.

"That was you!? How---What the fuck---"

"You need to check ya' panties angel face." She looked down at her pussy and undid her pants. I leaned against the door and watched her.

"Mackenzie why the fuck did you switch my panties? You almost gave me a heart attack."

"Naw the question is who the fuck is that you sitting across the table from and why the fuck did you lie to me?" Her face went pale, and I snatched her jeans from her hand.

"Talk Hazel because after I kill that old ass nigga, I'm fucking you up, and then we going to sleep." Her eyes bucked.

"Mackenzie I'm not cheating on you. That's my dad."
I grabbed her arm.

"You just gone keep lying to me." My anger was indescribable, and so was my expression.

"I'm not lying to you I swear."

"So why didn't you tell me you were meeting with him. Why'd you tell me you had some work bullshit to go to? You ashamed of a nigga or something?" She dropped them eyebrows, and her free hand went on the side of my face.

"Mackenzie I would never be ashamed of you baby. I just wanted to tell my dad about you and then introduce you guys face to face." A knock came at the bathroom door.

"Hazel honey are you ok?"

"Uh yea dad, it's just cramps. I'll be out in a minute." She looked at me and smirked.

"Told you. I'm sorry I lied, I knew you would have wanted to come to lunch with me if I told you where I was really going. It's not easy to say no to you, so I lied." She wasn't wrong about that. Hell, I never take no for an answer especially from my woman because I'd never tell her no. Looking down at Hazel I was still mad, and my expression hadn't changed.

"Don't ever lie to me again," I said calm but forceful.

"I promise I won't."

"And I'm about to meet your pops now." She held her hand up.

"Deal, just don't fuck with my panties again." We both laughed, and she grabbed her jeans from my hand. I snatched them back and grabbed her neck.

"My dick hard." I already had my hard dick out, and it was pointed at Hazel's pussy.

"Mackenzie no, my dad is out there." She was saying no, but I already pulled her to me with her back to my chest. I was kissing on her neck, and my hand went between her legs. I bagged back to the wall and put a hickey on her neck.

"Babyyy, someone can just walk in here." Hazel started whining, but her pussy was soaking my hand up.

"Shut the fuck up and gimmie what I want." I bent her over a little bit, and my dick slid in from the back. Her head went back, and she moaned.

"Fuck Hazel, you always so damn wet for me baby." I had her between my legs with her legs closed and that round ass slapping against my pelvis. I wrapped my hand around her neck and pulled her to my back.

"You bet not ever fucking lie to me again. You my bitch and you always keep shit G with me. A'ight?" I pumped her harder, and she started trembling like she did when she had them panties on.

"Y-Y-Yes daddy I won't ssss I won't lie again." I smiled with my lips on her ear. I sucked on her cheek and then kissed them soft lips. I swear when I was ruff with Hazel she got wetter. She loved that choking, biting and talking shit type of fucking. Watch how I make her cum harder. My hand went tighter on her neck, and I pulled on her bottom lip.

"That's my good bitch. Look at'chu cumming all on daddy dick."

"Ahhh...ahhhh...ahhhh." Her nails dug deep in my thighs as we both came together. I kissed her so nasty, and she sucked on my tongue.

"I ain't never letting you go, Hazel. Believe that shit." She smiled looking me in my eyes.

"I don't want you to ever let me go. I ain't never letting you go either." I pecked her again, and we got cleaned up.

"Tell your dad you called me up here." She nodded, and we made it back to the table.

"Dad, I apologize I just had to get myself together. But um, this is Mac, the guy I was telling you about. I figured I might as well call him up here so you guys can meet." Her pops stood up looking at me and then at her.

"Nice to meet you, Mr. Monroe." I may be a rude nigga, but my mama raised me to show respect. He shook my hand and nodded his head.

"Nice to meet you Mac young man."

We all set down and started talking. He did the typical father shit. Drilled my ass with questions but me being me and never getting intimidated by anyone. I answered whatever he threw my way. He asked about my family, upbringing if I have a high school diploma. What I did for a living and of course I only mentioned working at Chrysler. And of course, he asked me what intentions I had for his daughter. I told him the truth. That I was digging Hazel tough as hell. She had my attention, time, effort and it was only reserved for her.

He wasn't really feeling the fact that I would be twenty-five this year and Hazel was twenty. I didn't think it was that big of a difference, but I guess to a father it was. But I assured him she was the youngest I had ever talked to. Our age never played a factor because she was legal and I had already staked claim. Yea I told his ass just like that, and he respected it. Honestly, what choice did he have. His daughter was gone off of me, and she had me by the balls, so we were tied. After Red Lobster I told Hazel I had some business to take care of and I'd get at her later. She started whining because she wanted me to go back to her crib and I could have, but Hazel still lied to me today.

Even though she had reason, it's still not what our relationship is about. So for that, she gotta get punished. I couldn't stay away from her a whole day but a few hours would be good. I was on my way to the crib when I decided to stop at Lee's Beauty Supply. I needed a wave cap and some line-up clippers. Since it was next to Jay's Liquor store, I figured I could kill two birds with one stone. Park at the beauty supply, go in to get what I need them walk next door to Jay's and grab my drink and junk food. I chopped shit up with the chinks for a second then walked out with a pregnant woman and little boy walking out behind me. Lil homie was talking to me, and I was laughing because he had to be around three. Short and chubby, he reminded me of Liam. I put my stuff on the front seat of my car and walked with them to Jay's. I noticed a black Charger rode past fast ass fuck then did an illegal U-turn. Coming my way I knew what was up when the windows rolled down.

TAT! TAT! TAT! TAT! TAT! TAT!

I grabbed the little boy and woman so we could dip quickly behind these two green metal dumpsters on the side of the liquor store. You could hear the tires screech loud as hell and the bullets hitting the garbage can. The shooting stopped after a while and commission could be heard next. I looked at the woman and her son.

"Y'all good?"

"Yes, oh my God thank you. You saved me and my children's life." She hugged her son and rubbed her stomach. I helped them up, and people were outside the stores looking our way and of course on their phone. I was glad no innocent people were hit, but those bullets were meant for me. Muthafuckas were gunning for me hard as fuck. I thought about Jermaine and how he was caught slipping. The child he left behind, I thought about my mama, grandma, my baby brother, Hazel. It would fuck all of them up mentally and emotionally if I would have died just now.

I got a feeling that Malcolm is behind this shit. It was time to crack down on this muthafucka. It was nine-hours since I had been shot at. I left the scene and went home to smoke, shower, eat and get a nap in. Sada was at work, and I knew he was going over Alyssa house when he got off. I would holla at him tomorrow about what went down. I woke up and looked at the cable box. It was midnight, I didn't want to sleep that damn long. I grabbed my phone and saw Hazel called me eleven times and I had texts from her cussing my ass out.

The last one said she was done with me and hoped I had fun with the bitch I was fucking. I cracked up mostly at the threating ones. This girl said she was going to slice my balls off and shove them down my throat. I cracked up, and muthafuckas called me crazy. I got up and headed to the bathroom to freshen up. I put on some grey sweatpants, matching beater, some black socks, and my black Jordan slides. Grabbing my fitted 313 hat and keys, I headed out the house on the way to my crazy ass woman.

I made sure to watch my surroundings like I always did. I would never move through my city in fear; niggas gotta come harder than that. Getting to Hazel and Alyssa crib, I saw Sada's Charger out front like I knew. I pulled my key out and unlocked the big door. First thing tomorrow I was getting these girls an alarm system. I knew they were in the suburbs but still. Since they didn't like guns, a security system was best.

I got upstairs, unlocked the door and walked to Hazel room. Her back was facing the door, and her TV was on the Nickelodeon channel with that cartoon she loves *Fairly Odd Parents*. Hazel had me watch so many episodes of that shit. If I'm high, the cartoon is funny. I took my slides, socks, shirt, and sweatpants off leaving my boxers on. Climbing in her bed, she had a thong on and a tank top. I wrapped my arms around her and was shocked to see her woke and crying.

"Baby, what's wrong?" She sniffed and said.

"Your cheating on me." She cried harder when she answered me. I held my laugh in.

"No, I'm not Hazel."

"Yes you are, it's midnight, and I called you all day. You didn't answer not one of my calls, or you didn't read my texts." I kissed her shoulder and the side of her wet face.

"Stop Mac, just get out. I'm done with you." I laughed.

"Oh, I'm Mac now? You ain't done with me and I ain't cheating on you. I was shot at today at Jay's. I'm good though. After it happened, I went home, showered, ate and then went to sleep. I didn't plan on being sleep that long." I turned her over, and her gorgeous face was wet and eyes puffed up. A female crying would never in a million years move me if you weren't my mama or grandma. But Hazel crying always fucked with me even though I knew she was spoiled. Sometimes she cries because she knows I'm weak to that shit.

"Were you really shot at?" I nodded my head yea, and she cried hard again.

"Why you crying now?" I couldn't help but laugh again.

"Because you're going to die and leave me." I hugged her crybaby ass tight.

"Angel face you wrong about a lot of shit tonight. I'm not cheating on you, and I am not going to die. I got everything out here handled. I need you to trust in your man, a'ight." I kissed her lips and wiped her tears.

"Ok. Are you in a gang or sell drugs?"

"No to both. I work at Chrysler, and I get money taking out the trash." She looked lost.

"What does that mean?"

"I handle people's problems. If they got the right money."

"Oh. Does Sada do that too?"

"Yea. Alyssa knows because Jermaine got down like that too. I know that's why you think I'mma get killed. But I handle my shit differently. I promise I'm good." She sniffed and wiped her face.

"You better be Mackenzie because I will beat'cho ass if you're not." I laughed at her threat.

"You talking like you love a nigga or something." She blushed and looked down.

"I do love you." Her eyes met mine and out of all the 'I love yous' a bitch has said to me. I believed Hazel when she said it.

"I love you to angel face." I kissed her soft lips and pulled her on top of me. I wanted to make love to her for the rest of the night and into the morning. Once we were naked, that's exactly what I did.

***

"What the fuck yo baby mama got to tell you that involves me?"

"I don't fucking know I think her being pregnant is making her a damn airhead. Swear to God I hope Hazel don't be this damn stupid." Me and Sada were at our crib waiting on Quinn to get here. This bitch didn't have long because I had better shit to do.

"Tha fuck you mean by that? Hazel pregnant?"

"Naw I'm just saying when she does I hope she not like this." He chuckled.

"Since when you want kids?"

"Since I had some life-changing pussy nigga." He laughed, and I did too, but I was speaking real shit.

"You a fool bro. But I'm so ready to kill Malcolm and them Schoolcraft niggas he got working for him. We not about to have a repeat."

"You right bro, that's why I got Clip coming over too. I'm ready to talk to y'all and get this shit going." A knock came at the door, I looked outside and saw Quinn's car. Opening the door, she was standing there with her round stomach in some leggings and a strapless shirt. She rolled her eyes and flipped her hair.

"Can I come in or no nigga?" See, why the fuck do people wanna keep fucking with me.

"Not like that, fix that funky ass attitude."

"May I come in please?" I moved, and she came in standing in the living room.

"So what the fuck you want and why I gotta be here?" Sada ass cut straight to the point. A knock came at the door again, and it was Clip.

"I said just you and Sada." Quinn turned her nose up when she saw Clip.

"You don't run shit but what'chu about to do is run yo' ass outta here if you don't start talking." I was running out of patience and was ready for her to leave so I could holla at Clip and Sada.

"Ok so let me cut straight to it. Malcolm had Jermaine killed by his guys he has selling for him." Me, Sada and Clip just stared at her.

"How the fuck do you know that? It's in the streets?" I asked because if this nigga was bragging about this shit, I was about to go kill him now.

"I'll get to that once I finish. So he's been selling drugs and wants to run Detroit. Him and his crew are talking about doing a sweep on these east side niggas. Bodies, drugs, and money is what he said. After they do that he's offering the three of y'all a chance to get on and if you say no then he's having y'all killed." We still were quiet, and I glanced at Sada and Clip.

"Ok before I take anything you say seriously tell me how you know all of this?" I asked for the last time. She looked down, chuckled and then flipped her hair again.

"Because I'm fucking him."

"Aww hell muthafuckin' naw!" Clip shouted and started laughing. Sada shook his head laughing too. I just stood there leaned against my wall looking at Quinn. She looked everywhere but at me.

"I knew you were a slut ass bitch but damn Quinn, you had to go and fuck my uncle?" Her eyes shot at me then, and this hoe had the nerve to cry.

"So fucking what! He gave me something you wouldn't! I'm number one in his life, he made me his woman and put me in his bed every fucking night!" She pointed at Sada.

"And what room do you have to even judge me, nigga?" He still laughed and put his middle finger up at her.

"Yet here you are giving us information on him knowing we gone kill his ass. You a trick ass hoe for real." I laughed now because this bitch was really pathetic.

"I'm a hoe, but you fuck anything with a pussy. Yo' bitch is stupid as fuck if she think you'll be faithful."

"I'm not about to argue with you. Since you sucking his saggy balls and got all this information what day are they talking about doing this sweep on the east side?" I was tired of going back and forth. Quinn was a hoe, traitor and now a fucking rat and I was ready to throw her out my shit once she tells me what I need to know.

"I need insurance. My grandma lives in North Carolina, and I'm going to move there with her. I'll need money to hold me over while I get a job."

"Hold the fuck up, you want us to give you money for being a rat? How the hell do we know you not gone run to the police after you have your bread." Sada asked, but that was the least of my concerns.

"I got a better question, if this is my child, he's not moving that far from me. You can go, but he will be staying here."

Why so your bitch can be his mother." She started that crying shit again.

"He's not yours anyway Mac. He's Malcolm's"

"DAMN!" Sada and Clip both jumped up and started acting wild.

"You stopped fucking with me after Jermaine died. I was out with my sister and girls drinking, and he was there. We hooked up and were on and off because I was stuck on yo' ass. Me and you fucked raw one time that night you were drunk and high. I found out I was pregnant after and I wanted bad for you to be the dad. I already knew the truth, but I still tried to show you that I could be your woman." Quinn broke down, and I wanted to kick her ass in the face.

"What is the day they are all meeting at his crib to do the sweep?" I asked calmly, and she flipped out.

"See what I fucking mean! You just don't give two shits about me!! I---" I snapped and slammed her against the wall. In her face, I looked at her like the trash she was.

"Lower yo' fucking voice before I pull that baby out through ya' throat. You standing here telling me you been fucking my uncle, lied and told me this baby might be mine, wasted my time and money on you because I believed what you told me. You not gone say shit to no police because you know I will hunt you down and kill yo' ass. And I won't stop there, I'll kill ya' mama, yo' fat ass sister and her bastard ass kids. With all of y'all dead including Malcolm ya' kid will end up in foster care all fucked up. Now give me the date, and I'll give you your money. Keep yo' ass outta Detroit though." Her tears were rolling down her face fast as hell.

"Had you giving me what you so easily gave her we would have never been here." I turned my nose up.

"Ain't shit about'chu special enough to be my woman. Now I'm gon' ask you one more time, what is the day?"

"Saturday at ten o'clock at night. Malcolm said one of the trap houses they were hitting first was on eight-mile and Dequindre."

"Who is Malcolm's connect? I know you know since you know all this other shit."

"His name is Jimmy, and he lives in Cleveland Ohio. Malcolm meets with him once a month or sometimes once every two months. That's all I know about him, oh and that he's Mexican." I looked at Sada because we knew who she was talking about. Last summer him, me, Clip and Jermaine did a hit for him. Our pops name had a lot of respect in the streets. Jimmy heard about what we did and hit my burner up. I focused my attention back on Quinn.

"And how are we supposed to get in the house?" I asked her while I still had her against the wall.

"I'll leave the side door unlocked for you. Malcolm doesn't have an alarm or any pets." I let her go.

"You'll get your money after we handle this shit. Get the fuck out." I was serious as hell, and she knew it too.

"Mac pl----"

"I said get the fuck out Quinn." Crying hard she walked out my front door.

"This shit crazy as hell bro, all this shit wild. From Jermaine to that slut bitch and now this sweep." Sada spoke first, and Clip agreed.

"We gotta make a trip to Cleveland. Let me pick my girl up from work and then we heading out tonight. Now that I know who Malcolm connect is, I can put my plan in motion. We about to get paid and put them muthafuckas in the ground." We dabbed each other up and went our separate ways until tonight. This shit was all coming to a head in three days. My dick hard just thinking about it.

Malcolm

(Three days later)

"This is bullshit! He's living in luxury, and I'm cramped in a one-bedroom apartment."

"Please let my wife know that I work every single damn day. Something that she has no idea how to do. I'm living comfortably now not out of my means." I looked at my lawyer and told him. My ex-wife Shauney served my ass again. Basically, trying to sue me for more spousal support. This bitch didn't have to do anything when we were married. Just keep my house clean and fuck me when I wanted to, and we were good. Now that she wasn't my wife anymore I didn't give a fuck about her.

"Did he tell you that he has a young bitch living in his house?" She looked as if she had just dropped a bombshell.

"She's young enough to be his damn daughter."

"My personal life has nothing to do with her." I looked at her lawyer and stated.

"I'm in a relationship with a legal younger woman, but I am not hurting anyone. We have only been together for a few months, and she is over twenty-one years old. I don't even talk to Shauney at all. She only knows about my life because she is stalking me and stalking my woman."

"Do you have proof?" Her lawyer asked me, and I pulled my phone out. Shauney stupid ass followed Quinn on all her social media. She sat outside my home, and I was able to take pictures of her staking out my home.

"I was only driving by." I chuckled when she said that.

"We are not paying more in spousal support. My client also will be filing restraining order papers against your client." Me and my lawyer stood up and fixed our clothes.

"Have a good day ladies," I said, and we walked out the mediation room downtown at the Wayne County Friend of the Court.

"Thanks for looking out." I shook my lawyer's hand with two bags of goodies in my hand for him. He was a good ass lawyer who didn't mind getting a little dirty for me as long as I paid and had that white powder magic for him.

"No doubt." He went his way, and I went mine.

"You really ain't shit." I turned around and breathed out hearing Shauney voice.

"How? Because I won't give you more money?" I leaned against my car with my arms folded. Shauney was a dead ringer for Alexis Skyy including that smart-ass mouth.

"Because you act like I didn't give you half my life. Like I didn't give you a son, or we didn't have a marriage. But you can let a preschooler have it all?!" We were in the parking constructor, and no one was in here with us. I walked up to Shauney and grabbed her under her arm.

"You betrayed me more than once and don't worry about my woman. She good and she appreciates the life you didn't." She snatched away from me.

"I hate you, Malcolm. I wish I never had met---" I cut her off when I kissed her deep and hard. I couldn't front, she was looking so good in this wrap around dress and ponytail showing her bare face. She didn't even fight me when I lifted her against my car. Shauney undid my pants, and I lifted her dress up and was pleased she had no panties on.

"Ahhh." She moaned out when I put my dick in her. We kissed while I fucked her good against my car. I stuck my finger in her mouth, and she sucked on it. I needed more, so I opened my car door and put her over my seat. Pulling her dress over her fat ass booty, I started eating her out from the back. Shauney pussy was so good like I remember and when she started rocking back and forth, I sucked on that clit harder.

"Oh shit. Oh shit. Ugh." She came, and I went in from behind and started giving her some good back shots. I slapped her ass as she moaned and came again. A few more pumps and I nutted all in her.

"Ughhhh. Shit." My head was back, and my eyes were closed. That was a good ass nut.

"Why did I just do that?" She shook her head as she fixed her dress.

"Because you miss this dick and tongue." I went to my back seat and dug under it.

"Here." I gave her two stacks.

"That pussy was well worth it." I kissed her lips again and walked over to the driver's side of my Lexus.

I pulled off in the direction to my house. I was about to chill with Quinn until I have to leave with my crew tonight. We were making our move on them east side niggas tonight. I was ready to take over Detroit and sad to say once I handle these east side fools. I was having Mac, Sada and Clip handled. I had no use for them if they didn't want to get down on my team. I was asking one more time then it was lights out. I tried to have Mac handled the other day, but my shooter failed. Shit was real in these streets, and either muthafuckas rolled on my team or rolled in the dirt.

"It smells good in here," I said when I walked in my kitchen. Quinn pregnant ass was fixing our plates. I see she mad bake chicken, mash potatoes and corn on the cob.

"Thanks. I figured you'd be hungry." She walked to me and kissed my lips. Something about Shauney pussy being on my lips and Quinn kissing them made my dick hard. I can see a threesome in my future. Quinn put our plates on the table, and I went to wash my hands, so I could eat.

"How'd it go with your ex-wife?" Quinn asked me.

"It went good, I laid down the law." She nodded her head not even knowing what I meant. I fucked with Quinn, hell I loved her. Shauney is my ex-wife, so I don't look at that as cheating. Me and her ate and had some decent conversation.

"I'm about to go shower," I said while putting my plate in the sink. I needed to get clean and have some chill time until tonight.

***

"Can y'all muthafuckas be a little quieter. My woman upstairs sleep."

I walked downstairs in my all black. My crew was in the dining room setting up, and they were loud as hell. Abe and Clem were the only two missing, but they texted me and said they were on their way. Right now I only have five members on my team but once I do this takeover. I'll have such a spread on my team that I won't have to do shit except collect my money. After a while of running things, I was gunning for my connect and taking over his operation. My number two would run shit here, and I'd move to Ohio.

Me and Quinn gon' be sitting on top of the world in no time. By then she will have had my babies and taking care of my home. I pulled out the blueprints of the two trap houses we were hitting tonight. I didn't have a clean-up crew yet, so we had to handle the bodies. Trap had brought tons of 60-gallon trash bags, duct tape, and some saws. We were dumping the bodies in the Detroit River. I had bricks in my truck.

"I'll be back," I said while going towards the back to my downstairs bathroom. I probably shouldn't, but I need some of that magic powder. My connect had been down my throat because I have been short twice.

I made up some bullshit about business being slow, but after tonight I was going to have money for my connect and then some. My high was coming on strong and I should have stopped, but I needed a little more. Taking a sniff, I leaned my head back and closed my eyes. I felt my body lifting and that trip coming on. This was like an energy drink and an expresso at the same time. I stood up high as hell and turned the water on in the sink. If I splash some cold water on my face, it shocks me, and I'm more aware. Grabbing a towel, I wiped my face and put my little glass bottle back in the medicine cabinet. I opened the door, and a big ass fist came at me straight in my nose.

"Ugh fuck!!" I fell backwards into the tub. Holding my nose, the hits started coming to my face. I couldn't even open my eyes and get a clear look because the punches came fast, I was high and a little dizzy. Then I heard that voice.

"Punk ass muthafucka." It was my damn nephew, Mac.

"What tha fuck you doin'?!" I finally got out. I could feel my eyes swelling and my lip bulge out. Then he grabbed me and dragged me out the tub. I knew I shouldn't have got this damn high. I opened my eyes as much as I could, and I could see my crew laid out dead with two holes in their heads. Abe and Clem were dead in my kitchen. Getting thrown on the floor, Sada came over and started kicking me in my ribs and stomach.

"Argh!" Once Sada was done kicking me, and Clip sat me up on this chair, I was duct taped to it leaving my face free.

"Aw shit." I groaned out and then spit out blood on my floor.

"What the hell is wrong with you bastard muthafuckas?" Mac laughed and looked at his brother and Clip.

"Come on uncle Malcom, you ain't uh clueless bimbo. You know what the fuck this is." I looked up at him with a bloody face and my left eye completely shut.

"Still acting stupid. A'ight, let's start with the least to the greatest." He leaned on my wall.

"You had me shot at. Your crew in the same Schoolcraft niggas that we got beef with and you had your own son killed. Any of that shit ring a bell?" I laughed hard as hell and spit some more blood on my floor.

"I did all that shit. And so fucking what?! Y'all pussy ass babies came to my crib crying about some east side muthafuckas. You think I was about to let'chu get me??!! Naw, and as far as Jermaine. I gave that fucking boy every damn thing, and I gave his mother even more. Only for that bitch to tell me he wasn't my son, he was Randall's." Yea, that hoe told me that the day her and Jermaine got into it over Alyssa being pregnant. The three of them looked dumbfound as hell.

"She wasn't lying, and the more I thought about it, the more I knew she was telling the truth. She didn't even make him a junior. My son wouldn't have fought me about joining my team and taking over Detroit. So I had him, and his bitch ass friends handled. You muthafuckas was supposed to break and come work for me. But you got too much of my brother in you." I tilted my head towards Mac. He looked at me like the devil himself, and for that, I smiled.

"Thank yo' bitch for setting this shit up."

"Shauney helped you do this?" I was killing that bitch.

"No, I did." I looked towards the steps and saw Quinn coming down the stairs. I couldn't do shit but laugh. She stood at the bottom with her hands on her hips.

"Naw, I'on believe that shit," I said and then she giggled.

"I'm just looking out for me and my son well, our son." I was straight face then.

"That's my son?" When she said yea, I wanted to break free and kill that fucking girl. I was so hot I felt the tears fall from my face. Mac, Clip, and Sada cracked up laughing. I just stared at Quinn, and she didn't even look bothered.

"She a hoe ass bitch right?" Mac said between his laugh.

"I know when she told me y'all were fucking I was shocked as hell. I mean I didn't cry like yo' Cinderella ass, but I was shocked as hell. That's a rat for you though."

"I don't need to stand here and listen to this shit. I did my part, where is my money so I can go." I couldn't believe Quinn was saying this shit. Sada passed Mac a black bookbag, and he gave it to her and said.

"Twenty G's. Stay the fuck outta Detroit or you know the consequences." The look she gave him was one that she had never given me. Wiping her face, she walked to the kitchen and out the side door.

"Damn unc she didn't even say bye to you." Sada joked, and they laughed again. I snapped.

"FUCK YOU MUTHAFUCKAS!! Since we telling some truth, I had Randall killed in jail. He was my brother and took everything from me including my first child." Mac charged at me and hit me two times in my face with a closed fist. I laughed hard both times.

"Y'all some stupid muthafuckas if you kill me. I got a connect that won't be too happy with your decision. You'll be dead by the time my body can decompose."

"Oh you mean you're connect in Cleveland? Jimmy right?" This nigga looked at me like he was waiting for an answer.

"Yea big fella, ya bitch spilled all the beans to us. We took a little trip to Cleveland to visit Jimmy. You see it seems my pops made a bigger impact on the streets then you ever will. Ya' own team was crooked as fuck to. Abe been Jimmy's eyes and ears seems you got a problem dippin' yo hand in the product. Or shall I say your nose." He flicked my nose like I was a kid.

"We made Jimmy a deal. Kill you and your crew, bring him back the rest of his product and money you have."

"You think that nigga won't kill you after you deliver. You don't know Jimmy like I do." These little ass babies were fucking fools.

"Why would he kill his new hired hitmen? He already paid us for our first job." Mac looked around at the dead bodies and started counting.

"That's five, and you make six. Damn! That's sixty-thousand."

"Don't forget apiece bro," Sada added in smiling, and so did Clip. Then Mac pulled his gun out and put it to my head.

"Hell is too good of a place for you."

"And I'll be sure to see yo' ass there." Those were my last words before Mac put two in my head. Wanting it all cost me everything.

Damn.

Hazel

"I can't believe you, I told you to take off work today?"

"I apologize baby, but I gotta get to this money." I smacked my lips as I came to my exit from the freeway. I was on my way home from Walmart getting everything I needed for tonight's dinner. Tomorrow was my twenty-first birthday, and tonight I wanted to cook a big dinner for me, my baby, Alyssa, Sada and I even invited Clip and his new girl of the week.

I didn't think Mackenzie or Sada would be up for it considering their uncle Malcolm was murdered a few weeks ago. His funeral was day before yesterday. Seems he was mixed up in some drug-related shit, him and a few other dudes were killed at his house. Me and Alyssa were there for our men and they seemed to be doing ok. Anyway, my annoying boyfriend didn't even take off like I told him to so this is why I had an attitude.

"What time do you get off?"

"I don't know I'll let you know around four." See this shit was starting to really piss me off. I almost slammed on the brakes.

"The dinner starts at six."

"I will make it on time I promise baby. I gotta get back on the floor though I'll hit'chu up later."

"Whatever Mac." He started laughing like this shit was funny.

"Every time you mad I'm Mac? Stop being a crybaby, you know I gotta chase this bag."

"I hope you run into a wall." He cracked up, but I still didn't think it was funny.

"I love you angel face I'll see you tonight." He hung up, and I wanted to throw my phone out the window.

"He can't make it tonight?" Alyssa asked me She came with me to Walmart to help me shop and to get my widdle Liam some stuff. He was at our house with Sada.

"If he doesn't I swear I will kill him." We both laughed as I turned down our block. I was excited about this weekend. My dinner was tonight, breakfast with my parents tomorrow and my party that night. I wish my sister Goldie could have made it, but her new job wasn't giving her the time off.

We got home and since the kitchen downstairs was bigger and so was the dining room. I decided to cook and host down there. My menu wasn't anything special just my favorite meals and dessert. Spaghetti with giant meatballs, garlic bread, fried catfish, broccoli with cheese and corn on the cob. I was making a caramel cake because it was my absolute favorite cake. Alyssa went to the back to put up Liam stuff, and I got the kitchen ready for me to start cooking.

"Damn sister-in-law you gotta cook me for a meal for my birthday." Sada came in holding Liam and looking at what I brought.

"You know I got'chu." I washed my hands and played with Liam for a minute. Alyssa came back in the kitchen and got all on Sada.

"Liam tell these nasty ass people to stop before you throw up." I joked when her and Sada kissed, and he grabbed her booty. I kissed on him a few times and then gave him back to Sada so I can go change so I could cook. Walking upstairs I opened my door and put my purse on the couch grabbing my phone out if it. I was about to text Mackenzie telling him how I was mad at him. I turned my light on in the room and almost shit myself when I saw him sitting on my bed. But that wasn't even all. There were balloons in my room saying 'Happy Birthday Princess'. Shopping bags from Victoria Secret, Pandora, UGG store and Bath and Bodyworks. My mouth was open, and I looked at him smiling big. He walked towards me with that sexy smile, and he hugged me.

"I thought you were at work." I hugged him tight and kissed his lips.

"I wouldn't do you like that angel face, I took off the whole weekend." I looked at him with infatuation.

"This is the sweetest thing anyone has ever done for me. Thank you so much." I hugged him again, and I happened to look at my accent wall.

"What's this." I held his hand and walked over to it. He had money and a note taed to the wall. Two-hundred-dollar bills had the word 'shoes' written on the note. Three-hundred-dollar bills had the word 'outfit' written on the note. There was four twenties with the word 'nails' written on its note, the word 'hair/makeup' was written on another note with four-hundred-dollar bills taped to it. And finally there were six-hundred-dollar bills, and on that note, it said 'just because I love you.'

"Mackenzie," I said his name then turned to him with my lip poked out smiling.

"Aww babyyy. Thank you so much, I love you too." I hugged him again so tight because I really appreciated this.

"You two knew he was upstairs?" We walked downstairs with his arms around my waist.

"Yes, we did. You were at work yesterday when we got everything together. While me and you were shopping, it gave him a chance to set up."

"Well thank all of you I was really surprised." Alyssa and Sada went in the backyard to smoke while Liam slept in his swing in the house with us.

"So how do you feel about everything with Quinn?" I was in the kitchen starting up the cooking. Mackenzie sat on the bar stool, and when I asked him the question, he shrugged his shoulders. He told me Quinn admitted to him that he wasn't the father. Malcolm was. I thought that was the nastiest shit ever.

"I don't feel shit about it. I mean if it was mine I would have been there. But now that I know it ain't my baby it's like it never happened." I nodded my head and took a sip of wine while chopping peppers.

"If the baby was yours do you think you guys would have worked out?" He sat there calm, but the look he gave me was like 'shut the hell up'.

"I'm just asking because I know how a child can pull two people together. Look at Sada, he loves Liam like his own. You and Quinn would have had a bond and---"

"Hazel." I looked at him once I realized I was rambling.

"Can you shut yo' Mac suckers up." I giggled and dropped my mouth.

"What the hell are Mac suckers?!"

"If you were a random bitch, I was talking to I would have said dick suckers but since you'll only be sucking on my dick from here on out you got Mac suckers." I laughed and threw a piece of pepper at him.

"For real though you can kill all that talk. Me and Quinn would have been nothing but parents. Ain't no moment or nothing like that we would have shared. If I didn't have you, I probably would have had hit again, and that's only if I'm horny and all my bitches busy. Since that never happens, then we would only have our child in common."

"You think you just all of that huh? Every person goes through a drought." He shook his head.

"Not me. I had a bitch leave a funeral because I wanted some head and just because it's me she hopped to it." I turned my nose up, and he shrugged his shoulders.

"Well, you'll never get that type of dedication from me."

"Woman if you don't shut the hell up lying to yo'self. I had you bent over in Red Lobster while your daddy sat and waited. I'm that fuckin' nigga just admit it." I cracked up and kept talking shit.

"I will do no such thing. You're delusional." He licked them sexy ass lips and bit that bottom one. Those dark eyes were on mine.

"I'm delusional angel face? I ain't that nigga?" He walked around the counter that cologne and hard body was in front of me.

"Stop Mackenzie. Sada and Alyssa can come back in any minute." He lifted me up and put me on the counter ignoring me. His lips grazed my neck, and his hand went up my cami dress and brushed against my pussy.

"Say I'm that nigga and I'll stop." Two of his fingers went inside of me, and I arched my back. He started tongue kissing my neck, and I couldn't stop my body from grinding into his fingers.

"Oooo you that nigga baby. Sssss." He pulled his fingers out smiling big."

"I hate you so much." I giggle and put my head on his chest.

"I love you to baby." We kissed, and then he let me down so I could finish cooking.

***

Look, my bitches all bad, my niggas all real
I ride on his dick in some big tall heels
Big fat checks, big large bills
Front, I'll flip like ten cartwheels
Cold ass bitch, I give Ross chills
Ten different looks and my looks all kill
I kiss him in the mouth, I feel all grills
He eat in the car, that's meals on wheels (Woo)

Cardi-B Money joint was playing, and I was rapping along to it having the time of my life. My dinner yesterday went excellent. The food came out so good, we talked and had good music playing. Clip came with his new flavor, and she was cool. We all threw down on the food and the cake. I had a good time being around them and just enjoying ourselves. The breakfast earlier today with my parents and Mackenzie went great too. My mama likes him and told his ass all about how she hated Kahlil. Then her ass came with these baby pictures and embarrassing stories about when I was little. Mackenzie found that shit so funny.

After we left from my parents, I took the money my baby gave me and went to the mall. Me and Alyssa went to her boutique and picked me out a bomb ass outfit. I got a full crystallized mini skirt and puffer jacket with a strapless bustier top. Alyssa had on a mocha colored mini apron dress. She slayed and her chocolate skin complimented it perfectly. We went to The Hair Boss of Detroit in Greenfield Plaza and got long thirty-inch genie ponytails. The Queen of Nails hooked our hands and feet up as well. I was feeling good, my man was by my side looking so damn sexy and just like money. He has made my entire birthday amazing.

"Hazel!" We all turned around when my name was called.

"Goldie!!" I ran to my sister hugging her so tight. I could have cried because I didn't think she could make it.

"When did you get in?" I asked holding her hand tight and loving how bad my sister was looking tonight.

"Daddy picked me up from the airport around four this afternoon. You know I wasn't missing my baby sister 21st birthday!" She hugged me tight again, and we went back to my VIP section.

"Everyone this is my big sister Goldie. You already know Alyssa." They hugged, and everyone spoke to her. Clip looked at my sister like she was a whole damn meal even though he had a date sitting next to him and no it wasn't the one from my dinner.

"This is my baby Mac the one I been calling you all the time about." They spoke and then Alyssa introduced her to Sada.

"So guess what baby sister?" She whispered in my ear over the loud music.

"What?"

"I got my job to transfer me here." She grinned at me bright, and so did I.

"I was missing home so much, and Beaumont Hospital in Farmington Hills accepted my transfer. Next month I'll be home for good. I want you to go condo shopping with me."

"Of course, I will. I missed you so much Goldie this is such a good birthday gift." Hugging again we danced for a while, and then we all stood for my birthday toast. It was such a good ass night, and I wish I could relive it again and again.

"Happy birthday angel face." Mac wrapped his arms around me rocking me slow to *Bryson Tiller Don't* song. I tilted my head back smiling at his now low red eyes.

"Thank you, baby." I kissed his soft lips, and we went back to turning up.

The End (Not Really!)

I hope you guys enjoyed this book like I did writing them. I absolutely fell in love with them and with that being said they WILL BE BACK!! Let me get the rest of these projects out, and then my crew will be back with so much more drama and chaos. My December book will be a two-part series. Thank you all so much for all the love and support.

XOXO-Londyn Lenz

Keep up with me

YouTube Channel- Through The Lenz Of Londyn

Instagram: londyn.lenz.authoress

My Facebook Reading Group: Through Londyn Lenz

Facebook Author Page: Author Londyn Lenz

Email: *Londyn_Lenz@yahoo.com*

CPSIA information can be obtained
at www.ICGtesting.com
Printed in the USA
LVHW032058090119
603317LV00001B/29